CW00705029

DUNCAN'S BOOTS

and the
Field of Broken Dreams

By David Gardner

Immediate Books

Laguna Beach, California

Published by Immediate Books,
Laguna Beach, CA

ImmediateBooks.com
DuncansBoots.com

First published in 2018
ISBN: 978-0-9985957-4-0
© Text copyright David Gardner, 2018
Cover design: Keith Groshans, Rocket Juiced

For more information: admin@immediatebooks.com

Acknowledgements: Michelle Gardner, Duncan Edwards Tribute, Jim Cadman, David Harrison, Paul Burns, Keith Groshans, Mickey, Jazmin and Savannah Gardner, Martyn Christian and all at the Field of Broken Dreams

"We don't stop playing because we grow old; we grow old because we stop playing."

George Bernard Shaw

For my Dad, who was always there.

PROLOGUE

14:59 GMT : Munich, February 6, 1958

Duncan Edwards' ankle was throbbing. He stretched out in his seat, pressing against the lap belt, trying in vain to get comfortable. The plane, an Airspeed Ambassador, had been used to ferry Queen Elizabeth around Europe and there was plenty of room, with seats facing back and front like a First Class train carriage. But it wasn't designed for footballers who'd barely survived a 3-3 European Cup tie on a bone-hard pitch in Iron Curtain Yugoslavia and been booted to kingdom come in the process.

Duncan closed his eyes and dreamed of his comfy single bed back at his digs in Manchester. His mind drifted to thinking about his girlfriend, Molly, waiting for him. The two thoughts mingled and his eyes snapped back open. He was trying to divert his mind but not like that, not here with the lads.

They'd just got back on the plane for the third time. Duncan wore a big Crombie overcoat walking across the tarmac but the icy wind cut into his bones and he shivered, unable to shake off a sense of dread that compounded the chill, even inside the plane with the heaters full on.

He'd been so sure the flight would be delayed he'd sent a telex to his landlady. It read: "All flights cancelled, flying tomorrow. Duncan."

But here they were. Back in their seats. Waiting for take-off.

The previous night after the game he'd sat on his bed talking with Bobby Charlton, deciding together that they weren't Busbies Babes any more. They were men. And they were ready. Their time was now. Mighty Real Madrid had beaten them last season but the hard-fought 3-3 tie against Red Star Belgrade had won them a place in the semi-final, squeaking through thanks to a 1-0 win in the home leg at Old Trafford. Revenge was theirs against the giants of Madrid. They were sure of it.

Duncan looked down the plane to where Bobby was sitting. They were fast friends but Duncan had heard Frank Swift, the old England goalkeeper now writing for the *News of the World,* saying it was safer sitting at the back. Looking out into the darkness, the storm still swirling like a Christmas snow globe, he worried about ice building up on the wings and thought again about the girl waiting for him at home. He wasn't a good flyer at the best of times. And this wasn't that.

Munich was supposed to be a quick refuelling stop on their way home from Belgrade but they'd tried two times to take off and both times the pilot had aborted. The card schools had packed away their cards and the banter had faded into an uneasy silence. Eddie Colman, the ebullient winger sitting next to Duncan, was nursing a hangover from the post-match celebrations. He looked pale earlier; now he was ashen.

Harry Gregg, the keeper, had his head down and his body tucked into a ball. Liam Whelan, the Irish striker, was an even worse flyer than Duncan and he looked panicked. "This may be death, but I'm ready," he whispered, although everybody heard.

He didn't look ready at all, thought Duncan. But he was saying out loud what everybody else was thinking. Matt Busby, the manager, sat at the front, never looking around. Duncan doubted he could tell anything from his face anyway. The dour Scot rarely gave anything away.

Roger Byrne, their enigmatic captain, at 28 the second oldest on the squad and the one they all looked to in a crisis, wasn't much help this time. "It's now or never," he said, staring blankly out of the window.

It was 15:03 and the engine roared into action, drowning out everything but their fears. Duncan caught the eye of Tommy Taylor, the centre forward, who'd also moved seats to the back. They shared a thin smile.

The plane jerked and launched bumpily down the runway. The lights were dimmed in the cabin and Duncan saw the banks of snow falling away outside. They'd be home soon, he thought. He must remember to stuff his boots with newspaper so they'd by dry for the league match with Wolverhampton Wanderers on Saturday.

Then he thought of Molly again. And relaxed. They'd be in the air any moment…

CHAPTER ONE

Jimmy started running as soon as he heard the flat dink of plastic on aluminium, just as he'd seen the pros do countless times on TV. From the bleachers, he'd shouted at his own kids in Little League to watch the ball, watch the ball. He wheeled backwards and the spotlights filled the warm autumn evening. Time slowed down so he could sense the expectant eyes of his teammates, all on him.

As the ball arced through the night sky he decided that this was what it was all about, living the American dream.

Then a dull thud that only he could hear exploded to his right and for a fleeting moment he thought perhaps someone had thrown something on the field. All the eyes were no longer on him but on the three guys shuffling around the bases.

"Pick up the damn ball, Jimmy!"

He looked into his creased glove. There was nothing there. He stared back at the capped silhouettes on the sandy diamond, reaching out with their own gloved hands, all beseeching him now.

Jimmy scrabbled down in the dirt to grab the ball, dropping it in his haste and then throwing it just hard enough for it to dribble somewhere between second and third.

~~~~~~~~~~

"Good game, darling." Zoe smiled as she pecked Jimmy on the cheek, knowing it was the kind of lie they told to their kids to make them feel better about sucking. "At least you're making some new friends."

"I've probably lost them the way I played tonight. It looks easy when you watch the kids do it." Jimmy kicked the tires on the mini-van. "I can't do this any more; I'm too old." His t-shirt felt tight across his stomach and his hamstrings groaned as he bent to peel off his trainers and slip on his Rainbow flip-flops. A bald spot was feasting on the hair on the back of his head.

"What do you mean, too old? You're 47. You were probably the youngest out there." Zoe had enough to worry about shepherding the kids into the car without soothing her husband's bruised ego. "We've been in America three years now. It's about time you started to settle in."

"Dad, dad, I need to tell you something."

Zoe was trying to wrestle their daughter into the back seat and fasten her belt. "Just one minute, Charley! Give us a chance to get into the car."

"Dad," insisted Charley, irrepressible at 5, "listen."

"What's up, sugar?"

"We need to tell you something."

All three kids were in the car now. Charley was sitting next to her older sister, Grace, 8, and Tyler, their brother, was in the row behind, his head buried in his phone.

"Let's get going first. We need to get to In-N-Out and we have to get homework done before bed." Three years after finally persuading Jimmy to move the family from England to live in Orange County, where she grew up, Zoe still felt she had to make sure everything was okay. On a rainy day, and there were few enough of those, she felt guilty, as if somehow it was her fault.

"But mum!"

"Okay, okay," Jimmy knew Charley could be relentless. "What is it?"

"WATCH THE BALL!" All three kids shouted in unison, erupting into giggles. Even Tyler, self conscious at 11, joined in the laughter. It was the line Jimmy would always shout at them from the bleachers in Little League.

Zoe reached across and squeezed Jimmy's hand. She'd been worried about him; it was why she'd persuaded him to sign up for the softball team run by an old schoolfriend. The kids loved living in California, but Jimmy sometimes looked out of place. It was so different from where he was from. She worried he'd get so caught up in his own thoughts she'd lose him.

"Do you mean when I was supposed to be catching the ball as a fielder or hitting it as a batter?" Jimmy looked over his shoulder from the driver's seat.

"BOTH!" they all chimed in again.

"Dad, you were terrible." Grace could barely get the words out she was laughing so much.

"Tyler, you've got to defend me, here. Those pitches were really fast."

"They were throwing underarm, dad." Even Tyler wasn't going to come to Jimmy's aid. "And they were fat."

"I probably should have worn my glasses."

"You don't wear glasses!" said Charley.

"Well, I guess I should."

The laughter gradually died down and Zoe told Jimmy quietly that one of the guys on the other team was so drunk he could hardly stand up. That hadn't stopped him hitting two home runs.

Jimmy was hungry but he knew even a double-double burger wouldn't fill the emptiness he felt inside. He turned the corner to join the take-out line and a set of floodlights across the street caught his eye. A soccer game was going on. It was too far away to tell for sure but it looked like co-ed adult teams playing rather than kids. He felt a pang of regret for everything he'd left behind and a momentary tightness in his chest for the years and the dreams that had passed him by.

CHAPTER TWO

Jimmy knew he was in trouble the moment he realised the cop in too-tight shorts on a sand buggy was heading their way. He'd opened the Fosters can using the lid of the picnic hamper as a shield and poured the beer into a red plastic cup, much more discreetly than the mum mixing tequila and orange juice in a Tupperware.

He'd barely taken a sip when the cop stopped in front of him.

"Is that an alcoholic beverage, sir?"

A bunch of families from the kids' elementary school were celebrating Father's Day on the beach and, as far as Jimmy could work out, everyone was drinking alcohol. He even had his suspicions about some of the teenagers' water bottles.

The problem was that Jimmy had been playing soccer with the kids and that had made him thirstier than the others roasting around the sandwiches gossiping about the parents who hadn't come. Consequently, his judgement might have been slightly addled.

"No!" It was the first answer that came to mind.

He'd made the snap decision to lie rather than risk embarrassing Zoe and his children by getting a ticket for drinking on the beach. But he hadn't realised the cop had seen him pouring the beer.

"Can I take a look, sir?"

He didn't just take a look; he sniffed disdainfully at the cup, as well. Then came the lecture on lying in front of the children. "If you had told me the truth I wouldn't be giving you this $100 ticket for drinking on the beach."

Jimmy was still taking occasional mouthfuls of beer as he waited for the cop to write out the citation.

"Would you please pour out the alcohol, sir? Right now!"

Zoe looked mortified even though she was drinking a vodka and orange through a straw in the same kind of red plastic cup. Charley was hanging onto her waist crying because she thought her dad was being arrested.

A football rolled over from where Jimmy had left the other children playing on the hard sand by the water.

"I'll tell you what," Jimmy was emboldened by the three beers he'd sunk earlier, "if I can kick the ball into the trash bin over there by the boardwalk will you let me off with a warning?"

The distance was a good 60 yards and there was maybe three or four families huddled around beach umbrellas in the space in between. "Double or nothing. You let me off if I make it and double the fine if I miss."

He could feel Zoe's stare boring into his skull, but he didn't turn his head. For some inexplicable reason he thought the cop would go for it.

"Sir, if you do not pour out the contents of that cup right now I will arrest you and the ball and you'll both be coming with me to the drunk tank."

The officer's attitude turned a little switch in Jimmy's psyche and he was suddenly sick of all the rules and being told how to behave. "So how do we get there? On the back of your little scooter?" He knocked back the rest of the beer.

"Jimmy, enough of…." Zoe knew the warning signs. She moved across to her husband with Charley still hanging onto her. "Let's go. We should go."

The other parents were all suddenly very aware that they, too, were illegally drinking. One mum started packing away and surreptitiously tipped a flask of suspiciously red liquid onto the sand.

Zoe was pulling at Jimmy's t-shirt. His hair was long and uncombed and his four-day stubble set him at odds with the other 9-5 dads in the party. He knew he should keep his mouth shut and walk away but their passiveness only fuelled his irritation. "Exactly what harm was I doing here to make you feel it was necessary to embarrass me in front of my family and friends?"

"No drinking is allowed on the beach."

"I know that. We also all know that pretty much everyone on the beach today is drinking. What are you going to do? Arrest everyone?"

"Jimeee!" Zoe screeched her whisper. A black and white SUV pulled up from a side road and waited just across the boardwalk. The officer didn't actually put his hand on his gun but he was warier now and his partner closed in on his buggy.

"I'm going to have to ask you to leave, Mr. Keen," he said, lifting his shades to squint at Jimmy's driving license. He reached out his hand with the citation. "I suggest you take this and go home and sober up. This may be appropriate behaviour in your country but it certainly isn't here."

"But I'm not…"

"Thank you, officer, we're going now." Zoe grabbed hold of Jimmy's arm and yanked him in towards the boardwalk in the opposite direction to the police truck.

"I'm not drunk," he told Zoe as she led him away, turning to apologise to a couple of mums.

"I don't care what you are. I don't want you hauled off to jail in front of our daughter. Now shut up!"

He pulled away from his wife but didn't attempt to go back to where the cops were slowly driving away back down the beach. The football was just to his right. He lifted his head for a moment in the direction of the trash bin. Then he took one step and launched the ball into the sky with his bare left foot. It sailed over three colourful umbrellas and appeared to be landing plumb in the middle of the open bin but the topspin left the ball just a few inches short and it crashed noisily off the edge and clattered a bowl of guacamole laid on a picnic blanket a few feet away.

"Great!" Jimmy stepped back. "Just great."

The kids he'd been playing with burst into laughter loud enough for the cops to look back. By then Zoe had hold of Jimmy again and was pushing him away with Charley dragging alongside.

The minivan was parked on a meter across the boulevard on the bay side of the peninsula and the three of them were waiting for a space in the traffic to cross when an English voice asked them to stop. Zoe carried on across the road, holding Charley's hand. She wasn't speaking to Jimmy.

"Excuse me. Aren't you the guy involved in that little situation down by 11th Street?"

"I may have been." Jimmy didn't need another lecture. He already knew it was a long road back into Zoe's good books. The tension had been growing between them in recent weeks and this hadn't helped.

"Was that a fluke?"

Jimmy really wasn't in the mood for strangers. Just because he was English didn't mean he wanted to talk to everyone he came across. "Was what a fluke?"

"Your lucky shot into the trash." The guy smiled. He was younger than Jimmy, perhaps in his early 40s. He was totally bald and carrying a surfboard under his right arm. "Nice left foot."

"Thanks." Jimmy took the guy's outstretched hand, shook it and went to follow after Zoe and Charley. "But you can't have been watching closely. It missed."

"It was close enough. A bunch of us play on Sunday mornings at Vista Park in Laguna Beach. Brits, South Americans, Europeans, Americans - whoever turns up. Come along…we could use that left foot."

He insisted on getting Jimmy's number and texting the details.

"What kind of game is it?" asked Jimmy, intrigued in spite of himself. "Are you part of a league?" He didn't wait to hear the answer; Zoe was waiting by the car, her face as dark as thunder.

"No, it's just a pick-up game — anyone can play," the guy shouted after him.

"We call it the Field of Broken Dreams."

CHAPTER THREE

Jimmy had worked his fair share of building sites when he was an apprentice footballer with Leyton Orient FC in East London, but this was the first time a foreman had asked him if he had a degree.

"Degree in what?" Jimmy had given the suntanned guy in board shorts and a Volcom t-shirt the resume Zoe helped him write the previous night. It listed the kind of buildings he'd worked on in the past and his talents for drywalling, painting and brickwork. He hadn't thought to include his education, such as it was.

"Anything? The boss likes the people working for him to have degrees. Could be in surfing big waves for all I care." The foreman shrugged his shoulders. "Sorry, brah."

"I played some pro soccer in England when I was younger." There was a connection in Jimmy's mind; it was the reason his formal education ran aground at the age of 16. Informally it ended a couple of years before that.

"They give you a degree for that?"

"Well, no. They didn't give me anything much at all."

"Sorry then, brah. I already got a couple illegals on this job. Maybe next time." The foreman waved the next guy over. There were about a dozen waiting, all of them younger than him. Jimmy assumed his interview was over.

He walked back to his truck, stopping briefly to look across the rooftops to the Pacific sparkling in the early morning sunlight below. It was just past 7am. Another long day ahead without a job to go to or much hope of finding one. Zoe was taking the kids to school on her way to work and he didn't have to pick them up until 3.15pm. Then he'd have to go home and tell his wife he wasn't sufficiently qualified for the most menial construction work on the ocean-view mansion her friend was building.

Jimmy called his brother Carl in London. He knew exactly how the conversation was going to go but dialled the number anyway.

"Come home. I can get you plenty of work. I've got a bunch of mates in the building trade. I can get you a job tomorrow." Carl had the same answer every time. "You've got to tell Zoe that it's time to come home. What's so great about California anyway?" Carl was dead set against anywhere that wasn't Plaistow in East London.

"You mean apart from the sunshine and the beach and the girls in bikinis?"

"Exactly. Apart from the sunshine and the beach and the girls in bikinis."

"Well, Disneyland's just up the road, Mexico's about two hours away and so's the nearest ski resort." Jimmy couldn't help getting defensive.

But his brother liked to have the last word. "None of it's much good if you don't have any cash though, is it Jim?"

"You're supposed to be making me feel better." Jimmy slumped further into his seat. The waves were picking up and he could see a couple of young surfers jumping the wall onto the sand. He had a longboard back at the house but felt guilty using it on a weekday.

"We lost again at the weekend." Carl still played for the pub team they'd both joined when they moved to London from the Midlands. "Shame you hung up your boots."

Jimmy realised with a start that he'd need boots if he was going to check out the pick-up game in Laguna that Sunday, but he didn't want to ask Zoe for the money. He'd wear trainers for now. It was probably going to be crap.

"Actually, I've been invited to play this weekend. I can't remember the last time I was actually involved in a game. Probably the weekend before we came over here."

"Yeah, I think we lost then as well. Who you turning out for over there then? The LA Galaxy? Mickey Mouse All Stars?"

"This is just for fun, a kick-about." Jimmy wasn't even sure he'd go. It was a horrendously early start for a Sunday, but the possibility cheered him enough to head home and check out Craigslist on the computer to try and find some construction work that didn't require a Bachelor of Science degree.

CHAPTER FOUR

The road wound up from the coast and kept going, a view of the ocean way below filling Jimmy's rear view mirror every time he straightened up towards the clouds. He passed a woman in black Nike running up the hill, her gears clearly working better than Jimmy's groaning red Nissan. The shrill GPS instructions ordered him to turn left at the T-junction even though it appeared the route was going to take him over the edge of the cliff.

Just before the end of the road, a parking lot opened up to the right and he pulled in, still thinking that perhaps it wasn't such a good idea, after all.

A couple of guys were stretching out of their cars, rummaging in trunks for boots. One of them was wearing a red Liverpool shirt. He looked about Jimmy's age but his friend, who was struggling to clamp what looked like callipers to both legs, could easily have been 70. They both waved cheerfully at Jimmy.

"Lovely morning," one smiled, the refrain of morning people everywhere. Jimmy was wishing he was still tucked up in bed.

A truck not dissimilar to Jimmy's screeched into a spot, a surfboard tied in the back, followed by a black Rolls Royce Phantom. The two drivers jumped out, embraced, and hurried over towards a couple of picnic table benches next to a kiddies swings and slides where several other men were chatting and nursing Starbucks cups.

Jimmy was still considering turning around and fleeing but a giant of a guy, all of 6ft. 7ins., was following kitted out in full German national team gear.

"Hi, is this the soccer game?" One of the Starbucks guys looked up and reached out a hand. "We try."

"I'm Jimmy."

"Bill. Good to meet you." The smile faded. "I'm sorry, but are you English?"

"Yeah, I suppose I am."

Bill was wearing a bright yellow soccer shirt and green shorts. He looked embarrassed. "I'm afraid we've already reached our full complement from the UK. Maybe next week?"

The Rolls driver shouted over in a London accent. "Leave him alone, Bill."

"I'm just kidding." Bill wrapped Jimmy in a bear hug. "Welcome to the Field of Broken Dreams."

The parking lot was filling up and there was a hive of murmured conversation as the players converged on the picnic benches. Four goals were scattered haphazardly around a bumpy, yellowing field dominated by a baseball diamond and the low hum rose a decibel as Bill and a couple of others discussed whether there were enough players for two games.

"The cut off is 24 and we're at 25 already with the new dude." A thin guy with an Eastern European accent nodded over towards Jimmy.

"Burdie's on her way. I saw her running up the hill. She'll be here any minute." It was the bald surfer from the beach. "Jimmy's with me. He can play." He shook hands and ran off to help push the goals into position.

Jimmy was wishing desperately he'd swallowed his pride and asked Zoe for some cash to buy a pair of boots. Most of the players were wearing team uniforms from various countries and everyone was wearing boots. The grass was wet with dew and as he ran around the perimeter the dampness soaked through into his socks.

Nobody was in much of a hurry. They were stretching half-heartedly or rubbing various ointments into knees and backs.

It was easy to see why it was called Vista Park. The canyons cascaded down from the grassy plateau, banks of cloud captured in rafts of green, like something out of 'Lord of the Rings,' thought Jimmy.

A Scot in a Barcelona shirt was standing in the middle of the field with a scrap of paper reading out a stream of names. Another Londoner, introducing himself as Martyn, pointed towards the furthest pitch, now set up with cones. "You're in the first game, mate."

"Jimmy."

"Good to meet you. I hear you can play."

"The big question is whether I can run."

"That may take a little longer." Martyn smiled and ran over to the opposing side. He was wearing white; Jimmy had on a navy t-shirt and grey basketball shorts. He felt all wrong.

The bald surfer, Dom, asked Jimmy if he was okay in midfield. "You're going to be slipping all over the place in those, son."

"Perhaps I should start out as full back." Jimmy wanted to ease himself back in as quietly as possible.

"You don't want to play out there." Sand from the baseball field covered the entire right side of the pitch. "Better you use that foot of yours to get Ken and Paul the ball up front."

There was no referee, no whistle and not a lot of rules other than that the game stopped every time anyone fell over to make sure nothing had broken, slipped or sagged. Randy, the central defender behind Jimmy, mentioned he had a hip replacement four months earlier. It seemed to be working.

The first touch was fine. Jimmy played it down the line well enough, but Paul tapped it back into the space and moved on for the one-two. Jimmy knew exactly what he was supposed to do and the message his brain sent to his feet was precise. But the thought process didn't take into account his burning lungs. He had just enough energy to put the ball into space allowing Paul to launch a cross to the far post but absolutely no clue how he was going to make it back to the halfway line as the whites seized on the lost opportunity and counter attacked.

His right hamstring waited another ten minutes before screaming for a chair. By that time, Jimmy had twice ended up on his backside as he turned on the wet grass to watch the opposing central midfield player, Martyn, flash by him. Nermin, the lofty Croatian, had accidentally stepped on his left foot and it was quite possible he'd broken a rib slipping on the lumpy border between grass and sand with the nearest player a full 20 yards away from him.

Half time, randomly called apparently at the whim of John, the septuagenarian goalkeeper, couldn't come soon enough. Jimmy wondered if anyone would notice if he creaked over to his car and left.

"Well played, Jimmy. Good game." Bill patted him on the back. "You clearly know what you're doing."

"Yeah, nice," added Dom. "It'll take a few weeks for your body to get used to it again but you're doing great."

So much for sneaking off. The early morning mist had burnt off and there was no shelter from the blazing sun. The players ambled back onto the field in a jumble of colours and there had been a slight adjustment with a young striker swapped with an elderly defender to try and even up the sides.

The second half began with a more measured approach. Ken and Paul shuttled the ball back and forth before pulling it back to the edge of the penalty box where Jimmy was admiring the movement and enjoying another breather.

He could see the keeper out of position, the right half of the goal completely open. He remembered enough to keep his head down and not try and hit it out of the park. It was the same advice his friend Dave always gave him when they played golf back in England at the course behind his old school pal's house in Upminster, Essex. It never worked in golf; the ball invariably screamed wildly to the left or right and usually so far he never found it. But in soccer Jimmy's body was rehearsed enough as a boy to deliver. The ball fell so cleanly on his laces he hardly felt it loop off his foot high into the right corner.

The keeper had so many braces wrapped around his knees you couldn't see any flesh and he didn't even bother trying to jump but it wouldn't have mattered anyway. There was the slightest chink as the ball touched the underside of the bar. It was virtually unstoppable; maybe not for a keeper playing for Real Madrid or Manchester United, but certainly for a Sunday morning pick-up game where every player on one side had to do a ten-minute stint between the sticks for the sake of fairness.

Running back to the halfway line with a new spring in his step, Jimmy got a couple of high fives from the opposition defenders. He didn't need to chase around like a wounded rhino any longer; he felt accepted.

"I told you he could play." He heard Dom telling Martyn.

"No argument from me, mate."

The game restarted and Jimmy found himself isolated on the left with two players bearing down on him and nobody else defending the goal. Jockeying backwards, he tried to turn, slipped and lost his balance. The onrushing striker didn't need to pass the ball. With Jimmy squirming on the floor he slowed down, took aim and slotted it in the left corner outside John's valiantly outstretched boot.

"Mind the bumps in the grass," said the forward, leaning down to help Jimmy up. "And you could probably do with some boots. This ain't Wimbledon. My name's Simon, by the way. Good playing with you," he added, offering a handshake.

Jimmy had lost count of the score but someone shouted that it was close — 9-8. The exuberance of his goal baked out by the sun, Jimmy was daydreaming about softball. Perhaps it wasn't so bad.

He tried a couple of cross field balls that barely made it halfway and blundered late into a tackle, tumbling over his opponents legs.

"No slide-tackling." The cry echoed around the pitch. "We've all got to work in the morning," yelled Sean, a friendly American who'd been among the first to welcome him.

Lucky you, thought Jimmy. He tried to explain that it wasn't really a tackle and that he'd simply fallen over near the ball but his throat was dry, his head was pounding and he no longer had any feeling below his waist.

There has to be a final whistle soon.

When the end of the game did finally come it was by consensus. Pete, the watch keeper, was overruled when he called

23

time. The others — everyone other than Jimmy, it seemed — wanted to play an extra five minutes.

In that short extra time the other side scored another three times and Jimmy was reduced to a bystander. He tried to hide at left back but they kept coming at him. *What are these old guys on?* he thought.

Finally, the game was over. He couldn't be sure, but Jimmy thought his team had lost. If that was the case nobody really seemed to care.

"Nice game," said Paul, coming over to him. "That was a cracking goal. You'll be living off that all week."

"Field of Broken Dreams," said Martyn, shaking Jimmy's hand. "Better than sex."

"You'll be lucky to have the choice," quipped Mark, another Englishman. "Go home looking like that and your wife'll think you've aged 20 years."

"And she'd be right." Jimmy promised he'd return the following week and stumbled off towards his truck and some shade.

His knees were throbbing and the aching in both legs was just as painful when he was sitting down as when he walked. It was quite possible he'd fractured a rib and the thought of a single, simple, cold lager trumped any thoughts of goals or intercourse but perhaps for the first time since he'd arrived with the family in America Jimmy felt like he was in the right place.

He felt like he was home.

CHAPTER FIVE

The 25-minute journey home along Pacific Coast Highway was torture. Everywhere Jimmy looked he saw smiling, blonde people carrying surfboards and exuding health and optimism. Even the MAMILs on their road bikes looked less ridiculous and more admirable. They had legs that worked!

He turned right away from the beach and the million dollar mansions and towards the West side of Costa Mesa where his apartment block was squeezed into a corner behind a charity shop and a taco restaurant. He spent 10 minutes searching for a parking space and dragged himself out of the truck wondering how to suggest to Zoe that 9.30am was a perfectly appropriate time of day for a couple of Coronas.

Negotiating the two flights of stairs up to the front door was like climbing Mount Everest. Jimmy summited to find Zoe bent over the computer in the living room holding a small piece of paper.

"How was your game?" She looked up and smiled but she wasn't happy.

"Good. Really good, actually. Bit tough on the old legs and I don't think I'll be wearing those sneakers again at the gym. They're wrecked." He grinned. Jimmy never went to the gym.

Zoe's smile was fleeting. She turned back to the screen. "The drinking ticket came in the mail. I've just been checking our accounts. We don't have the money to pay for it."

Jimmy's stomach turned. The feelings of helplessness returned. But he knew he couldn't let Zoe see his panic. It scared her.

"Don't worry about it, babe. It'll wait a while. I'm still owed some money from that last job and we've got our savings." He put his arm around her shoulders, wincing as he bent down. "Everything will be fine."

"We haven't got any savings left, Jimmy. I told you last month; it went on the rent."

"I told you, we're okay. Stop worrying your pretty head." He knelt down in front of her, ignoring the excruciating pain, pulling her tightly towards him, marvelling at the way she always smelled so good at the same moment he remembered his shirt was still wet with dirty sweat.

He kissed the top of her head and held her face so he could look into her glistening eyes. "You have to trust me on this, Zoe. Everything's gonna work out. Do you trust me?"

Zoe nodded slowly, her eyes as large and as sad as Jimmy had ever seen them.

"Now let's get the kids away from their bloody computers and take them down to the beach."

The Coronas would have to wait.

But much later, several hours after they'd gone to bed, both of them exhausted after a day of forced jollity, Jimmy woke to hear muted sobs from Zoe lying face turned away from him. He feigned sleep, not wanting to face his own nightmares but feeling cowardly as well as inadequate when he heard her getting up and padding quietly out of the bedroom.

Consumed with guilt, Jimmy followed her a few minutes later. Zoe was sitting, head in hands, over the computer. The sound of her muffled whimpers broke his heart but, knowing there really was nothing he could say to ease her fears in the silence of a long, harsh night, Jimmy turned and went back to bed where he waited open-eyed until his wife, her tears spent, returned to her side of the bed.

Jimmy waited until he was absolutely sure Zoe was asleep before he allowed his own tears to come. It wasn't so much that he'd failed to provide her with the security she craved so desperately; it was the knowledge that he didn't have a clue what to do about it.

CHAPTER SIX

Zoe would have told Jimmy to research football boots online before going to the store but he hadn't told her was going to buy a pair. He'd kept back a few dollars here and there and continued playing on Sundays in his trainers.

Now there he was in the shoes section at Dick's Sporting Goods looking at a pair of Adidas Copa Mundials. Unlike most of the others on display, they looked like soccer boots. Black leather with the requisite three white stripes, they were perfect. They even had them in his size.

There was just one problem; they cost $145.

"Have you got any that look like these, but are cheaper?" he asked the store assistant.

"Of course," the young man smiled broadly. "These are tremendous value and a very durable shoe." He held up a green, yellow and orange splashed boot with laces precariously balanced along the side.

"I'm sorry but I can't wear those. It looks like someone's puked up all over them."

The clerk looked mortified.

"I'm sorry, it's just that I'd prefer a more conservative look."

"Would these work any better?" He reached up for a red and blue shoe. "They're in your price range. They're only $29."

"I'm sorry, but do you perhaps have a single colour shoe? Preferably not in yellow."

The assistant went away for what seemed an age and returned with a box and an uncertain look. He lifted the lid to reveal a pair of white boots covered in black strands resembling a spider web and a purple blob.

"These are on sale — just $25. Down from $29.99. Lionel Messi wears ones just like it."

Jimmy tried them on and tried not to look at the Copa Mundials still in their box on the floor. The spider boots fitted pretty well. "Are they leather?"

"Man made, sir."

"So plastic then?"

"Yes, I suppose so, sir."

"Any particular cleaning instructions?" It was the sort of question his dad used to ask when buying him football boots back home when he was a kid. Cleaning boots then involved something called Dubbin and rags and you had to break in the boots for a couple of games, playing through the pain of blisters.

"Probably just run them under the tap, sir."

"Okay, I guess I'll take them then."

Mission accomplished, Jimmy threw the boots in the back of the truck. With money so tight he didn't want Zoe to think he was frittering it away, but he was getting sick of spending half the Sunday morning matches on his bum.

He'd tell Zoe once their money problems had eased. It's not like he was going to wear them in public anywhere else.

CHAPTER SEVEN

Jimmy was one of the first to arrive at Vista Park the following Sunday; he didn't want an audience when he took his shiny new boots out of the bag. Driving up through the clouds he could hardly see the road, but the sky was cobalt blue by the time he reached the T-junction on the brow of the hill and his dashboard already showed the temperature at 23 degrees.

There were a couple of early morning dog walkers and a lost looking guy who may well have been there all night hanging around outside the public toilet fronting the park.

Jimmy pulled into a space and reached into the messy glove compartment for the bottle of Jameson he kept for life's little emergencies. The longer he'd been out of a job, it seemed the more little emergencies there were. He didn't take a swig, but he felt reassured by the fact that he could.

He felt a trickle of sweat down his side a few minutes later as he walked from the parking lot past a couple of fully helmeted mountain bikers looking strangely ominous in the dawn light. It was still only 6.35am. Back in the day, when he was playing football seriously, it was about the time he'd roll back home after a Saturday night out with the lads.

Sitting down on the hard metal picnic bench, Jimmy groaned as he bent over to pull on the left cleat. His legs had ached virtually non-stop since he first played a month earlier. At least he'd found an old pair of soccer shorts he'd had for about 30 years. They were tight but he didn't feel like he was going to sail over the fence every time there was a puff of wind.

"Nice boots…"

Jimmy lifted his head to see Dom.

"…way to go Peter Parker."

The Spiderman jokes continued as the FOBD regulars ambled over to the bench.

"I was going to call you Spidey, Jimmy," said Stuart, a Glaswegian rock promoter, "but the others said it wouldn't stick." Not for the first time, Jimmy thought how much easier his life would be with money in his bank account.

The early risers headed over to the first field discussing the pros and cons of various professional teams with someone cutting in every so often with another jibe about Jimmy's boots.

"Don't worry," Simon said, running past, "We'll get the guys that sold them to you. Or are they paying you to wear them?"

It didn't bother Jimmy; the jokes were nothing compared to the hard time he got as an apprentice in England, but he was still glad when the game finally kicked-off.

He'd given up playing defence and settled up front in his old No. 9 position. The boots felt good, but they weren't the answer he'd hoped for. Jimmy knew where to run and how to be in the right position for a shot at goal and more often than not, legs willing, he could get there in time. The problem was that his feet still weren't in tune with his head. He'd scuff the shot or blast it over the goal, over the fence and halfway down the canyon; his passes were hit and miss and even though he was fully aware the goalkeeper was physically unable to bend over he still kept blasting the ball right at him when a dribble into the corner would suffice.

"I thought it'd come back quicker than this," he said to Sean after apologising for a misplaced pass.

"It's not your fault, man," said Sean, a muscular engineering shop owner who was wearing a thick jacket to sweat off some extra pounds, "haven't you noticed...we're getting old."

Jimmy had still scored a couple by half-time and was enjoying staying on his feet. The studs may have been cheap moulded rubber but they worked. He grabbed his water bottle and, out of habit, picked up his iPhone to check his new messages. There was just one from Zoe: *Call home*, it said, with a sad face emoji.

Jimmy turned away from the field and dialled Zoe's number.

There was silence at the other end at first when she answered and Jimmy thought it was the reception but then he heard a sniffle and his wife's fragile voice.

"It's your dad," she said. "He's dead."

She couldn't get out anything else as she fought with her emotions.

"...in a car crash."

So Jimmy was going to get to take his family back to England after all, but in the worst way possible.

CHAPTER EIGHT

Jimmy cried when his mother died five years earlier, but his tears were for his father; he couldn't see how his dad could exist on his own and the pain he felt was for him and not himself. He'd left the Field of Dreams at half time without explanation. Not because he wanted to but because he thought that was what he should do. An extra 45 minutes relieved of the burden of grieving would have been just fine but it's hard to laugh at superhero jokes when your last surviving parent has just died and he didn't want to have to explain himself.

There was a brief moment of confusion as the others tried to reconfigure the sides after Jimmy said he was leaving, but it wasn't anything out of the ordinary. Rarely a week went by without at least one player tweaking a hamstring or pulling up with some sort of injury brought about by age.

Driving down the hill, Jimmy called his brother to find out more.

"He had a heart attack driving back from the shops. Nobody else was hurt. It could have been worse." Carl was being all stoic but Jimmy caught the tremor in his voice.

"When?"

"This morning, so it was in the middle of the night for you over there. I called early but you were already out so I told Zoe." Carl hesitated. "Are you coming back for the funeral?"

"We'll try and get a flight today." Jimmy's eyes were dry; he could feel the friction in the sockets. "Are you up in Dudley?"

"Yeah, we drove up as soon as we got the call. We've been here a couple of hours now. I guess we'll see you tomorrow. Text me your flight details."

"I'm sorry, Carl."

"Me too, Jim. Me too."

Jimmy said goodbye. He'd felt guilty enough leaving Carl and his wife, Sarah, to keep an eye on their dad after moving halfway across the world. Now he was worrying about the cost of the flights.

All three kids were in tears when he got home and Zoe was trying to be practical, urging them to pack their bags while arguing on the phone with the airlines. Jimmy limped into the living room and she ran to put her arms around him. Her emotional levy broke and she sagged into his chest. "I just can't believe it; he was doing so well. It's just not fair."

Jimmy had to be the strong one.

He went with the kids to try and get their stuff together. Grace had filled her bag with stuffed animals, Charley packed the house phone so she could keep trying grandfather's number and all Tyler wanted to take was his skateboard. Jimmy didn't try and dissuade them. The flight was in just four hours and they had to drop their dog, a soppy black Labrador named Snoop, off at the kennel on the way to LAX.

"I've booked us return flights for the same day next week," said Zoe, her eyes red. "We'll have to help Carl and Sarah clear out your dad's house in Dudley after the funeral but after that…."

Jimmy nodded. He was thinking about how excited his dad had been at the prospect of him playing for one of the big clubs. When it didn't happen he felt bad more for his dad than for him. He'd spent years telling all his pals how good "young Jimmy" was and it all came to nothing. They never talked about it again and his dad never bought Sky or BT Sport. As far as Jimmy knew, he'd never watched the game again once Leyton Orient decided not to renew his son's contract. He certainly never discussed it with his son.

Carrying the luggage to the truck, Jimmy felt a twinge in his right hip from the morning's match. He couldn't imagine going back there now. What was he thinking trying to play at his age? It was ridiculous.

As far as Jimmy was concerned, the California dream was dead. Zoe may have booked return flights but he'd be happy never coming back.

CHAPTER NINE

The funeral was as bleak as Jimmy feared. Both he and Carl had given brief eulogies and Charley and Grace, looking tanned and healthy and out of place at the old mahogany lectern, read lyrics from 'Borrowed Angels,' a song they'd sung at Christmas for their grandpa.

There wasn't a dry eye in the place, except for Jimmy's.

The red brick St Francis Church was in Laurel Road on the Priory Estate, where Jimmy and Carl grew up. The estate in Dudley, about 8 miles from Birmingham in England's West Midlands, was as dilapidated as the rest of the crumbling market town, with it's feeble heart, already slowed by chronic unemployment, crushed by the 2008 recession. The flowers and incense couldn't hide the smell of stagnation and the pews were half full with old friends who'd known Jimmy's parents most of their lives. His dad had still been living in the same corner semi-detached house a five-minute walk away in Elm Road that they'd bought when they married in the 1950s. Jimmy wasn't even sure they'd changed the wallpaper.

Jimmy had been to the church dozens of times as a kid, but never with his parents. His dad would never allow them to go to St Francis and Jimmy's mother would often take two buses to another church across town on a Sunday morning. But his dad had been emphatic in his will that the funeral service would be right there in the Assisi Chapel of the local church that Jimmy had never seen him ever set foot in.

Being back there felt claustrophobic to Jimmy. He'd sat in the pews as a boy staring at the two stained glass windows dedicated to Duncan Edwards, the former Manchester United wing half who was one of the eight Busby Babes who died from injuries sustained in the Munich plane crash.

There were two windows, one of Edwards in his Manchester United strip and the other in a white England shirt. They were inscribed: "Thanking God for the life of Duncan Edwards. Died at Munich February 1958."

When he still had hopes of becoming a professional footballer, Jimmy had prayed to those windows, shutting his eyes tightly and wishing with all his might that Duncan Edwards, the great Black Country hero, would somehow make all his own dreams come true. He'd even gone down there the night before he left for London, sneaking in through the church cafeteria to get Duncan's blessing. But none of it had worked; sitting there again for the first time since that last visit a lifetime ago, Jimmy felt stupid at believing a memorial to a player who died before he was even born could make any difference to his life. Of one thing Jimmy was certain; his prayers had not been answered.

Tyler and Grace were unusually quiet afterwards as everyone gathered again outside the church. The sun came out from behind the clouds to torture the mourners in black and

Charley wondered loudly whether grandpa would be back in time for tea.

The little girl kept wandering off around the graveyard as if she was looking for something. "I'm looking for nana," she finally told Zoe. "We left her here last time we came to England."

Jimmy remembered most of the people there from his own childhood, although more than a couple looked a wrinkled, much frailer imitation of their former selves and had to remind him who they were.

"Your father always had such high hopes for you," said one old man Jimmy couldn't place. "He hoped you'd be playing for the Baggies one day, he did. Such a shame."

Jimmy didn't wait around to ask whether the shame was his dad's passing or his own aborted football career. But he couldn't escape the past that easily.

"Well, if it isn't our favourite Dudley Schoolboys number nine." Wally Stamford had lived next door for 40 years. With his rumpled, ill-fitting brown suit and white shirt, the edges yellowed with age, the old man looked hardly changed, but then Jimmy thought he was ancient when he was a kid. He never remembered seeing him wearing anything other than that brown suit. "I could never get your old man to stop going on about how you could have been the next Bobby Charlton. He said you should have been better than all of them if you'd stuck at it."

Jimmy started to explain that if it wasn't for a certain thug of a Hull City reserves centre back raking through his ACL like a fork through spaghetti he would certainly have "stuck at it" but the grizzled old retired milkman wasn't listening.

"Your dad was only telling me the other day how you were wasting your time over in California without any money. All the cash those footballers earn these days. You'd be made for life. Broke his heart, it did, you giving up like that. You should a never gone down to London, not with all the teams we've got up here. Villa are looking for some fresh blood; you should hit them up while you're here."

Jimmy didn't have the heart to tell him he was 30 years too late, nor that he'd spent the majority of his adult life ruing the injury that wrecked his dreams. He smiled and shook the old man's hand. "Good to see you, Wally. I'll see you back at the house for the reception."

Back at 34 Elm Road, Zoe didn't seem to be having any problems with his father's Black Country pals. She had refused to dress in black, arguing that blue was her father-in-law's favourite colour and that was what she was going to wear, and was orchestrating the reception like it was a kid's birthday party, making sure everyone had a drink and some food, clearing up the mess and comforting the mourners when they got a little maudlin. She may have been an exotic American to many who considered Birmingham a trek and London a southern cesspool to be avoided at all costs but her raucous laugh and lack of pretentiousness made her one of their own.

Carl's wife, on the other hand, grew up a block away on the Priory Estate, and she couldn't wait to get out. She carried her Chanel handbag like a shield to fend off her past. "Do we really need to brew up another pot of tea?" she asked Zoe. "You know they'll never leave, don't you," she whispered. Almost all trace of Brummie was gone from her accent, which sounded like it originated somewhere halfway down the M1 motorway.

"I'm worried about Wally." Zoe nodded over towards the old neighbour, who was cradling a glass of whiskey and staring out of the window to the narrow lawn where the kids were playing with a ball. He was looking into a space way beyond the children.

"They were friends a long time, a lifetime really."

"Yeah but dad was always moaning that Wally would never shut up and he always outstays his welcome, always has."

"I know but he's lovely really."

Sarah rolled her eyes and filled the kettle and Zoe went to answer the doorbell. People were still arriving at the two-storey semi, its brown shingle walls stained black with time.

Charley still hadn't quite grasped what was going on and ran into the hallway every time the bell rang asking: "Is that grandpa?"

"It's not like she doesn't understand," Zoe told Sarah, "it's just that she doesn't want to."

"Sounds like Carl when I tell him every Sunday that he should come home for lunch after football instead of going down the pub with the team," said Sarah. "He understands what I'm saying but does he ever come straight home? Does he heck?"

A few minutes later Carl came over and put his arm around his wife. "Time to go, beautiful. We've got to get back to London. Work in the morning."

Sarah didn't need to be asked twice and took her bag off to collect her coat and their two daughters.

Carl hugged Zoe tight. He didn't have the physical presence of his brother but they shared the same intense blue/green eyes. Carl was a sub-editor for The Sun national newspaper and Sarah was a columnist on the same publication which didn't always make for an easy life at home, especially because she was paid almost twice the salary of her husband.

"So are you going to start clearing out the attic, Jimmy?" Carl shouted across the living room to where his brother was napping in an armchair.

"I guess so. We'll make a start in the morning." Jimmy answered without opening his eyes.

"Good luck with that. I don't think anybody's been up there since the mid-60s," Carl went over with Sarah and gave Jimmy a hug. "Good to see you brother."

They bundled out of the house leaving an eerie silence behind them. Jimmy helped put the kids to bed and left Zoe trying to explain to Charley again why grandpa wasn't at the funeral.

Then he went downstairs for a nightcap with Wally.

CHAPTER TEN

Coming back home had always been a complicated affair for Jimmy, especially since his mother died. He'd arrive with all good intentions but the one thing he had in common with his dad was football and his father never wanted to talk about it, not since the injury. So the conversation would lull into a stony silence and it would invariably be left to Zoe to take up the slack. The old man would come alive to her; Jimmy would hear them chuckling together in the kitchen and he could see the glint in his eyes when they talked. But when Jimmy was with his dad, especially when they were alone together, the weight of failed expectations was just too heavy to overcome.

It was different with Wally. He'd always been there and you couldn't stop him talking if you tried. And tonight, Jimmy didn't try. He wanted to know more about his dad, to try and understand him and, perhaps, to understand a little more about himself.

William Keen (it always sounded strange to Jimmy to hear friends call his dad, Will) had grown up in a rough, tough area of the Black Country. The family lived in a terraced house where every penny earned was used for a hand-to-mouth existence. A good week would be one when they didn't have to water down the milk.

If that was tough, then it was nothing compared to the harsh life which Jimmy's dad's father, Josh, (Jimmy's paternal grandfather) and his family had to endure. At that time, Wally's parents lived in the next street, although the tiny homes were so packed in that everybody knew everybody else's business.

Josh was raised in a terraced back-to-back house in Tipton with one room downstairs and one room upstairs. The downstairs room was effectively the living room, dining room, kitchen and bathroom combined. Bath time would be one night a week - usually a Friday - with the water boiled on the black-leaded fire range. The whole family would share the same bath, one after the other, with the water occasionally topped up from saucepans and pots boiling on the fire. There was no room for personal modesty.

The pecking order was defined. The cleanest went first, working up finally to the dirtiest, usually Josh, who would be covered in dirt and grime from his work at the nearby Baggeridge coal mine.

The one bedroom was divided by a blanket down the middle to allow Josh and his wife, Selina, a modicum of privacy. The children, all ten of them, would share the bed on the other side of the room, sleeping top to tail.

The toilet was outside in the garden and was a simple affair. It was a plank of wood embedded into the closet wall. A hole had been cut into it and a bucket was placed underneath. When it became full during the week, the toilet contents would be hurled onto the garden as fertiliser. It was known as bucket-and-chuck-it. One day a week a couple of men would call with their horse and cart to collect any surplus toilet contents. They were known as night soil men and their job was to collect the human waste and take it to a nearby tip.

To save the children having to go down the garden to the toilet on a freezing winter's night, they had a chamber pot to use. It was kept under the bed and in the Black Country it was known as a "gazunder" (because it goes under the bed). The job of one of the children in the morning was to empty the contents, either in the toilet or on the back garden. Usually it was the child who was last to get up who had the dubious task of emptying it. If nothing else, it was an incentive to get out of bed early.

Josh was a troubled soul. He had survived the horrors of World War One, having enlisted as a teenager to fight "the war to end all wars." He went to the front and obeyed orders, witnessing the slaughter of fellow soldiers, and never spoke about it to a soul, not to his friends, his priest and certainly not to his wife and children.

His only physical wound was the loss of his right thumb. Mentally he was shot to pieces. Today they would call it post-traumatic stress but back then it was put down to his "moods". The men were told to get on with lives. They were told they were returning to a "land fit for heroes." In truth they came back to squalor, depression and social devastation as Britain struggled through those troubled years of the twenties and thirties. Josh went to work down the pits in Wales for a while and took part in the General Strike, before returning to the Black Country and Selina.

By then, he had turned to drink to blot out his memories of the war. He was a bright man but had no outlet for his intelligence. He took on an endless sequence of menial jobs in factories and on building sites, gradually losing his identity along with his youth.

The local pubs were his escape from that drudgery. Often in a state of inebriation, he would get involved in regular fist fights, fuelled by copious amounts of ale. His wife bore the brunt of some of this aggression but she soldiered on uncomplainingly, rearing her children, including Jimmy's dad, with love and affection. Eventually she embraced her grandchildren, including Jimmy, with that same unconditional love.

While Jimmy's dad was too young to be called up for World War Two, his older mate Wally joined up voluntarily as a 15-year-old. He lied about his age and signed up for the Staffs Parachute Regiment. After his training, Wally went into active service and was parachuted into German-occupied France in 1941. On landing awkwardly, he broke his ankle and limped away to hide in a nearby wood.

The Germans eventually captured him and whisked him away to a prisoner-of-war camp. Back home in Dudley, Wally's whereabouts were unknown. His mother eventually received a telegram to say her son was missing in action and presumed dead.

As the war was drawing to a close and the Allied troops advanced into the German heartland, Wally and his fellow prisoners-of-war were taken out of their camp and marched down a dirt track.

They knew not where they were heading. For all they knew, they were being taken away to be shot.

Wally fell behind the line of marchers, struggling to keep up because his broken ankle had not been set properly. Grasping an opportunity to escape his captors, he rolled into a ditch, crawled across a field and found himself in a small German village where a family took him into their home, clothed him, fed him and kept him safe.

Months afterwards, a group of Allied servicemen arrived in the village. Wally stepped out in front of a vehicle, waving his arms and shouting: "I'm English."

He explained his amazing story to the driver who said: "Blimey mate, where are you from?"

"I'm from Dudley," said Wally.

"That's good, maybe you know this bloke then," the driver replied.

Half-asleep, the passenger blinked up from his prone position with his legs up on the dash. "It's the Wall! How're you doing Wally?" Will Keen jumped up in his seat. "Hop on board. We'll give you a ride home to Tipton."

Jimmy had heard this punchline before, many times. He knew it was apocryphal; his dad would have still been a kid when the war ended, but he never had the heart to contradict Wally.

Eyes wide in the dark, sunk deep in his father's battered brown leather chair, Jimmy watched Wally's face lit only by the yellowing bulb of a solitary table lamp.

The years had fallen off the old man and he went quiet; he was back there now, living his past, interrupted only by the occasional sip of whiskey. Jimmy waited, hoping Wally would talk some more about his dad, but his neighbour's soft Birmingham burr was replaced by the purr from the slightest of snores.

Wally was asleep and the ghosts had settled back into his dreams, where his memories were alive again, lost to all but himself.

CHAPTER ELEVEN

Sitting precariously in the attic with his backside on one wooden floor beam and both feet planted across a dirty sea of insulation foam onto another, Jimmy felt the sobs wracking through his body as he delved through his own past in a pile of crumpled cardboard boxes.

He still wasn't crying for his dad; this was for himself, or at least the past versions Jimmy recalled in school books graded in lazy red handwriting, broken plastic trophies and yellowing photo books.

Just as he pulled his emotions back tight, they spilled over again at the sight of a fresh-faced schoolboy in blazer and striped tie, smiling confidently at the camera with all the arrogance of youth. It wasn't the poignancy of the photo that upset Jimmy, more the realisation that the future didn't mean any more than the past at that age. All that mattered was right then. It was only when he was on the downward side of 40 that he started wondering about what might have been. Before that, pretty much anything had seemed possible, even when it was patently clear that it wasn't.

He'd used a tire lever to force the ceiling door to the attic and it popped open in a shower of dust and debris, covering Jimmy and Zoe and the threadbare bedroom carpet. There wasn't a ladder and he had to move a dresser to climb on top and pull himself into the darkness with Zoe nervously watching from below.

"Can you hand me a torch, love?"

He looked down to see his American wife looking blankly back up at him.

"Sorry, I meant flashlight. Have you got one? I can't see a thing up here and if I'm not careful I'll be coming down a lot quicker."

The dim light helped a little. There was no floor but boxes were balanced across the wooden beams right up to the slanted roof.

"I don't think anyone's been up here in years," shouted Jimmy as he caught the sight of a kid's bicycle at the back by some lagged pipes.

"My bike's up here! You know the one I asked dad about for the kids. I knew I hadn't thrown it away like he said." Jimmy looked down but Zoe was gone. He was alone with his memories.

He'd been up there going through his old belongings for a couple of hours, his hair full of cobwebs and tears tracked down his face, when he heard Zoe calling him. He hadn't really done much clearing. If anything, there was more of a mess with the contents of the boxes scattered around him.

"Wally and a few of the lads have come over to help." Jimmy shuffled over so he could see Zoe.

"They thought you might need a hand."

Jimmy looked down to see Wally, who sat down on the bed rubbing his knees, along with Bill from up the road, who was about 5ft. 2ins. tall and wore a one-size-too-big cap covering half his head. Craning his neck, he spotted Brian, the wiry gardener who hated to be cooped up inside and was famous for marching around the neighbourhood whistling late at night. The story went that he'd served time as a young man for assault and had hated being inside ever since. At least he could carry something, thought Jimmy, even if it wasn't a tune.

"Great, thanks lads," he said, self-consciously wiping his face with the back of his sleeve. "If I pass some of these boxes down to you perhaps you can stack them over in the corner."

"I'll bring you boys up some tea and cookies." Zoe left them to it.

As he distilled the boxes down, he decided to keep just one with his old stuff. Marking a bunch for Carl to sort through he finally came to a couple of planks placed across the beams with some old luggage on them that he didn't recognise.

Lugging them nearer to the entrance he took a look inside the biggest one and it was full of really dated, mothballed clothes. They looked drab and grey, perhaps from the 40s or 50s. There was nothing to identify them so he told his ageing helpers to put them with the trash.

Reaching down with the second-to-last case, the bag flipped open just as he was handing it to Brian and the contents rained down on the old man.

There was a bunch of shorts and socks and what looked like a medal hit Brian just above the eye causing him to cry out in alarm. Then a pair of studded boots clobbered him on the head and crashed onto the floor.

A pile of newspaper cuttings pinned together with a giant silver paper clip fluttered down onto the bed and Jimmy picked them up.

They were football reports from the Dudley and the Worcester and Birmingham combined schools teams and at first Jimmy thought they were about him and that his parents must have kept them.

But he quickly saw they dated back to before he was even born. Leafing through them, he also saw they included reports from Manchester United and England matches. Jimmy looked on the floor and saw a box half open with some old photographs spilling out. Almost all of them were of the same footballer, tall and striking with a slight, bemused smile and tousled dark hair atop his side parting.

"That's Duncan Edwards, boy." Wally was leafing through an envelope full of photos. "The great Busby Babe."

Jimmy knew that the Manchester United player had lived in the house before him. It was one of the reasons for his furtive visits to St Francis and his one claim to fame at school, but he couldn't believe the treasure trove of memorabilia had been in his attic all these years.

"The best who ever played the game," said Bill, leaning down to pick up a dusty England football cap. "You can ask anyone who saw him play. Sheer brilliance."

"We all hate Manchester United, always have," Wally took up the story. "But when that lad joined United at 16 or 17 or whatever it was, then all of Dudley became Reds fans. He was that good. I once saw him score four goals for Dudley schools when he was 12-years-old - and he was playing centre-half! He was incredible even then."

"He was 21 when he died with the rest of 'em in the Munich plane crash in '58," chimed in Brian. "I'll never forget hearing about it on the radio. We were sitting in the living room listening to the light program and they interrupted it to make the announcement. It was a national disaster."

Jimmy was trying to scoop up all the mess before Zoe arrived with the tea. "But what's his stuff doing in dad's attic?"

"Don't you know, son?" Wally looked surprised. "I'd always assumed your dad must have told you."

"Told me what?" Jimmy was even more confused. "My dad didn't tell me much about anything."

"You must have known that your mum and dad bought this house from Gladstone and Sarah Edwards, Duncan's parents. The Edwards moved here from number 31, just up the road." He gestured towards the yellow terraced house across the street. "They couldn't bear to live here after he'd gone. Terribly sad."

Wally went quiet for a moment. "Lovely people," he almost whispered. "Lovely."

"I knew he lived in the house, but I don't know why his stuff would be here," said Jimmy, confused.

"Your dad was his best pal, son. They grew up together. He was absolutely broken up when Duncan died."

Jimmy looked closer at a sepia-faded clipping and thought he recognized one of the other boys with Duncan in the 1949 Dudley Boys' team photo. Duncan was looking straight at the camera, tousle-haired and serious faced, with a smaller boy looking up at him with a beaming, adoring smile.

"You know who that is, don't you son?" Wally was leaning over Jimmy's shoulder. "That's your dad."

Stunned, Jimmy looked closer at the other cuttings and saw the same face staring out at him, as if for the first time. The match reports weren't all about Duncan Edwards either. Some of them featured William Keen.

"Will was a fine player, almost as good as our Dunc," said Wally, sitting down on the bed. "I was a good few years older but I remember watching them play together in the old Priory School team in '49. I even played with them a few times over the park when they were teenagers. They'd call me "The Wall"; it was a play on my name, you see. But I was about as fast as a pile of bricks while those two were like terriers, both of them. They'd have that ball off you and in the goal before you knew what day it was."

Jimmy sat down beside Wally, trying to figure out how at the age of 47 he was finding out for the first time that his father was almost the equal of the great Duncan Edwards. He turned to Wally, the tears finally working their way loose. "How come I don't know any of this?"

Wally's eyes suddenly watered up, too, milky tears glistening the deep, baggy lines. "It was all so long ago, Jimmy boy. Remind me to tell you about it before you go." With that, the old man slumped slowly out of the bedroom, one arm over Bill's shoulder, looking every one of his 91 years.

CHAPTER TWELVE

It took three days and an ugly skip parked on the pavement outside the terraced house before the junk was cleared.

"Don't you want to take anything, Carl? There's all your old school reports."

"Why would I want them? They all say the same; lazy, could do better if he tried."

Carl and Sarah had driven back up the previous night from London to check through a few boxes that Jimmy had set aside. It didn't take long. Sarah stuck her nose up and refused to even look, claiming "allergies," and Carl's interest was only piqued very briefly by an old record player and a couple of Rolling Stones LPs.

"Wasn't that yours, Carl? You played that thing to death." Jimmy expected his brother to be excited at the discovery at the back of the attic.

"Yeah, that's why it got dumped up there," said Carl, plugging the power cord into the wall socket. "It stopped working." He clicked the power switch and a red light came on.

"Looks all right to me," said Jimmy.

Carl slowly took one of the records from its sticky sleeve and plonked it carelessly onto the turntable. He lifted the needle and put it on the smoother groove around the platter's outside edge. Nothing moved.

"I told you," said Carl, smirking. "I wanted to throw it away back then after I bought a cassette player but dad said he'd fix it."

"So he put it up there with all the other things he was going to fix," said Sarah. "Can we go and get a drink now? I'm gasping."

"What about that case full of old football stuff from the babe guy?" Zoe had never understood Jimmy and his family's fascination with soccer. "Shall I put that it the trash, too?"

"I was going to keep it." Jimmy looked sheepish. "If that's okay?"

"But how are we going to get it in our cases?" Zoe looked exasperated. "As it is we came over on the cheapest airline and brought carry-ons so we didn't have to pay another fortune on top of the tickets. You know how things are…"

Jimmy gave his wife a sharp look that he instantly regretted as he knew it would upset her. He just didn't want Carl and Sarah to be any more sanctimonious than they already were about his reduced circumstances.

"Tell you what," said Carl, feeling the tension. "I can take them over to the Duncan Edwards museum in town. They'd love to have this stuff and we could get them to write a little card saying it was donated by dad. Kind of like a nice memorial for the old man."

Everyone agreed it was a great idea but Zoe was still confused.

"You mean they have a museum for some soccer player who died at 21? What could he have done by that age?"

"We never had much to shout about in Dudley," said Carl, "but this guy was supposed to be really something. Bobby Charlton said he was the best player he had ever seen bar none."

"Who's Bobby Charlton?" Zoe was suddenly feeling very far from home.

"He's a bald guy who some other people think was the best player that ever lived. He's still involved at United," Jimmy explained patiently.

"Does he still play?" Zoe couldn't understand why the others, Sarah as well, burst into laughter.

"He's about 70 love," said Jimmy, putting his arm around her.

"Well, you're nearly 48 and you think you're still a player." Zoe looked up at him and smiled. Then she leaned over to pick up the old pair of football boots that had fallen out of the case. "I'll chuck these in the skip and we can get that drink. I think we deserve it."

"I'll find room for those in my backpack," said Jimmy, grabbing the boots and looking under the tongue for the size.

"They're so old," said Zoe. "And they're falling apart. We'll get you a new pair, Jimmy. These aren't good for anything." She reached out for the boots but Jimmy wouldn't let her take them.

"Look," he showed Zoe, "they're eleven-and-a-half. They might even fit!"

CHAPTER THIRTEEN

Jimmy peered into the darkness of The Wren's Nest, knowing instinctively where to find Wally, Bill and Brian huddled on stools at the end of the bar. The old pub on Priory Street had seen better days and the younger clientele had long abandoned it for a gastro pub just up the road. The worn red tapestry carpet had turned orange with age and there was a faint smell of toilets. Nicotine-stained net curtains hung limply across windows that were rusted closed and hadn't been opened in decades, but Jimmy felt strangely reassured by the familiar grunge. His father had been one of the ageing statues propping up the bar, ever present following the death of his wife. Everything else in life moved on but The Wren's Nest remained resolutely in the past, as did all of the conversations there.

"It was like the ball was tied to his foot with a piece of string," said Wally, lost in his story. "He must have beaten three or four players before he was even out of his own half and then he put his head down, I can remember like it was yesterday. He put his head down and hit that ball so hard I thought it was going to break into a million pieces."

Bill and Brian looked gobsmacked, even though they must surely have heard the story a hundred times.

"Everyone on the touchline was craning their necks watching the arc of the ball through the clouds. It went so high you couldn't see it for a moment and then it dropped out of the sky," continued Wally, his head moving in time with his mind's eye. "The keeper was a tall lad, probably 6 foot one, which was tall for those days, and he never saw it coming. There was a shout from one of the coaches and he looked around just in time to see the ball landing behind him, right on his goal-line, and bounce into the net. It was the most incredible thing I've ever seen on a football pitch. I'll never forget it."

Wally hadn't seen Jimmy coming over. He wore a pair of specs but they'd been calibrated to his last optical exam a couple of decades earlier and required holding anything an inch or two away to be discernible at all.

Bill and Brian smiled at Jimmy and Wally turned around, peering into the near darkness that always reigned in The Wren's Nest.

"Are you talking about Duncan Edwards, Wally?" Jimmy could see the old man relax when he knew who it was?

"Jimmy?" Wally reached out a hand to reassure himself.

"Yeah, Zoe wanted me to let you know lunch'll be on the table in a couple of minutes." They'd downed a quick glass of wine at the gastro pub. Even Zoe, who felt comfortable in any company anywhere, couldn't quite face a drink at The Wren's Nest. Jimmy wasn't even sure they sold anything but a pint of mild.

"Oh! Okay lad. We'll be right there. Just let me finish this last drop of mild." He picked up his half-pint glass and downed a backwash of murky brown liquid. "We were just taking a little trip down memory lane."

"It must have been amazing to have actually seen Duncan Edwards in action." There was some old black-and-white footage of the Manchester United legend on YouTube and Jimmy had seen most of it over the years, but it didn't really do him justice. "It sounds like he could do some amazing things with the ball."

"He could indeed, Jim old son." Wally's watery eyes dimmed again, looking inward. "One of the best there ever was, maybe the best of them all." The other two old men sagely nodded their heads in unison.

"But I wasn't talking about Duncan then, Jimmy. We was talking about your old man when he was playing for Dudley schools."

Jimmy was exasperated. "How come I didn't know my dad had ever played for Dudley Schools, even though I played for Dudley Schools, and then twice in two days I hear how good he was?"

"He didn't like us to talk about it," said Wally. "But now he's gone, well, it seemed a good time to remember what old Will could do."

"So what could my dad do then Wally?" Jimmy sat on an empty stool. "Tell me."

"After he got injured he didn't like to be reminded," said Wally. "Gladstone and Sarah, Duncan's parents, were also at that game I was talking about. They were standing right next to me, they were." Wally went quiet for a moment, lost in the memory. "Duncan was the same age as your dad and they absolutely adored each other. Like I told you earlier, they were great pals."

Jimmy was trying to process this new information. Had his dad never told him because he'd never asked? Or was there some other reason he'd kept his friendship with one of the greatest footballers in history from his football-loving son?

"Why didn't he ever say anything?" Jimmy asked Wally. "Something…anything?"

"He wasn't one to show off," Bill interjected. "That's how he played, too. He didn't like to talk about it; he let his feet do all the talking."

"You knew all this as well, Bill?"

"Of course. Brian and me were at the Dudley schools game Wally was talking about. Brian was one of his coaches."

"So everybody knew all this except me?"

"It was a long time ago." Wally's voice was so soft Jimmy hardly heard him. "Such a long time ago."

"But my dad could play like Duncan Edwards? That's what you're telling me."

"He could, son," said Wally. "But we never really knew for sure."

"What do you mean? You all saw him, didn't you?"

"We did. Yes, we did and it was special." Wally suddenly looked every one of his advancing years. "But he was injured in the game after that one. A horrible knee ligament injury; went down like he'd been shot. It was different in those days. They couldn't fix that stuff like they can now. He never played another match and he would never hear a word about it. All he cared about was Duncan and then about you."

Wally creaked off his stool and reached unsteadily for his jacket hanging on a peg behind him. "Then Duncan died and you got yourself injured down in London. He wouldn't talk about it after that. Too many memories, too much heartbreak and now he's gone, God rest his soul."

Wally brightened. "Maybe he's up there right now, playing football with Duncan, just the two of them like they was in your back garden; all that youth and promise.

"Now, where's that lunch? Nothing like funeral leftovers…"

CHAPTER FOURTEEN

There wasn't much more they could do in Dudley; Carl and Sarah had already arranged for the house to be put up for sale and they all had to leave early the following morning because Jimmy had promised to take Tyler and Grace to a football match before they flew home.

The choice of a match to watch hadn't gone down well with Wally.

"Your dad would have wanted you to take the kids to the Hawthorns. Just because your brother's gone all soft down south doesn't mean you have to." The old man was still arguing as the family climbed into their rented Ford Mondeo.

"I told you Wally, I still support West Brom and I always will but Carl's got us all tickets to see West Ham against Manchester United," said Jimmy. "He's a season ticket holder and we've got great seats down by the halfway line. It's their last home game at Upton Park. There will be fireworks for the kids."

"It's not right son. Your father'll be turning in his grave." Wally hugged Zoe and the kids and stood waving them goodbye with Bill and Brian as Jimmy pulled out into the street.

"Don't be a stranger," he shouted after them. "You all know where I live."

Carl and Sarah had gone ahead to pick up their kids from a sleepover. Sarah and her youngest, Emma, were going shopping later with Zoe and Charley while the dads took the older kids to the football.

"Why do you go all quiet with Wally when he talks about your dad like that?" asked Zoe as they battled through the Midlands traffic.

"I don't want to upset him." Jimmy was lost in his own thoughts.

"What do you mean? He just likes to talk. It probably makes him feel better about losing his best friend." Zoe didn't like things to go unsaid. She was all about getting all the emotions out in the open. Most of the time Jimmy didn't mind; the fact that it was so much the opposite to what he'd grown up with at home was, after all, one of the attractions. But sometimes Jimmy wished she'd just let things go, especially when it came to his family.

"I know, but he talks about dad and West Brom as if we'd been there every Saturday like some happy family. Dad didn't take me even though he went to every single home game with his mates, and he never came to watch me play. He didn't even want to sign the papers allowing me to go down to Leyton Orient, like they were beneath him."

"I know, Jimmy. But old people like to remember the good things." Zoe put her hand over Jimmy's.

"That's why I don't say anything," said Jimmy. "And to think that my dad was best friends with Duncan Edwards and I didn't even know. That just kills me. We never talked about anything."

"Nobody knows this Duncan guy, sugar. It was so long ago. Your parents probably didn't know who he was either." Zoe squeezed Jimmy's hand, trying to reassure him. She hated seeing him like this and it had been happening more and more lately. The spark that she loved about him; the confident glint in his eye; it had been dulled by worry and she felt helpless to bring it back.

"Dad would have known for sure how much it would have meant to me. I knew the story. Every football fan knows about the Busby Babes and the Munich air crash and everyone back home knew we were living in Duncan's old house, but my dad wouldn't talk about it. He said that was all in the past. Imagine if I'd known as a kid that Duncan Edwards and my dad were close?"

Jimmy edged onto the crawling southbound lane of the M1 motorway and tried to shake off his past.

"But you know what really got me?" he turned to Zoe. "Wally kept saying how dad was always telling everybody how good I was. He never told me that, not once."

CHAPTER FIFTEEN

Jimmy had forgotten why people ever ate hot dogs. Walking down Green Street towards the Boleyn Ground and catching a whiff of the fried onions from the stands lining the crowded street his mouth started watering and he found himself asking the kids if they were hungry.

"We just had dinner, dad," said Grace. "How can you want more food? I'm so full."

"Can't you smell those hot dogs?"

"I thought you hated hot dogs," said Tyler. "You never let us have them because you say they're full of cardboard."

"That's your mother."

"You, too," said Grace, in rare agreement with her brother.

"Okay, okay, but can't you smell them? That's the smell of Saturday afternoon football right there."

"But dad, it's Tuesday night."

"Whatever, I'm getting a hot dog."

They'd arrived early for the game to avoid the traffic but the streets all around the ground were full of chanting Hammers fans. Jimmy didn't care what anyone said; he was having a hot dog and he joined a long line waiting patiently in the evening drizzle outside a bed store. When he asked this time, everybody wanted one.

The drab shops, their white walls blurred dirty grey by years of decay, were at odds with the bright uniforms of the fans outside. The odd red-shirted Manchester United fan walked by but the whole area was awash with claret and blue. Jimmy thought the kids would be intimidated by the noise and the dirty streets and the edgy excitement in the air, but they didn't seem fazed.

"It looks like people started drinking early tonight," said Carl, pulling his daughter, Jade, out of the street. "Stay close to us, kids," he shouted over the soccer chants.

Just then a big black coach rounded the corner mobbed by rowdy fans banging on the sides and jeering. There was the sound of glass breaking as bottles and other missiles were lobbed at the roof.

"I think it's the United players' coach." Jimmy said. "Let's get out of here." He grabbed Tyler and Grace by the arm and tried to push them away from the road towards a side street. It was impossible to get across to the stadium entrance. Carl and Jade followed but the crowd was surging the opposite direction towards the bus.

Grace fell and Jimmy lost hold of her. Unable to reach him as she tried to get back on her feet, Grace screamed out, "Dad! I can't get up."

Jimmy could hear Grace but he couldn't see her. "Grace! Grace!"

"Dad! Dad! Where are you?"

There was a ripple in the crowd and both Carl and Jimmy were trying to push back while still keeping hold of Tyler and

Jade. Jimmy could see a bigger man heading towards them from where Grace fell.

Bottles were being hurled over their heads, hitting the side of the coach and smashing in the road and Jimmy was getting increasingly desperate. They were hemmed in, unable to move. "My daughter," he shouted at the top of his lungs. "Grace!"

The crowd parted and a bald man, tattooed to the top of his neck and wearing a West Ham shirt, was carrying Grace, her hands wrapped around his shoulders. "Here you go, mate. Here she is. She's golden."

Jimmy reached out gratefully and Grace climbed into his arms. She was upset but otherwise unhurt. "Thank God." He turned to thank the stranger. He was gone but they were able to edge back the way he'd come to break free from the melee just as a squad of riot police moved in.

Jimmy, Carl and the kids watched from a safer distance as the United coach was finally allowed to finish its journey to the stadium a few hundred yards away. Grace seemed none the worse for her scare.

"Give it a minute to settle down and we can go in and sort out our seats," said Carl. "It's not normally like this."

"How long before kick-off," asked Tyler.

"Why do you want to know?" asked Jimmy. "Are you looking forward to the game?"

"I am," said Tyler, "but I was hoping we'd still have time to get that hot dog."

CHAPTER SIXTEEN

"I'm forever blowing bubbles, pretty bubbles in the air,
They fly so high, nearly reach the sky
Then like my dreams they fade and die
Fortune's always hiding, I've looked everywhere
I'm forever blowing bubbles
Pretty bubbles in the air.
UNITED! UNITED!"

Carl had been drilling the kids on the words of the West Ham United anthem and even gave Tyler and Grace a lyric sheet to study on the way down from the Black Country. As a lifelong West Bromwich Albion supporter, Jimmy didn't know quite what to make of it, but he looked along the line of seats at the Boleyn Ground to see his two children, and Carl and Jade all singing their hearts out. The noise was deafening and Jimmy's eyes prickled in spite of himself.

"Incredible atmosphere." Carl shouted across to his brother.

Jimmy felt a tug at his sleeve. "So this is the last game ever for West Ham?" asked Grace with a frown. "What will they do?"

"It's not the last game for the players; it's the last game here at this ground.The club's moving to a bigger stadium not far away."

Grace clearly wasn't pleased with his explanation. "I don't want them to leave."

"A lot of people here probably feel the same," he said, putting a hand on her shoulder, "But I'm sure they'll be okay. They really want to beat Manchester United."

"Are they the ones in red?" she said, clapping as a buzz reverberated around the stadium with the referee's whistle starting the game.

Tyler leaned over to tell Jimmy that the visitors were looking good. "Why are they booing Wayne Rooney?" he added, but the answer never came. Everyone bar the fans in red in the Sir Trevor Brooking Stand were on their feet. West Ham were one up.

Ten minutes in and the Hammers were in charge. Carl smiled at Jimmy with a two thumbs up. Now their father really would be turning in his grave. Jimmy felt guilty just being there. He tried not to appear too enthusiastic but the kids were loving every second.

At 20 minutes, Carl, his face ruddy with excitement, said: "We should be five up by now. They've barely had a touch."

"Will West Ham be moving to West Brom?" Grace's brow was furrowed with concentration. "That would make sense, wouldn't it, dad? Then you could support them, as well."

"It doesn't really work like that," said Jimmy.

"But they're both from the West. They must be close together, right?"

Jimmy leaned over and hugged Grace. It was the best reply he could think of. Looking at his daughter's innocent, intent face he was overcome with emotion. He bowed his head so she wouldn't see his damp eyes, but it wasn't quite in time.

"You okay, dad?" Grace looked worried.

"I'm fine, sugar. Honestly, I just got something in my eye." Jimmy smiled, but he couldn't quite shake off the sense that he was somehow failing his family. His helplessness, his inability to earn enough to pay the bills to raise his family; the despair washed over him as it so often did these days. The players were out for the second half and a loud whistle punctuated the songs from the crowd.

"Is it because you're missing grandpa?" Grace asked. She paused and turned her head back towards the pitch before adding softly: "I miss him, too."

Moments later Grace was back on her feet. "Goal!" Her clear, high voice rang across the silent terrace.

"Sit down, Grace." Tyler grabbed his sister's arm and pulled her back into her seat. "Man United scored, not West Ham."

"Oops, sorry."

They may have moved a long way from Dudley, all the way to California. But Grace's big loopy smile reminded Jimmy just when he needed it the most that none of it really mattered as long as his family was together.

He looked back down the line to see Carl gesturing to him.

"You okay?" Carl said.

"Yeah, of course, just had something in my eye."

"That's good, I was going to ask if you wanted a game with the boys on Sunday but not if you're getting all soft," said Carl. "The legend of Jimmy Keen, the Eric Cantona of Sunday football, will be shot forever."

CHAPTER SEVENTEEN

Jimmy was having trouble reaching his borrowed boots to tie them up. He could feel every muscle in his back shriek the further he reached towards his laces.

"LA life been good to you, then?" Alf Larcombe was the tough as nails right half for Plaistow Irons FC of the East London Conference League. "Looking a bit soft around the middle, Jim. All those burgers and pizzas."

The changing rooms at the Manor Park Recreation Ground smelled like a mixture of urine, horse liniment, sweaty armpits and the previous night's curry.

"It's good to be home," Jimmy smiled up at the muscled, greying welder. "Not suspended then, Alfie? I heard you were out for 10 games for having a whack at the ref."

"Finished last month. I'm on my best behaviour now, aren't I. Been playing in this league for 30 years — they're giving me a medal if I can stay out of trouble until the end of the season."

Balancing on the wooden bench to wind duct tape above and below his shin pads, Alf was suddenly shoved from behind by a balding giant with scouring brush stubble. "No chance of that, mate. You've got as much chance of staying clean as I have of winning the world limbo championships."

"Hello Colin! Long time no see." Jimmy stuck out his hand and it disappeared inside his friend's huge mitt.

"Yeah well who's the one who deserted us in the middle of our best ever cup run to piss off to America then? Now nobody can shut Carl up."

"Give it a rest, Col." Carl was pulling on his shorts across the room. "If you played half as tough as you talked we'd be unbeatable. Since you left, Jim, Colin's been taking the corners. I ask you, why is the tallest bloke on the team taking the corners."

"Because he can't head the ball," piped up Nigel, the polo-playing goalkeeper.

"Fair point," said Colin, "but at least I don't have to stop to comb my hair every time I touch the ball."

"At least I have hair, unlike some I could mention." Nigel's green kit was ironed immaculately. He was putting a glob of gel in his jet black, perfectly manicured locks.

"Well, I can see nothing has changed here." With one last tummy lunge Jimmy pulled the bow tight on his bright Orange Nikes and jumped up. "I feel like a bloody clown in these."

"You got the right boots then," said Dave, the captain. "We don't want none of that fancy stuff today, Jim. Just get rid of it, preferably in the direction of their goal."

"Alright, Dave." They bumped fists. Dave was Jimmy's closest friend from their comprehensive school days and they'd kept in touch. He was the only one other than Carl who knew life wasn't exactly roses in California.

"Just give me the ball, mate. Let me do my magic."

"With my eyes, I'll be lucky if I can see who wins the toss." Dave's age - he was 47, the same as Jimmy - was a running joke with the team. Every game brought a new ailment.

"It was your knees last week," said Colin.

"Them as well. But I don't need them to toss a coin, do I?"

The referee popped his head around the door. He looked about 12. "Okay then lads, let's be having yer."

The players groaned out onto the muddy pitch. Carl jogged up to Jimmy. "Enjoy the Hammers game. Jim? The kids are still raving about it."

"It was all right."

"All right! It was bloody wonderful. 3-2 against Man United on the last game ever at Upton Park. Bloody brilliant it was."

Jimmy was determined to brighten up. Carl was right. The kids had loved it. "Yeah, yeah, Carl, it was pretty good, I'll give you that."

Carl smiled, always the younger brother looking for approval.

"What I wouldn't give to be playing out on that pitch rather than this shit-hole. Look at the mud bath in the goalmouth." Jimmy pointed to the end of the pitch, one of about half a dozen lined up across the windy park, each one as poorly maintained as the next.

"This is pretty good compared to last week at the Hackney Marshes. We almost drowned," said Carl, pulling his shirt out of his shorts and tapping a spare ball towards Jimmy. "How's Grace doing?"

"Not great." Grace had been sick since the morning after the West Ham game. "She was throwing up half the night again. Tough leaving her really but Zoe said I should come. The other kids seem okay."

Dave ran back from the centre circle. "Lost the toss. We're playing into the wind; we've gotta swap ends. You okay up front, Jim? We'll need some goals to beat this mob."

Jimmy was glad he'd played a few times with the FOBD in California but the first tackle reminded him this was a very different proposition. He trapped a pass from Carl with his back to goal just outside the penalty box and his legs were scythed away from him almost immediately.

Jimmy screamed in pain and rolled over clutching his ankles. He looked up to see the game had moved on. No ref's whistle, no team doctor rushing on to check if anything was broken.

"Jim, get up," Tim, the brickie who played left midfield, shouted at him. "We need a little help here."

"But my ankles…"

"Anything broken?"

"No, but…"

"Well, get up you lazy bastard. We're getting overrun."

Either the game was much faster than Jimmy remembered or he was slowing down. He just couldn't get a fix on the ball.

When it did finally land in front of him inside the box he snatched at his shot and it flew a mile over the bar.

They went into the dressing room at half-time 2-0 down and Jimmy could feel the accusing eyes wondering what had happened to the Irons legendary goalscorer. "Sorry lads, I'm a little rusty," he said to nobody in particular.

"Don't worry," said Colin, bending down to get in the door. "It's not like we've got any subs."

Dave's two daughters handed out some oranges and slapped down the lads trying to chat them up while their dad delivered his version of a team talk.

"We need to get more stuck in. We're losing far too many 50:50 balls. And Gerry, for God's sake man, stop being a wanker and punting the ball up the pitch every time you get it. We've gotta give Jimmy some kind of service up there. Col, you're tip-toeing around like a big fucking fairy. How many times do I have to tell you to throw your weight around out there. You should be bossing it."

He put an arm around Jimmy's shoulders as they walked back out. "Just relax, mate. I'll make sure you get the ball and you make sure you put it in the net. Keep it simple."

This time when the centre back came for him Jimmy was ready. He let the ball run past him and sidestepped the lunge. In one quick movement he was the other side of the defence with just the keeper to beat. He thought for a moment about dribbling around him — it was what he always used to do — but the fear of failure hung over him, even there. He picked a spot in the corner and put his head down to shoot. By this time the goalie was so close there was no way around him. An outstretched boot sent the ball spinning sideways into the mud where it stuck, waiting for the keeper to pick it up and thump back down the field.

Jimmy was having trouble keeping up and the one-size-too-small boots were crushing his toes. The football pitch was always the one place he could forget all his worries and just play. But with every lost opportunity he felt increasingly down, as if the game he loved was mirroring the life he was trying to escape.

There was one bright spark towards the end. He chested the ball down, pretended to go one way and cheated to the other, hitting the ball low into the corner of the unguarded net. They did the old Eric Cantona kung fu celebration but it felt hollow. The Irons were five down at the time and it wasn't much of a consolation. Even his teammates looked like they were going through the motions. Jimmy was just happy when the final whistle blew.

Perhaps I'm just too old, he thought. They were flying back to the States the following day. He decided not to return to the Field of Broken Dreams on Sunday. He'd broken enough already.

CHAPTER EIGHTEEN

The arguments had started long before they got to Gatwick Airport. He'd persuaded Zoe and the kids to bring carry-ons to save money with the Scandinavian airline that charged for every bag, drink and packet of peanuts. They even had to pay to reserve seats next to one another.

"You can't bring them, Jimmy. Not when Charley's having to leave her sneakers behind because you're so paranoid about the extra weight. We're all wearing two jackets, for heaven's sake."

Jimmy wanted to take the football boots he found in his dad's attic back with him. "But honey, they belonged to Duncan Edwards."

"I don't care if they belonged to David Beckford or Beckham or whatever his name is, there's no room for them. You want the kids to dump stuff that belongs to them and for you to fill up half a case with a smelly old pair of cleats sworn by some soccer player nobody's ever heard of." Zoe's patience with Jimmy was fast running out. "I just don't understand you these days. All that fuss about just bringing the essentials and now this. It just doesn't make any sense."

Jimmy had insisted, the kids had complained and Zoe had finally relented with a compromise — if Jimmy wanted the old boots so much he'd have to wear them around his neck and Charley would bring her sneakers home in the luggage.

Grace had stopped vomiting but the little girl was a pale shadow of her usual tanned, bubbly self. She slept most of the flight, as did an exhausted Zoe and Charley and Tyler, who were both unusually quiet, more than likely fighting off the same bug.

Jimmy was wide awake trying to work out in his head how they were going to pay the next month's rent with credit cards that were already right up to their limits. By the time the plane was taxiing to the gate at LAX, he'd drunk the bottle of Belvedere that Zoe bought at duty free.

On the shuttle home from the airport, Grace could barely open her eyes and Jimmy finally fell asleep. Zoe had to shake both awake when they stopped outside the house.

"Jimmy! Jim! I'm worried about Grace. She won't wake up."

Jimmy forced his own eyes open and turned his head so Zoe couldn't smell his breath. "Don't worry, babe. She's probably just tired from the flight. She'll be okay"

"She slept the whole flight. And the way there and the way back in the shuttle. She hasn't said a word since we left London. I'm really worried." Zoe pushed the hair out of her face and Jimmy couldn't help thinking how beautiful she looked.

Her eyes brimming with tears, Zoe insisted: "We've got to take her to the hospital. We probably shouldn't have taken her on the flight. We should have waited."

"It's fine, baby. Don't worry." Tyler and Charley were looking scared now. Grace was laying lifeless on the couch. "Sleep will help get back her strength."

"Jimmy, she's been sleeping for the last four days, pretty much non-stop. There's something wrong. She won't eat or drink anything."

Zoe leaned over to put a cushion under Grace's head. The stuffed toy bison the little girl was holding dropped to the floor and she made no attempt to pick it up.

"Okay, okay, it'll be okay." Jimmy pulled Zoe to him in a bear hug. "I'll take her over to Hoag Hospital and get her checked out. Just to be sure." Even as he was saying it he was wondering how they were going to pay the medical bill without insurance.

"I'm coming with you. I'll get Nancy in from next door to look after Tyler and Charley. We need to go." Zoe was already on the phone.

Jimmy carried Grace out to the truck and lay her on the bench seat. Moments later, Zoe squeezed in next to her and put her daughter's head on her lap. "She's burning up," she said, looking over, a hint of panic in her voice.

"We'll be there in just a couple of minutes." Jimmy pulled out into the busy evening traffic.

"Hurry. Please Jimmy, I'm really worried."

Jimmy shuffled through the traffic trying to find the fastest route. Seeing a gap he edged right into the slow lane without checking his mirror. In England, it was illegal to pass on the inside but a sickening metal thud reminded him too late that such a law didn't exist in the United States.

"Shit!" The open-top Mercedes trying to pass had been shunted off the road and plowed into the front of an Italian restaurant. Luckily the people lining up to get in were on the other side of the entrance.

"Shit, shit, shit."

Zoe screamed as Grace, who wasn't wearing a belt, slid onto the floor. She hardly reacted at all. She wasn't hurt but she was still half asleep.

"What are we going to do?" Zoe looked to Jimmy for an answer he didn't have.

The Mercedes driver, who only looked about 20, was climbing out of the driver's seat and looked uninjured. Jimmy checked again that no pedestrians or diners had been hit. He looked in the wing mirror. No cars. He gunned the accelerator pedal and hurtled up the street. He'd have to sort out this mess later.

The hospital was only five minutes away and the traffic miraculously cleared to make it a straight run. Pulling up outside the entrance, Jimmy left the engine running and carried Grace into the ER with Zoe holding her hand by his side.

Just for once, there was no waiting and the triage nurse quickly directed them to a bed and had Grace hooked up to a saline drip. They stood on either side of the bed to wait for the doctor. After about five minutes, Grace opened her eyes and said: "Dad, I'm worried about the homeless West Ham players." She drifted off and whispered: "We should let them live with us." Then she closed her eyes again, a slight smile playing on her lips.

Jimmy went around the bed and hugged Zoe. "I told you it would be okay."

She brushed back tears with the sleeve of her jacket. "Yeah, but what about you? The cops will be after you. I saw that guy writing down our license plate as we drove off."

"I suppose I'd better sort that out now. Are you okay here?" Jimmy looked in Zoe's eyes. "I don't care what happens as long as you and the kids are okay."

He squeezed Grace's hand, kissed Zoe on the lips and went off to call the police.

CHAPTER NINETEEN

Jimmy was back a few minutes later. With a police officer.

Zoe, stunned, raised her hands to her mouth. "What's happening?"

"He's let me come over to give you the car keys." Jimmy turned around to show his wife the handcuffs. "Can you get them out of my pocket."

"But you called them," she said, her eyes filling with tears. "Officer, he had to get our daughter to hospital. It was an emergency."

The male cop stood impassive by the door. Zoe could see a second officer, a woman, further down the corridor.

"It wasn't that, babe." Jimmy's voice was flat and unemotional. "They were okay with the hit and run. I explained all that."

"So why are you in handcuffs?"

He shrugged. "They breathalysed me. I'm getting done for drunk driving."

"But how?"

"The booze on the plane."

"What booze? We slept the entire journey, pretty much."

"I couldn't sleep. Ended up drinking the vodka."

"What vodka?" Zoe was looking more and more confused and upset. "What's going on?"

"The Belvedere you bought at Duty Free, Zoe. That vodka. I drank it on the plane but I never thought I was going to drive, did I?"

"Why would you drink the whole bottle? I don't understand." Zoe put her head in her hands. "I can't deal with this, not now."

Just then the doctor came in to check on Grace.

The cop finally moved. He gestured with his head that Jimmy had to go with them. "You'll be able to pick him up from the station on Jamboree Road in the morning, ma'am," he said, taking Jimmy by the arm and leading him out.

"How's my daughter?" Jimmy asked as he left.

"She's going to be fine," the doctor replied, seemingly unmoved by the drama in the room. "She just got dehydrated on the flight. Once she's got sufficient fluids in her she'll be back to normal. We'll probably keep her on the drip overnight to be certain. You may even be able to take her home in a couple of hours. Well, your wife can take her…"

Jimmy looked back at Zoe hoping to catch her eye.

But she was tucking in the blankets on Grace's bed and didn't look round.

CHAPTER TWENTY

The desk sergeant gave Jimmy back his cellphone along with a pile of legal looking papers after waking him in the drunk tank and telling him he was free to go. He tried not to think about how much this was all going to cost.

Jimmy had spent most of the night worrying over how he was going to explain drinking the bottle of Belvedere to Zoe. It was so out of character. He didn't even drink vodka. Jimmy tried to rationalise it in his frazzled mind. He hadn't really mourned his dad's death, not properly. So many mixed emotions and he was returning to more doubts and questions over his future in California. He felt irrelevant. Lost. He'd started the bottle and it had seemed easier to finish it than to stop.

Walking out into the bright sunlight, Jimmy blanched and covered his eyes, squinting out into the parking lot hoping Zoe might be there. He tried to turn the phone on to call an Uber but the battery was dead. *I guess I'll walk then*, he said out loud.

Forty-five minutes later, he got back to the apartment to find the front door locked. The cops had impounded his car but gave him his key ring and he opened the door to find everything as it was when they'd left for the hospital the previous night; cases abandoned in the hallway, a mound of unopened mail on the side table and Grace's stuffed bison lying upside down by the empty couch. The ancient football boots were next to it, their thick, flat laces ribboned across the fake wood floor.

"Zoe!" Jimmy shouted, thinking they'd perhaps gone straight to bed, exhausted.

"Tyler! Charley!" He paused. "Grace!"

There was no reply. He ran up the stairs but it didn't look like anyone had been up there since they'd left for England.

"Zoe!"

It was still 6.30am and he hadn't wanted to wake up Nancy, their neighbour, but there wasn't a lot of choice. The lights were all out and Nancy's front door was locked. He tried the doorbell and then hammered on the window, softly at first and then more urgently. There was no sign of life.

Jimmy suppressed a growing panic. *Had Zoe left him and taken the kids?*

The only thing he could think of to do was to walk to the hospital, which was a couple of minutes in the car but a good 30 minutes away on foot, and see if Zoe was still there with Grace.

Jimmy suddenly felt terribly alone. Back home he had family and friends he could always call on in an emergency. People were there for him and he was there for them. Here, he wasn't so sure. He had nobody outside his family…and now he wasn't even sure he had them.

The more Jimmy walked, the more he worried. The money problems had put a strain on his marriage that was never there before. It was quite possible that Zoe had finally given up on him. What use did she have for a jobless, failed footballer? His mind raced through all the possible explanations for her absence and they were all bad.

By the time he reached the ER at Hoag Hospital he was convinced that Zoe had gone back to live with her parents and taken the children.

Jimmy was surprised when the reception nurse looked so pleased to see him after he told her who he was looking for.

"They're waiting for you inside," she said. Leaving a line of people waiting by her window, she came around and led Jimmy through the double doors towards the room where Grace was being treated the previous night.

At the other end of the corridor, he saw Zoe and the kids sitting on a bench. Nancy and Zoe's parents were standing up talking to them. The moment Zoe saw Jimmy she got up and ran towards him, throwing her arms around his neck.

"It's okay," he said. "Everything's going to be okay." He hugged her tightly, really believing it for the first time in a long while.

"No," she sobbed into his shirt. "It's not."

An icy realisation shot down Jimmy's spine. The kids, Zoe's parents, it didn't add up.

"Where's Grace?"

"The doctors are in with her now doing more tests." Zoe could barely speak she was crying so much.

"What do you mean tests?" Jimmy fought to keep his legs from buckling. "What tests?"

"It's Grace," said Zoe. "They think they've found a melanoma."

"Melanoma? Is that bad?"

"It's cancer, Jimmy. They think Grace has skin cancer."

CHAPTER TWENTY-ONE

Grace was sitting up in bed when Jimmy and Zoe were finally allowed in to see her. She looked tiny in the frigid room filled with metal apparatus and white sterility. She smiled bravely as her parents hugged her. Only her eyes gave her away; they were wet with tears but Jimmy saw behind them to the terror she was trying desperately to hide.

"Can we go home now?" she said softly.

"Not yet baby," said Zoe and Jimmy marvelled at his wife's strength. She appeared calm and unworried although he knew she was unraveling inside. "The doctors say they need to do a little operation."

"But dad…" Grace turned to Jimmy. "Please take me home. I'm fine, honest. I don't feel hot any more. I'm not tired, I promise."

There was nothing Jimmy wanted more than to sweep his daughter in his arms and take her far, far away from this hospital and this life. But he knew running away wasn't an option when a tumour was growing on your daughter's skin like a ticking time bomb. "It'll be over before you know it, Gracie. We just have to let the docs do their thing and then we'll get you back home as soon as we can. I promise."

He could see any hopes Grace was clinging onto that she could wake from the nightmare evaporate that moment.

"It's going to be fine, I promise you. Don't worry."

But Grace had given up any pretence of stoicism and buried her head in her mother's arms.

The oncologist had spoken earlier to Jimmy and Zoe after leaving Grace's room. The tumour had been discovered by chance when an ER nurse who fitted the saline drip noticed a mole on the little girl's back.

"Something about the look and the feel of the blemish worried her," he told them. "It really was just a hunch but a biopsy shows it to be a rare and aggressive form of melanoma.

"She's really lucky," he told them. "It has been growing really fast and, if left untreated, would have spread to other parts of the body. We're waiting to find out for sure, but we don't think that's happened.

"So what are her chances?" Zoe squeezed Jimmy's hand and held tight.

"Good," said the specialist. "Very good, in fact. She's young and we've caught it early. I really don't think her tiredness yesterday had anything to do with it. That was just dehydration caused by the virus. But we should go in as early as possible to see what's going on. With luck, we can get it all out before any real damage is done."

"And if we don't?" The thought of his little girl in the operating theatre all alone was killing Jimmy. "What will happen if we just take her home?"

"Maybe nothing right now," said the oncologist. "But a melanoma can spread very rapidly. Everything may remain completely normal for a while but left untreated the cancer will grow and it will become harder and harder for us to do anything about it."

They all fell silent. There was another issue that neither Jimmy or Zoe wanted to raise right then but Zoe asked anyway.

"Do you know how much it's likely to cost?"

"Well, it's not for me to discuss, to be honest." The specialist squirmed. "The billing department is on the 2nd floor."

"Can you give us an idea?"

"It depends on a number of things. You have medical insurance I hope?"

"We do, but we recently downgraded it to emergencies only. There's a $10,000 deductible." Zoe hadn't told Jimmy they couldn't afford the higher premiums.

"There will be the surgery and we may have to follow it up with radiation treatments." The oncologist started edging away. "Would you like to take a little time to think?"

"No," said Jimmy. "We'll sort out the money. You just take care of our Grace. That's the only important thing right now." He smiled at his wife and held her hand as the oncologist backed off down the corridor.

"Is it okay if we go in and see her now?" Zoe asked the nurse.

CHAPTER TWENTY-TWO

The alert chimed on Jimmy's phone but by the time he'd stopped washing the dishes and dried his hands a second text was coming through.

Can I have a drink of water? :)

No, make that a cuppa t

Grace had taken to texting her demands from her bedroom where she was well on her way to recovery three weeks after the melanoma was removed.

"Give me a minute, Grace," Jimmy yelled up the stairs. "Make that five minutes."

But dad, the text came through, *I'm Thursday*

"Thirsty!" shouted Jimmy.

No - it's Friday :0)

Just then, Tyler and Charley burst in the front door, both throwing their backpacks on the floor and demanding snacks.

"I hate carpool," said Charley, "Ashleigh's mum is so mean. She told Tyler to turn off his phone because he was watching a surfing video and didn't answer her and she had a go at me because I don't play lacrosse. I hate lacrosse."

Tyler grunted hi and sat down still staring at the screen on his iPhone. "They're streaming the Pipeline Masters," he said without looking up. "It's awesome - some Brazilian just broke his board."

Jimmy's phone was buzzing every few seconds now. Grace was getting too used to having a servant, he thought.

"Tea anybody? Cold drink? Fruit? Cookies?"

"Cookies," Tyler and Charley shouted in unison.

"Your mum told me not to give you cookies."

"But you asked…" Charley wasn't going to let him get away with anything.

I'll have a cookie as well plse, Grace texted.

"Grace, if you can hear why don't you just tell me and stop with the texting." Jimmy could feel his hackles rising. He wasn't cut out to be a full-time carer.

I can't hear you

Jimmy sorted out Tyler and Charley with tea and cookies and insisted they started their homework before taking a snack upstairs for Grace. She couldn't have looked more different from the distraught little girl in the hospital a few short weeks earlier. Her white pillows were plumped up behind her, a yellow daisy-covered duvet was pulled up to her waist and Snoop was curled at her feet. She was reading a book and the branches of an orange tree pressed against the window behind her.

About time!

"How did you do that?" Jimmy spluttered.

Grace lifted her phone up from behind the book and laughed, throwing her head back like she didn't have a care in the world. If it wasn't for the wad of gauze bandaged on her back Jimmy could have fooled himself into believing the family's world hadn't been turned inside out since they returned from England.

"How are you feeling?" Jimmy sat down on the side of the bed and fended off the dog.

"I'm good." She smiled. "The doctors said it's all gone, right?"

"They were really happy with how it went and the way you've been so brave." Jimmy put his open right hand to the side of Grace's flushed red face. "They think they got it all but remember they said we'd have to wait a little longer to be really sure."

"But it's going to be all right, though, isn't it dad? That's what you said."

"Yes, baby, it's going to be all right. You'll be back in school bugging the teachers in no time."

Jimmy heard the front door and looked at his watch. "That must be mum. I'll make her a cup of tea and we'll be right back up."

He went downstairs to find Zoe hugging the kids. He could see that she was fighting to control her emotions.

"Let your mother get in guys," he said, taking her bag and steering her into the kitchen. "I'll be checking on your homework in a minute."

"Is it okay if I…" Tyler started to ask before Jimmy interrupted: "You can go surfing once you're done, Tyler, and not before."

Zoe sat down on the bar stool and Jimmy put on the kettle. "I don't think tea is going to solve this one," she said finally, her lips quivering.

"What's up, babe? It can't really get any worse, can it?"

Zoe shrugged her shoulders. "I called the insurance people today." It took her a few moments to get the words out. "They said the bill so far is $25,100 and they haven't got it all in yet."

"But what about our insurance? Aren't we covered?" Jimmy felt like he'd been punched in the gut, but he didn't want to show any weakness to Zoe. He knew he somehow had to stay strong.

"Most of it will be covered, but we still have to pay $10,000 and I don't know where we're going to find that kind of money. We've got all the bills and your DUI and…"

"Shh, stop worrying. I told you that we'll find a way. The important thing is that Grace is safe and she's going to be okay." Jimmy ignored the ring from a new text and held Zoe close.

"But how, Jimmy? How? I just can't do this any more. It's too hard." Zoe sobbed so hard her head banged against his chest.

When she finally fell still, he sneaked a look down at the text and his own eyes filled with tears.

Tell mum it's all going to be all right :(

CHAPTER TWENTY-THREE

The days when Jimmy slept in until lunchtime on a Sunday morning were long past. It was 5.30am and he'd already been awake for a couple of hours. Zoe was lying upside down beside him, a sure sign that she'd also been struggling for sleep.

Jimmy's court case was Monday. He'd decided to fight the DUI at his attorney's suggestion. He was going to argue that as far as the cops were concerned, he may have downed a bottle of vodka after arriving at the hospital and parking his car. He hated the idea of lying but his lawyer didn't appear to have such qualms and an acquittal would save him a ban, a fine upwards of $5,000 and a heavy hike in car insurance. For a family on the brink of bankruptcy it was a lifeboat in a storm.

All this was churning over and over in Jimmy's mind. It was only when he realised it was a Sunday that he came up with a way out, at least for a couple of hours. Martyn and Paul and a couple of the others from the Field of Broken Dreams had texted him since they'd been back but Jimmy couldn't get his head around playing soccer when there was so much happening at home.

He got up thinking perhaps that 90 minutes of not worrying about anything but who to pass to would be the perfect escape right then. He quietly searched in the cupboard for his kit and scribbled a note he left next to the bed: *Gone to play soccer — back for breakfast!*

Coming downstairs he saw Tyler and his friend, Kyle, waxing their surfboards on the living room carpet. They smiled guiltily and took the boards outside. Even at 11, Tyler was ripping up the waves and was way better than his dad. Jimmy tried to surf with him as much as possible anyway, all too aware of his own feelings when he looked for his father on the touchlines and he wasn't there.

"Be careful," Jimmy shouted after them as they put the boards in the back of Kyle's dad's truck. "The waves are supposed to be big today."

He looked at the clock on the stove and realised he had to get a move on to get to Laguna Beach in time for the early kick-off but he couldn't find his spider pattern boots anywhere. The plastic had become smelly really quickly and Zoe wouldn't have them in the house, but Jimmy couldn't see them on the deck. All he could find was the pair of trainers he wore when he first played at the FOBD and the antique Duncan Edwards boots. He threw them both in the car and drove down through the empty streets towards the Pacific Coast Highway feeling lighter than he had in weeks.

By the time he was getting closer to the field his initial optimism was fading. He hadn't exercised since arriving home and the memory of his last game in London wasn't a good one. He'd have to get used to the idea that his feet were never going to be able to do what his brain was telling them. It was pretty much all downhill from here.

Arriving at the Vista Park bench at just after 6.30am, there was already a huddle of players chatting. The field was above the mist and the sun was rising above the canyon that dropped down from all sides. The quiet buzz of conversation in the half light complemented the ethereal beauty of the scene. Jimmy took a deep breath, his first for weeks, maybe years.

"Jimmy, we thought you'd abandoned us." Dom, the surfer who'd first told him about FOBD, stood up and shook hands. "We've missed you."

"Good to see you back," said Nils, a skilled midfielder from Denmark, and Turan, who inherited his deft touch from his father, a former Turkish international player, reached out his hand to shake.

Jimmy rubbed some pain reliever on his knees and swallowed a couple of Ibuprofen, checking the label for dosage instructions. They were so small he couldn't read them so he took a third capsule just in case.

He had both pairs of shoes in his bag but was too embarrassed to try on the old boots. The sneakers were falling apart — the sole was coming away from the rest of the right shoe — but he figured they'd last one last game.

It was another 20 minutes before the game got started. They'd been about to kick off with 12-a-side when an extra four players dawdled along and the decision was taken to split off into two matches of 7-a-side.

Jimmy groaned inwardly. The smaller sided games meant a lot more running.

With his first kick, the right sneaker split a little further apart and the pass went straight to Martyn, playing with the opposition whites, who promptly blasted it into the net and ran past smiling. "Thanks Jimmy. Good to have you back!"

Jimmy tried kicking more with his left and the laces began to tear from their worn sockets. The field was uneven and two plastic water sprinklers jutted out from the worn turf. Small round cones were put next to them to keep players away. The match was delayed a couple of minutes in when a dog turd was discovered by the corner cone.

By half-time, the score was 6-0 and Jimmy was having a nightmare. His sneakers were flapping like drowning ducks and Phil ran to his truck to get some duct tape to hold them together. It was still only 8.30am and Jimmy wished he'd stayed in bed. It seemed like the harder he tried the worse he played.

"Let's get back at them, Jimmy." Simon patted him on the back. He'd recently returned after two years working as a missionary in the Philippines and Jimmy admired both his strength of belief and his soccer prowess. He was a former apprentice with Bournemouth in England and it showed.

"I'm really sorry," said Jimmy. "I just can't pass to save my life. I don't know what's wrong."

"Just relax," laughed Simon, still heavily tanned from his mission. "This ain't Wembley. The pitch is worse than a farmer's field and nobody's watching." He hesitated, peering across to the other side of the field where a man was desperately trying to prevent his German Shepherd from running into the penalty box. "My mistake, there's that old guy and his dog. Let's keep it simple and have some fun."

"Where can I get a pair of those boots?" Jimmy smiled ruefully as Paul trotted past in his Chelsea gear. He may have had a working class cockney accent but he was one of the most successful businessmen in Orange County.

"You mean my lucky boots?"

"If they're your lucky boots, I'd hate to see your unlucky ones!"

"They're in the car," said Jimmy. He still couldn't face trying on the old English boots, whatever the state of the sneakers.

It wasn't quite so bad as the game wore on, but Jimmy wasn't sure if it was because he was getting better or the others were getting worse. His passes were a little better but still nothing like as crisp as he would have liked.

The bonus was that his worrying was entirely about his footwear, a far preferable concern than the fears shadowing his weekdays.

The field was bone hard and with no foot support Jimmy was feeling every step in his knees and hips. He wasn't doing much attacking or defending; he just hoped that when the ball came to him in midfield he could make some use of it.

At one point, he jogged backwards and tripped over a grassy mound in the right hand corner.

With Andrew, a former English County cricketer, and Kirk, a marriage counsellor, keeping a tight rein at the back for the whites, Jimmy was having trouble finding a way through until, about halfway through the second half, Simon knocked the ball back to Paul who stepped over it to give Jimmy a clear view on goal. Head down, he struck right through the ball with his laces and it rocketed into the top left hand corner.

Unfortunately, so did his right shoe which disintegrated on impact.

There was nothing for it; he'd have to wear a pair of boots that were more than 50 years old for the remaining 15 minutes.

CHAPTER TWENTY-FOUR

Jimmy was acutely aware of the age of the thick, frayed laces as he pulled them tight. The black boots were surprisingly supple and slipped on easily even though they were a size larger than he usually wore and the metal studs were worn down to stubs.

He staggered to his feet on the sideline and looked down. They still looked half a century old.

Jimmy waited for a moment for someone to wave him on and quickly remembered there was no referee. He ran back to the right hand side and decided to stay out of the action as much as possible for the remaining minutes. The leather around his toes was fixed rigid so he had no idea what the ball would do if he kicked it.

He dropped back a little and saw John, the goalkeeper, gesturing at him. He wanted him to take the goal kick.

"It's okay," said Jimmy. "You take it. It's all good."

"No, it's not. I can barely turn my hip. It's killing me." John placed the ball for Jimmy to take the kick.

Other than the goal, Jimmy hadn't hit a clean ball himself all game. He shrugged and looked up to see Simon cutting in from the left towards the goal. It wasn't a full sized field but it would still take a mighty thump to make the other end.

Jimmy was worried that if he tried to pass it out to the flanks the ball could go anywhere. Thumping it seemed the better alternative.

Simon had his hand up as he ran. *You're hopeful*, thought Jimmy as he ran up for the strike.

He hardly felt it as his right foot swept through the ball, which fired into the clear morning sky with the trajectory of a finely hit golf drive. It rose just above Martyn's head on the edge of the penalty area and kept going up until, at about the two-thirds mark, the ball dropped, not like a stone but a looped softball, over the shoulder of the last defender and right into Simon's path as he continued his run towards goal. He hardly had to control the ball before side-footing it past the astonished keeper.

"Nice ball," said Martyn. "I thought it was going to take my ear off."

"Good stuff, Jimmy." Simon had a new spring in his step running back. "One down, six to go."

From the restart, Nermin passed wide to Ken, the young Ghanaian who had honed his skills in Italy and had scored four of his team's six goals. At 30, he was younger than most of the FOBD regulars and a better player, but he wasn't a show off and easily fitted in. That didn't mean he liked to lose.

He surged past a couple of players, beating them for speed and knocked the ball one side of Jimmy and ran around him. In the type of soccer Jimmy played as a kid, such audacity was repaid with a block that sent the attacker crashing to the floor, but he resisted the temptation, watching Ken race past him to collect the ball about ten yards from the goal.

Then, just as Ken was about to shoot, Jimmy found himself touching the ball aside just in the nick of time and turning with possession. Ken kicked thin air, suddenly looking confused. Jimmy looked up and none of his teammates were ahead of him so he started running up the pitch.

Normally as Andrew, a fierce tackler, approached he tried to offload the ball, but this time Jimmy rounded him with the faintest of sideways flicks and then turned two more defenders inside out as he mazed through their lunges. He lifted his head to see the keeper on the edge of his box, thinking about running out to challenge him. Before he could make up his mind to come or go, Jimmy threw up a backspin lob that spun over the keeper's head and kicked off the turf into the empty net.

There was a moment of incredulous silence and the spell was broken by the old man with the dog applauding from the touchline. "Well played," he shouted. "Well played indeed." Players from both sides ran over to congratulate Jimmy and even the dog started barking.

"Nice," said Paul. "That's 6-2. We just need four more like that."

He didn't know if it was adrenaline or simply being pumped by playing some decent soccer at last, but Jimmy felt invigorated. He didn't feel at all tired and the aches and pains seemed to have gone. He was playing without fear, letting it happen with the kind of confidence he'd thought was gone forever.

The ball was like a magnet to Jimmy and he lined up precision passes to Paul and then Simon to score easy goals. He took a corner that was so accurate that all Pete, the American left back, needed to do was stand still and let it hit his forehead.

A rare free kick, called after Sean bundled him over, was a good 40 feet from the goal. Jimmy stood up and brushed himself down. He took a three step run up and hit the ball with the inside of his boot. Initially, it was heading for the right corner cone but halfway through its flight the ball started moving back towards the goal in a steady semi-circle, as if Jimmy was drawing it with a compass. As it pulled round to the top right corner of the goal, the ball appeared to straighten out and speed up, hitting the net with such force it almost broke.

"How did you do that?" Sean stood open mouthed.

Jimmy honestly had no idea. "Just lucky, I guess. The wind?"

"There's no wind here. This is Southern California." Sean was still staring at the goal, wanting a replay to see if his eyes were cheating him. "That was awesome, man. Incredible."

Jimmy jogged back giving high fives. *What is going on?* He couldn't work it out. He felt like a teenager again.

"Two minutes left and it's 6 each," said Pete, the timekeeper.

This time both Ken and Martyn ran at Jimmy, daring him to take the ball from them as they passed it expertly between them. As they neared the goal, Martyn spotted Andrew backing them up in space and pushed a firmly hit pass towards him.

Jimmy was on it like a flash. The pass was strong but it looked to him like it was moving in slow motion. He intercepted the ball and knocked it past the last defender on the left, beating him handily for pace.

Knowing there was only seconds left, the white team charged back and there were three defenders in the box in front of Paul at the back. Jimmy took one quick look and hammered a pass low and hard just behind the defenders to find Paul at the far post. He stuck out a foot and the ball crashed into the goal.

7-6.

It may not have been Wembley. It may just have been a public park covered in ruts, lumps and bare patches.

But right at that moment, Jimmy felt like he'd won the World Cup Final.

CHAPTER TWENTY-FIVE

Jimmy was walking on air when he arrived back at the house. Zoe was out on the deck reading a book and the kids were inside playing video games.

"What's happened to you?" Zoe looked surprised.

"Nothing. What do you mean? I haven't done anything."

Zoe put down her book. "I don't mean anything. You just look so happy. It's been a while since I've seen that look in your eye. Was it a good game?"

"Great, actually." Jimmy had been trying to work it out in his mind the whole drive home, but it still made no sense. "Everything seemed to click."

"I'm pleased for you, darling. It's good for you to get out with some friends. I love seeing you looking happy for a change." Zoe picked the book back up and started to read. "I'm just taking a few minutes out before taking Charley over to dance practice."

Jimmy wasn't listening. He was still trying to understand. "It was like I was another person out there. I was always okay going forward but I was defending as well. It's like I could tell what was going to happen before it did. I felt so young and fit. I could have played on for hours. And I took this free kick…"

"That's great, baby, really great." Zoe didn't look up. "Can you check on the kids and tell Charley to get changed. There's a doll."

Jimmy limped back inside. Every muscle in his legs ached now and both feet were numb, as if they'd been in a pair of shoes three sizes too small. *I just don't get it*, he mumbled to himself.

"Oh! Jimmy," Zoe shouted after him. "I found those spider boots in the washroom. Can you put them outside or throw them away. They were stinking the place out."

Jimmy picked up his sweaty soccer kit to wash and threw his bag out the door with the old boots. *I won't be needing those again*, he thought. *How good am I going to be with decent modern boots that actually fit?*

He checked his phone and there was a bunch of texts from players congratulating him on that morning's game.

Last time I play against you, texted Martyn.

Awesome game, wrote Sean

I'll pay you $100 for those boots, messaged Paul

Pick you up at 7.30am

The last one was from Bill, from FOBD, who was a lawyer and had offered to go along with him for moral support at the DUI hearing in the morning.

And just like that, Jimmy's aura of invincibility was gone and he was back in full fight or flight mode. Football was just a game. This was real life.

CHAPTER TWENTY-SIX

Sitting on the hardwood bench outside Court 5 at Orange County Superior Court in Newport Beach, Jimmy gave the impression he was listening intently to his attorney but he wasn't hearing a word. He hadn't slept all night worrying about going on the stand and lying to the judge.

"There is a good chance you won't even be asked if you were drinking earlier. Everyone understands this is a technicality," said the lawyer, a rake-thin, meticulously dressed friend of a friend who was cutting Jimmy a slight break on his fees. "The point is that the police can't prove you didn't have a drink at the hospital or sometime after parking the car. It's a game really, but it's important you play along."

Jimmy nodded back but his eyes were blank.

"Do you understand, Jimmy?" The attorney was insistent. "I need to know you're going to say the right thing otherwise we may as well go in there, plead guilty and start racking up those Uber bills. There's even a chance you could do some jail time. This is not a time to flake out on me."

"So you think we've got a good chance of winning?"

"If you stick to the script you'll walk out of here without a problem." The lawyer looked up as the court clerk came outside and beckoned him over.

Zoe had been parking the car and walked in with Bill. Jimmy stood up and hugged her. Bill ignored his outstretched hand and hugged him, too.

"You'll be fine." Bill was wearing a navy pin-striped suit, a very different look from his colourful gear on Sunday mornings. "Just tell them straight what happened and it'll work out, believe me. Good things happen to good people. It's karma."

Jimmy's stomach lurched. So he'd be lying in front of his wife and a teammate he liked and respected.

The defence attorney was calling him in.

"I'll, er, see you on the other side." Jimmy smiled and hurried into the hushed mahogany courtroom.

He hesitated at the door, struck by the stuffiness. It reminded him of his kids' kindergarten classrooms and the thought hurt his heart. He walked slowly across to where his lawyer was sitting behind a long table. The clerk was surrounded by paper in the eves of the empty high bench that dominated the room.

"Where's the dock?" Jimmy wasn't sure what to do.

"You're not on trial for murder. The seat next to me is just fine." The attorney seemed relaxed. "If all goes well, we should be out of here by lunchtime and you can carry on with your life."

Jimmy looked over his shoulder and Zoe gave him a thin smile. She looked petrified. Bill was sitting next to her with three more FOBD regulars, fellow English expats Martyn and Paul, and Stuart, from Scotland. They had all offered to come in case Jimmy needed them to speak up for his character. He hadn't even known them that long and felt a stab of emotion that left his eyes glassy.

Pull yourself together, he told himself, blinking back the tears. *This'll all be over very soon.*

"All rise." The clerk's bark pulled Jimmy out of his reverie and he stood up as the judge came in from a door behind the bench and sat down. He'd been expecting a wig or a red gown but the elderly judge looked distracted in an unkempt brown suit. He peered down through his glasses at Jimmy.

"I have this trial marked down for just one day. Is that sufficient, counsellor?" he asked Jimmy's lawyer. "Are all your witnesses present?"

"One day should be quite sufficient, sir," the attorney replied, "and only the defendant will be giving evidence. It should be quite straightforward."

"Let me be the judge of that." The judge didn't sound friendly.

The prosecutor, a mild-mannered fellow in a foppish green jacket, outlined the case against Jimmy in a lot more detail than seemed necessary. He even gave the licence plate number of Jimmy's truck.

"In conclusion," he said. "Our contention is that Mr Keen was still inebriated when he drove his wife and daughter to the hospital. There is no evidence that he partook any alcohol after arriving at the hospital. He gave a full statement to police following his arrest and there was no mention of drinking anything other than 'a couple of vodka and tonics' on the flight from London.

"Considering the level of alcohol in his blood it was more than a couple of vodka and tonics. In fact, Mr Keen's alcohol intake is not the matter in doubt. The issue is that he knowingly put the lives of his wife and daughter as well as innocent members of the public in jeopardy by getting behind the wheel of a vehicle while dangerously impaired."

The prosecutor's opening statement had been so methodical Jimmy felt his eyes get heavier. He'd barely slept the previous night as much as he'd tried to divert his mind by reliving his heroics at FOBD. But there was something in the way the lawyer's demeanour had changed. His speech speeded up and he was clearly working up to his grand finale.

"Considering the danger Mr Keen represented both to his own family and to every other motorist on the road that night and his apparent lack of remorse we believe a prison sentence is appropriate in this case, along with a $5,000 fine and a driving ban of at least 12 months," he said, his voice getting faster and louder with every word. He sat down with a flourish.

Jimmy turned and looked at Zoe. Even in his worst nightmare, he hadn't seriously thought he'd be going to jail.

As shocked as Jimmy was, his attorney didn't bat an eyelid.

"As my learned friend told the court," he began, getting slowly to his feet, "this case is not about how much Jimmy drank - I think we'd all agree it was too much - but when he drank it. That is the crux of the case and all that concerns us here."

"I'm not going to waste the court's time by going into an elaborate description of the night in question. Suffice to say that Jimmy and his wife got their daughter to Hoag Hospital in time for her to get the medical treatment she desperately needed.

"That should be taken into account, should it not?" He looked from the prosecutor to the judge without getting any response.

The defence lawyer was unperturbed. "I'd like to call the defendant, James J. Keen."

Jimmy had been expecting another detailed run through of the events of the night. Taken by surprise, he rose unsteadily to his feet, unsure where to go.

"Over there," said the judge tersely.

Jimmy climbed into the witness box, vowed to tell the truth and looked over uncertainly at his lawyer.

"Let's get straight to it, shall we, Jimmy?" The attorney came over and leaned an elbow on the edge of the box.

Jimmy nodded. "Sure."

"Sometimes, to get to the truth, we have to acknowledge some uncomfortable things. You understand that, don't you?"

Again, Jimmy nodded his head, although he wasn't so sure.

"I don't think I'm revealing any real secret by telling the court that you are, indeed, an alcoholic. Is that right, Jimmy?"

Shocked, Jimmy looked again at Zoe. "Well, I er..I wouldn't say I'm an alcoholic. I like the odd drink but…"

"You had perhaps a vodka and tonic on the flight from London to LA, is that correct?"

"Well, yeah, but…" Jimmy didn't know what to say.

"Maybe two at the very most."

"Yes, but…"

"Is that right, Jimmy?"

"Yes, but…"

"So will you please explain to us how later, after driving your family to the hospital, after being involved in a minor road traffic accident, after parking your car in the hospital parking lot, you couldn't deal with the shock and stress of seeing your daughter so sick that you drank all the contents of a duty free bottle of Belvedere vodka before throwing it, empty, in the trash?" He looked meaningfully at Jimmy. "Take your time and then run us through what happened."

Jimmy stood there for a long while unsure what to do. He'd already fallen so much further than he'd ever dreamed possible. He couldn't find a job, he couldn't even pay the bills for his own family. He didn't feel like a man at all, certainly not the man that Zoe fell in love with and married.

But he could not lie in front of his wife and say that while she was holding Grace's hand and praying she'd live he was hiding in some corner drinking like a coward. He'd known he was over the limit when he drove and he'd do it again if it meant saving Grace. He'd do anything, but he wouldn't do this.

Yes, he had been a fool, but he wasn't a liar.

CHAPTER TWENTY-SEVEN

It turned out Jimmy's lawyer was right about one thing. The case did end before lunchtime.

All it took for his defence to collapse was Jimmy's admission that he didn't touch a drop after driving Grace to the hospital. His attorney made a faint-hearted attempt to persuade him that perhaps his memory might have been flawed, but Jimmy was unyielding.

"After the accident, I made sure there were no injuries and then I continued to the hospital because I was worried about my daughter's condition," he explained to the judge. "As soon as my daughter was with the doctors I called and reported the accident to the police and it was the decision of the officers who interviewed me to give me the breathalyser."

"So, just to be clear," the prosecutor asked, "you didn't drink anything at Hoag before meeting with the officers?"

"Just a cup of tea." Jimmy shrugged, unsure what was going to happen next.

He quickly found out.

"Does this mean your client will be changing his plea?" The judge directed the question at the defence attorney, ignoring Jimmy.

The attorney looked at Jimmy and he nodded.

"Yes, your honour."

"In that case, Mr Keen, will you please return to your seat next to your attorney and remain standing." The judge had his head bowed over a file and he was scribbling something.

Jimmy stepped out of the witness box and walked over to his attorney, who blanked him. He took his place behind the table and waited for the judge.

"Mr Keen, this could have ended very differently. With that amount of alcohol in your system you could very well have killed somebody and then we'd be looking at a murder case instead of a DUI."

Jimmy bowed his head and the judge continued.

"I am cognisant of the situation involving your daughter and the district attorney's office has agreed to drop the charge of leaving the scene of an accident, but I am less inclined to leniency on the charge of driving under the influence. You will pay a fine of $5,000, in addition to costs of $2,200 and you will be banned from driving for a period of 12 months. You will also register with a court-ordered Alcoholics Anonymous program."

Jimmy could hear Zoe sniffle behind him. He stared straight ahead; he didn't dare look up at the judge.

"I am also mindful of the time wasted by your misguided not guilty plea and as a consequence you are hereby ordered to serve a custodial sentence of three months…"

The judge looked down at Jimmy and then back down at the file he'd been writing on. Jimmy's head was in a spin. He couldn't take it in. Did this mean he had to go to prison?

"What's happening?" Jimmy felt sick.

"I told you," his attorney whispered. "Judges don't take kindly to being lied to."

"But I didn't lie."

"You pleaded not guilty."

"But I…"

Jimmy closed his eyes and waited for the sheriff's deputy to grab his shoulders and clamp a pair of handcuffs on his wrists. He looked helplessly across at Zoe and the FOBD guys and snapped back at the sound of the judge clearing his throat.

"…suspended for two years."

Jimmy felt his legs wobble beneath him. He wasn't going to go to jail after all.

He was free to go.

CHAPTER TWENTY-EIGHT

Jimmy took a long, cool drink from the bottle. It contained water. He hadn't touched any booze since his court appearance three weeks earlier. He'd run along the sand to the pier and back again, a distance of about three miles. He felt pretty good.

He'd been for the run on the beach before picking up the kids from school and drove home to find Zoe on the phone. Since the court case she'd been coming home earlier from work and Jimmy suspected she was worried about his so-called alcoholism.

He went into the kitchen to make a cup of tea and a couple of minutes later Zoe followed him in. She was beaming.

"Guess what?"

"I don't know," said Jimmy. He tried to make light of his suspicions. "How about you've come home early again because you think I'm going to get drunk and strip off all my clothes while the kids do their homework?"

"No." Zoe didn't always get Jimmy's humour and she did the same thing she usually did when she didn't find him funny. She ignored him. "I may have found you a job."

"Awesome." Jimmy tried to summon up some enthusiasm but he felt flat. As much as he needed a job, he didn't necessarily want his wife getting it for him.

He saw the danger signals as Zoe's lips tightened and blundered on. "That would really be amazing. Thanks Zo. What is it?"

"It's another construction job but this could be really good. Have you seen that big new development they're opening up at the Laguna Beach end of Newport Coast. You know, where the monster mansions are? Well, my college friend's husband's looking for a contractor." She paused a second to make sure she had Jimmy's full attention. "Not just a contractor but the main contractor to get started on the first couple of homes."

Now Jimmy really was interested. "So I'd be the boss? Like the old days?"

"Yes, you'd be the boss." Zoe was beaming again. "You can kiss me if you like."

Jimmy kissed her full on the lips. "I can do more than that."

"Jimmy! The kids are upstairs."

"So what's wrong with here?"

"Stop!" She pulled away but she was still smiling. "Later, you naughty boy."

"So what do I have to do?" Jimmy rearranged his clothes. "About the job, I mean."

"Sorry, but he wants to see you on Sunday morning. I know you were hoping to play soccer."

Jimmy cursed inwardly. *Only Americans would still be working on Sunday mornings*. "No problem, baby. What time?"

"10 am. You can't be late. He's meeting you specially."

"It'll work out fine." Jimmy had told all the FOBD regulars he'd be back this weekend and he really didn't want to miss it. "We finish at about 9am usually. I'll just make sure to leave the minute the final whistle blows."

"But what if you get hurt or something? This is the chance you've been waiting for isn't it?"

"Don't worry. I'll be there. That's amazing, thanks babe." Jimmy cuddled Zoe, made another playful attempt at seduction and went upstairs to get ready for the bar job he'd picked up to at least make a small dent in his fines.

"Maybe our luck is finally starting to change," he said looking back at Zoe.

CHAPTER TWENTY-NINE

When Jimmy arrived at the Field of Broken Dreams that Sunday the others were huddled in the baseball dugout by the neighbouring diamond, the only cover from the rain. The wind was whipping across the park and every so often a squall would send a sheet of rain hurtling along with it. The view across the canyons, usually so majestic, was shrouded in smoky, grey clouds.

Martine, from Costa Rica, and Jovan, from Chile, nodded hello and shuffled along the bench to give Jimmy room to sit down. Rather than put anybody off, the weather had drawn about double the number of players than usual.

"This is more like it." Mark, one of the English regulars, strolled over with his kitbag over his shoulder.

"If you like the rain so much," said Thor, an elegant German midfielder, "why did you come to California?"

"We like rain," said John, another Englishman and, at 63, the younger of the two goalkeepers named John. "Just not every day."

Jimmy banged his boots together to knock off some dirt.

"What happened to your grandpa boots, Jimmy?" Like most of the other more senior players, Greg wore Adidas Copa Mundials.

"If you wanna sell them, my offer still stands," piped in Paul. "A tenner to take them off your hands."

Jimmy laughed and laced up his plastic Messi boots. He'd brought the old pair just in case but he was really looking forward to seeing how he could play with some decent footwear.

The spider boots felt snug and he could sense the magic return as he started kicking a ball around outside the dugout while they waited for the stragglers to show up. Everything else may have been falling apart in his life, but after his last performance when his team won after being 6-0 down, Jimmy was brimming with confidence.

A couple of warm-up passes squirrelled off the side of his foot, sending Andrew running off towards the playground to fetch the ball. "Sorry, I'm a little rusty. Last week took a lot out of my legs," Jimmy apologised.

"Yeah, I remember," said Andrew, wearing a Port Vale shirt. "You killed us."

Jimmy tapped the ball back. He couldn't wait for the kick-off.

The wind had died off a little but they were all soaked by the time they started the game at 7.15 am. The ball went straight back to Jimmy standing on the edge of the centre circle. He didn't feel the same lightness in the legs he'd felt last time out but he put it down to the fact he wasn't properly warmed up.

Looking around for his options, Jimmy saw John, the Hungarian striker in white, dashing towards him. He wasn't concerned, feeling the same sense of time and space he'd felt before. It was all flooding back.

The next moment he was on his knees in the mud. John kicked the ball away the instant before Jimmy was about to send a raking cross field pass and the force of the missed swing threw him off balance. Scrambling in the mud to stand back up, he turned just in time to see John dash past Greg, the American full back, and easily slot the ball past the keeper. The old magic was going to take longer to kick in than he thought.

"You've got the wrong boots on, son." Paul jogged back to the centre spot with the ball.

"These are my new ones," Jimmy replied.

"You should give the old ones another try. More your style." Paul grinned and knocked the ball to Martyn on the right hand side. He took a big gulp of air and set off down the wing at speed, taking the Whites defence totally by surprise. He made for the corner flag like an arrow, leaving three defenders in his wake, but was so quick none of his teammates had caught up.

Like slow motion, Jimmy saw Martyn lift his head and see him. There was a space in front of goal screaming Jimmy's name. He started his run, knowing exactly where the ball was going.

Martyn's in-swinging cross was pinpoint perfect, arriving head height five yards out from the front post, right in the path of Jimmy's run.

Jimmy leaned forward. He'd already seen the goal in his mind's eye and all he needed to do now was to execute. That amazing feeling he'd had his last time at FOBD was back. Now he could take over the game.

But the ball flashed by with Jimmy a good 10 yards out still. He may have visualised the goal; he just couldn't score it. He wasn't even close.

Martyn trudged back, apologising to Jimmy. "Must have hit it a bit hard. Sorry Jim, I thought I had you."

But Jimmy knew better. The cross was perfect. He just didn't have the legs.

The Whites ran back down the field from the goal kick and scored another easy one. The score was heading in a depressingly familiar direction - 3-0 - but Jimmy didn't feel any energy in his legs. He was struggling to make the easiest passes.

Twice more he was caught in possession, once by Nermin, the Croatian, and the other time by Luis, a predatory goalscorer hailing from Columbia. Both times, the Whites ran on to score.

Dylan, who was only 17, was running rings around Jimmy in midfield. He nutmegged him one time before curling a beautifully struck shot inside the post. To make Jimmy's humiliation complete, the teenager ran back and helped pull him out of the mud and back to his feet.

Simon snatched back a goal with a clean strike from outside the box, but Jimmy's team still went into halftime 5-1 down and showing little likelihood of getting back into the game.

Jimmy was crushed. He'd been dreaming of coming back out and building on his last game but he'd barely put a foot right. Trudging back to the dugout, he saw a middle-aged man in a raincoat standing in the dugout with Stuart, the Glaswegian who was out for a few weeks after breaking two ribs. Both men walked towards him as he got nearer.

Jimmy went to say hi but they walked past him and he could see the stranger, an athletically built older man with a razor short haircut and boxer's broken features, introducing himself to Dylan.

After a few minutes they wandered over to where Jimmy was slumped on the ground impervious to the rain.

Stuart leaned over. "Jimmy, I want you to meet Neil Murray, a good friend of mine from Scotland. We grew up together in the Gorbals in Glasgow."

"What are you guys doing out in the rain at this time of the morning?" Jimmy put out his hand.

"I brought him to see Dylan. The boy's got some potential." Stuart shrugged.

"Nice one." Jimmy suddenly realised that he recognized the guy.

"Neil's the General Manager at the LA Galaxy," said Stuart. "He's looking for some youngsters for their youth academy and I've been on at him for a while to take a look at Dylan."

"Tough season, eh?" Jimmy said. "It's cool for you to still find the time to come out here."

"When you haven't won a game in two months and you're in serious danger of missing the play-offs, it's a real treat to get away for a morning and watch players actually enjoying the game." Murray spoke in a transatlantic Scottish burr.

"We spent a fortune on Francesco Torres, from Real Madrid, and he's crocked. So now I'm left with a bunch of kids. What can I say?" he laughed, "I'm desperate."

"We were out last night and I told Neil how you played the other week. If only you were 20 years younger, eh son?" Stuart watched as Jimmy dragged himself up.

"No sign of that today though," moaned Jimmy. "I'm playing crap."

"We've only been here for the last ten minutes of so," said Stuart, "but I'd say your assessment is pretty sound."

"It's probably the pitch. It looks awful." Murray was letting Jimmy down gently. "Do you mind if I ask how old you are?"

"47." Jimmy really couldn't think of anything to add.

To compound his misery, Jimmy felt water oozing through the sock on his left foot. He looked down to see a tear through the outside of the plastic boots from a raking tackle by Mark, the friendly, soft-spoken Englishman. The last thing he could afford was another pair. He had no choice right then, anyway. He'd have to wear the old ones again.

"I'm sorry guys," he said, pointing at his feet. "I'd better go and get my back-up pair."

Jimmy staggered over to the parking lot; his legs felt shot. He sat on the path to put them on away from the others. It was bad enough that Murray was seeing him play like a clown, now he was wearing boots to match.

The rain was coming down in sheets and Jimmy could hardly see as he jogged back on the pitch. He could just make out the two spectators taking cover in the dugout, peering out into the storm.

"Come on guys, let's do this." Jimmy clapped his hands, eager to get going. "We can get this back."

"Perhaps we should give you one of our players to even it out?" shouted Mark. "We don't want to run up too high a score."

"We're good," said Ken. "Or at least we will be if Jimmy snaps out of it." He passed to Paul who knocked it back to Jimmy. The ball barely rolled a couple of feet before sticking in the mud.

Jimmy could see John bearing down on him again with a hungry look, but this time it was the Hungarian who ended up in a heap on the ground. Jimmy was on the ball in a flash and knocked it sideways the exact moment John made his lunge.

Jimmy chipped the ball out of the mud patch with his right foot and lashed it on the volley with his left, slicing it across his laces. The shot spiralled like a corkscrew all the way from behind the halfway line. American John was in goal for the Whites team and was quick to catch the ball above his right shoulder, but the spin was so intense that it squirmed out of his grasp, dropped right on the goal line and the backspin kicked it into the net.

Jimmy checked across to the dugout to see Stuart was still there with Neil.

His second goal was from a towering header from a corner. From a standing start he felt like he had rockets in his heels and easily out jumped 6ft 7ins tall Nermin. The third, another header, was from a carbon copy cross Martyn had sent his way in the first half, only this time Jimmy was there in time to knock it into the goal. In fact, the had to arch back to reach the ball after almost arriving too early.

The other players, even those usually assured on the ball, were struggling to do anything. The downpour had turned the field into a quagmire and it was awash with standing water. A mist had also drawn in and it was hard to see from one end to the other. But Jimmy saw everything with a clarity he'd never experienced before. He could read the opposition passes before they happened. He wasn't even thinking about it; he just knew what to do. He felt like he could score with every kick but was wise enough to involve his teammates, spraying the passes around at will.

The Whites moved Dylan back to defence to try and stop him but Jimmy was unplayable.

The score wasn't even close. It was 11-5 when Pete shouted there were just two minutes left. It was raining harder than ever when Jimmy called for the ball from John the younger, his own keeper, who threw it at him at knee height. Controlling it without allowing the ball to touch the ground, he chipped it into the air in a small arc, running forward to kick it up a little further, he again caught it on the volley, hitting the ball harder this time over three defenders bunched in front of him. Darting past all three, he again reached the ball before it touched the ground about 5 feet from the opposition touchline midway between the goal and the corner flag. He then hit the ball from an impossible angle, cutting across it with a huge amount of slice. The ball flew in a semi circle ending in the top right hand corner.

Nobody moved. Even Jimmy stood still, stunned by what he'd done.

Then, through the steady splatter of rain on the puddles of water, he heard the sound from the dugout across the field of two men clapping.

CHAPTER THIRTY

Jimmy's goal was the final action of the game and the rain eased to a drizzle as the players walked off the field in a sodden congratulatory scrum.

Stuart and Murray were waiting for them on the touchline.

"That was quite some display out there, Jimmy." Murray's demeanour had completely changed. "In fact, I don't think I've ever seen anything quite like it."

There was so much adrenaline pumping around that Jimmy felt he could have played on forever. "I know this sounds daft," he said. "But I finally feel that my game is all coming together. I'm not even thinking about what I'm doing. It's instinctive." The words rolled out in a torrent. He couldn't believe it himself. "It's like I could go out and play another 90 minutes right now."

"I do believe you could." Murray looked equally stunned by what he'd witnessed. He repeated himself. "I don't think I've ever seen anything like that."

"Bloody hell, pal. That was amazing." Stuart slapped Jimmy on the back. "I told Neil that you knew what you were doing but, man, you were incredible."

The other players were all sitting and lying on the wet grass, shattered. Jimmy felt 20 years younger. He may have felt 30 years younger but he couldn't remember that far back. He'd taken a couple of Ibuprofen before the game and wondered if that had something to do with it.

Stuart clapped him again on the back and took Murray over to talk with Dylan and his dad, John, who'd been sitting watching from his truck. The teenager still looked fresh and Jimmy could see the old coach was interested. He looked over and gave the kid a thumbs up.

Jimmy sat down and untied his boots. They still had the original flat ribbon laces and he'd wrapped them several times around the cleat because they were so long. He pulled at the left boot, struggling to lever it off his foot. He had to force his thumbs behind his heel and as it pulled away the shoe suddenly felt like it was about two sizes too small. It had two stripes across the top, one less than the conventional Adidas, and the toe was hard, like it was made out of steel. It felt fine when it was on but turning the boot over in his hands Jimmy wondered how he'd managed to play in them.

An overwhelming tiredness overtook him and a pain in his right knee that had been bothering him for weeks knifed back in. The exhaustion doubled when he eased off the right boot. He tried to stand up but fell back; every muscle in his legs was crying out. Both feet were cramped up like a ballerina's.

"Where did you get those things?" Paul was standing over him and Martyn reached out a hand to help him up.

"Found them in my dad's place in England. I know…it's about time I got a new pair." Jimmy could barely get the words out. He was going to tell them about Duncan Edwards but it was too much effort. They'd probably never heard of him.

"Nah, I'd keep wearing them if I were you. After what you did today I don't want to face you in a pair of proper boots."

Jimmy heard Stuart's voice, calling him over. "You got a minute? Neil wants a word."

"Sure." Jimmy just wanted to get home but he didn't want to be rude. The thought of walking to the truck was as much as he could handle. He turned, slipped and almost fell as both Paul and Martyn reached out to save him.

"I just wanted to say again how much I enjoyed watching you play this morning," said Murray. "It almost made it worth Stuart dragging me up here at the crack of dawn. I don't know how you guys do it every week."

Jimmy shrugged and smiled. That was all he could manage.

"Anyway, I'll be off. The first team played like crap yesterday and we've got them in for extra Sunday training. Perhaps next time we'll get them in for 6.30am. That should get their attention."

"Nice to meet you, Mr Murray." Jimmy picked up his boots and went to shake the Scotsman's hand.

"You, too," said Murray. "Actually Jimmy, I have a question for you."

Jimmy stopped and turned, swaying slightly.

"Are you interested in a trial for the Galaxy?"

Jimmy assumed he'd misheard. "I don't know...I mean, you know how old I am right?"

"I know how old you are, but when did age have anything to do with it if you're good enough?"

Pretty much all the time, Jimmy wanted to say.

"To be accurate, it's not a trial per se. We're inviting a bunch of people to an open session we're holding at the stadium. They're all players we're interested in taking a closer look at. We'll run a few drills and a practice game, nothing too fancy. I'd like to see how you cope against some younger opposition, no offence."

"None taken." Martyn, Paul and Bill, who'd just walked over, said in unison.

"Let's be realistic," continued Murray, "the MLS is a rather different proposition than your FOBD, but I'd love to see you play again. No guarantees. Would you indulge me, Jimmy?"

"Yeah, I guess, if you're serious." Jimmy was stunned.

"Deadly serious. It's this Thursday at the stadium. 2pm. I'll see you there."

Murray left with Stuart and Jimmy got his phone from his bag to check his schedule. He saw the time and his first thought was that he was in trouble. The next second he remembered why.

It was 10 am and he was supposed to be meeting Zoe's friend to talk about the construction jobs.

He tried to run to the parking lot but his legs wouldn't allow it. Zoe was sitting at the wheel of the minivan waiting for him. She was in tears.

He tried to call the guy but the reception was terrible and he couldn't get through. There wasn't any time to change so they drove right to the address with Jimmy still in his football kit.

Wet with an equal amount of rain and sweat, Jimmy ran up the drive. He knocked on the door and knocked again.

There was no reply. He was screwed.

CHAPTER THIRTY-ONE

The parking lot attendant at the Carson, CA stadium was surprised to see Zoe driving with Jimmy in the passenger seat and three kids in the back of the truck.

"Nobody else brought their family with them," he said, ticking off Jimmy's name on a clipboard, "apart from maybe a couple of dads who came with the teenagers."

Zoe hadn't talked to Jimmy since he'd missed his interview but had told him through an intermediary (Charley) that she had agreed to take the kids to watch the trial. She'd remained silent on the way but the children were full of questions. What number would be choose? Would he be playing against Ronaldo? Did he remember his Zimmer frame?

Jimmy was nervous in spite of himself. "I'm way too old," he told Tyler, who asked if he would be playing in the English Premier League. "There's absolutely zero chance this is going anywhere, but it's cool to try out. I've just got to avoid having a heart attack."

Before they left, the children had surprised him with a gift. The $145 Adidas Copa Mundials were clearly bought by Zoe but she remained in the bathroom straightening her hair when the kids gave them to Jimmy.

By the time he'd tried them on and thanked everybody profusely they were running late, so he threw the new boots in his bag with the old ones and hurried out the door.

Having parked the truck, Jimmy was directed to the training rooms while the rest of the family were shown through the empty turnstiles to the bleachers at the South end of the ground where several earnest-looking middle-aged men sat sprinkled through the lower section.

Out on the grass, track-suited staff were setting out cones in lines leading out from the goal. A bucket of balls was emptied onto the pitch.

Jimmy followed a security guard down the player's tunnel and into a dressing room filled with kids in various coloured shirts.

"Oh! I'm sorry. Wrong room." Jimmy apologised and backed out of the room as Neil Murray was coming in.

"No, you're all right. This is the right changing room. How you doing, Jimmy?"

"I'm fine but this can't be right. They're all school kids."

"Not all of them." Murray had blocked Jimmy's exit. "There's a few in their 20s and a goalie who's 30. What did you expect? This is a soccer club, not a geriatric ward."

"I know but they're so young."

"Well, it's supposed to be a young man's game."

Jimmy was tempted to walk out but the thought of Zoe and his own kids sitting in the stands stopped him.

"Come on, Jimmy," said Murray. "Trust me, you'll be fine."

Awkwardly, Jimmy followed Murray back into the room and sat down on a bench closest to the door hoping nobody would notice him. It didn't smell anything like the dressing rooms Jimmy was used to growing up. No horse liniment, no unwashed socks, stale farts or people throwing up from the previous night's excesses.

Everything was gleaming and smelled of lemon.

"Hello everybody, thank you for coming." The room fell silent as Murray spoke.

"We're excited to see you new players and the Galaxy has organised this event to expand our talent identification efforts," he said, speaking slowly to ensure everyone understood his Glaswegian accent. "We want to find young talent who can enter our organisation and work their way up to the first team.

"This special try-out gives us a chance to evaluate some different players: hidden gems that may not have agents, players without a fair chance in the past, first time pros, or young pros who are not under contract. Some of you are still at school but haven't come through the club soccer system. Others are a little older and already in the workforce." He couldn't resist a sidelong smile at Jimmy.

"Most of you have already progressed from earlier tryouts. This is the last one; this is it. We want to make sure that everyone has a fair opportunity to be evaluated for a chance to earn a professional contract. No need to worry about anything. Just go out and enjoy yourselves."

The players clapped nervously.

"Now grab a shirt everybody and I'll see you out on the field in 10 minutes." Murray stopped by Jimmy on the way out. "Good luck, son."

Jimmy could sense the questioning looks as he checked through the white and blue LA Galaxy shirts on the dressing room pegs. He was looking for an XL but they were all small and medium. He finally found a large and wrenched it over his head. The shirt pulled tightly around his stomach, showing a slight bulge. Jimmy took a surreptitious look around. Everyone else was wafer thin and a couple of kids were moaning that the medium was way too loose.

At least his boots were new, although even they looked dull compared to the lime greens and oranges everyone else was wearing.

Jimmy jogged out of the tunnel with his heart in his mouth. His knees were hurting and he was already out of breath. From the bleachers, he could hear Tyler, Grace and Charley shouting, "WooHoo! Go dad!" All three kids were standing up, craning their necks to get a better view.

Assuming he was one of the coaches, a young, tufty-headed trialist asked him: "Do you have any balls we could play with, sir?"

His friend sniggered.

"Hey you!" Murray's voice boomed across the field. "Pay attention."

The general manager and three staffers were all standing on the sideline with notebooks and pens poised. Two coaches called the players closer to explain the first drill.

One of the coaches, who looked about 18 to Jimmy, led them over to the cones.

"We're going to warm you up with some simple running exercises," he said. "The cones are set at distances of 10 yards, 20 yards and 30 yards. I want everyone to take it in turns to do 10 then back, 20 and back, 30 and back and repeat 5 times.

"Then I want you to move across to the second set of cones. Criss cross through them at speed 5 times and then rest. When you've completed both courses just sit down and wait in silence."

Jimmy waited his turn as a line of young players took off in front of him, gliding across the grass and swooping through the cones with a studied intensity, the gaps between them maintained with practiced precision.

When the whistle blew for Jimmy he pushed off on his right foot and felt a slight twang in his hamstring. He pulled up, grimacing and saw Murray writing something on his pad. He assumed it wasn't a tick.

Every step was painful from then on and the skin tight shirt was sopping in seconds. He didn't swoop down to the cones; he ducked. He turned like a cruise liner. He was panting like a hungry dog.

By the time he'd finished he'd been passed by all the players behind him and they all sat watching his final sprint in silence. Several offered ironic applause and Murray nodded to one of his assistants to stop the clock. It didn't take an "A" license coaching badge to know Jimmy was dead last.

Jimmy wiped the sweat from his eyes and tried in vain to breathe deep enough to get his heart rate back in check. "Up you get, lads," shouted Murray. "Sort yourself out into teams of six."

He looked across at the bleachers and the kids were sitting in a row next to Zoe. They seemed small and far away.

Groaning up from the grass, he saw that his right knee had swollen to almost double the size of his left. He pushed down his weight; there was a shot of pain but it appeared to hold. His dad was in his head, *Gah'n you softie, give it up. Go back to your dolls. Who're you trying to kid, boy?*

The players quickly gathered into groups and Jimmy was left alone, like the odd man out on the playground, until it was clear that he had to join the only team left with five.

"All right, lads?"

A couple of them nodded; the others ignored him. They didn't want to be associated with failure.

"Three on three. Stay inside the boxes." Murray pointed to a bunch of cones shaped in squares across the other side of the pitch. "Go!"

The ball rolled to Jimmy and he shaped it off to a short, bearded Hispanic guy. His shirt was tucked in and everything about him was meticulous, including his trap and pass to a bullish, rectangular striker. Jimmy heard the player earlier saying he wore shin guards on the front and back of his legs so he could go in "where it hurts."

The pair of them passed it back and forth for a while until their three opponents, all wearing orange bibs, pressed so the only option was a ball back to Jimmy. The thuggish forward finally bowed to the inevitable and slotted the ball through to Jimmy.

The ball bobbled just slightly on the turf and Jimmy's first touch was bad. The ball came off his Copas too hard and he lunged to try and keep it under control but it was too late. It rolled outside the cones.

"Bibs get the ball." Murray passed it back in to a black player with a lightning pattern in his scalp and he chipped it delicately over Jimmy's head to a giant of a man with a bald head and teapot handle ears.

"Nice one."

The Hispanic glared at Jimmy and kept the ball away from him for the rest of the drill, losing the ball twice when he could have easily passed it. He wouldn't look at Jimmy when the whistle blew, perhaps realising that his selfishness had probably cost him a contract, as well.

Jimmy's new boots had rubbed blisters on both heels and his entire body hurt. Almost as much as his pride.

CHAPTER THIRTY-TWO

Jimmy was relieved to see the Hispanic player wasn't on his team in the scrimmage. Murray kept the team talks simple before the match started. "Both teams will be playing 4-4-2. Two halves of 30 minutes each. Let's see what you can do."

There were six substitutes for both teams and Murray explained that his assistant coaches were free to pull players in and out of the game but would try and give everyone an equal opportunity.

Jimmy wasn't picked to start and left his boots off, hoping to get some air to the blisters. One had popped; the other was an angry purple. He leaned back on his hands on the grass by the side of the perfect pitch.

His family had moved down to the front row and the kids were peering over the top of the wall. They waved but when Jimmy looked over Zoe was studying her phone.

The game was very different from FOBD and from the English Premier League. It was fast and athletic. The players were all so fit and mobile. Jimmy felt tired just watching them.

Jimmy's opponents, wearing the Galaxy's blue away strip, went up after about 10 minutes when the Hispanic guy that hated him gathered the ball on the left wing, played a tidy one-two with the centre forward and side-footed it past the keeper. His celebrations were as neat as his hair. He did a tight fist-pump and straightened his shirt as he ran back for the restart.

The football was all movement, give and go and go again. Both defences hustled and sent raking passes for their attackers to chase. When Jimmy was finally called on with five minutes left in the first half and asked to play centre midfield his neck was left aching from watching the ball fly over his head in both directions. He hadn't got a kick when the whistle went for the end of the half.

The young guy in charge of Jimmy's team called out the names for the second half and Jimmy wasn't one of them.

"Sorry dude," the track-suited coach said to Jimmy. "I'll get you back on before we're done."

"No worries." Jimmy just wanted it all to be over. He'd made a mistake coming. The kids would understand.

The score remained 1-0 and while the other players were being revolved in and out of the line-up, he was left sitting on the grass, forgotten.

With about 15 minutes to go, Murray stopped the game and ran across the field from his perch in the dugout. Jimmy could see him remonstrating with the young coach and pointing over at him.

Seconds later, the young coached shrugged and called his name. Jimmy was on.

He grimaced as he pulled his boots onto his bruised feet. Both blisters hurt like hell, his knee had blown up like a balloon, his leg muscles shrieked as he stood up and he thought for the first time in weeks how he'd really, really like a cold beer.

But then as he stood tall to look around the empty stadium the grunts and barks of the earnest young players faded into the background and the memories from a thousand football matches filled his head. The wins and losses all blended into one but the pure joy of playing the game, of living for that moment and leaving all else behind in the changing room, that had been one of the things that defined his life. The battles he'd fought with his teammates, the friendships formed through all those games over all those years, they were an integral part of who he was. He'd been chasing a dream when the dream had been his all along.

And with that sudden moment of clarity, Jimmy realised something else that had been staring him in the face for weeks but he'd been too caught up in himself to see. He'd been handed guardianship of someone else's dream and was in great peril of squandering it.

"You'll have to give me a minute, coach," he said, running back towards the tunnel, "I need to change my boots."

CHAPTER THIRTY-THREE

When he came back out a few minutes later, Jimmy was wearing the old boots from the attic. He rolled rather than ran with a long, loping stride that was in stark contrast to his painful shuffle off the field just moments earlier.

The young coach was indignant. "What the hell are you doing?"

"I had a problem with my boots." Jimmy felt like another man. "I'm ready to go now."

"So glad to hear it. Well, you'll have to wait until I'm ready."

"Put him on, Roy. I want him on now." Murray was emphatic.

"I just changed a bunch on his team."

"Put him on the other team, then." Murray threw a blue shirt at Jimmy. "Here, put this on."

"You can put Jimmy on for Hector. I've seen enough of him."

The coach waved at the Hispanic midfielder, who jogged slowly back to the sideline without acknowledging Jimmy.

"Show me something, Jimmy." Murray clapped his hands. "Don't make me look stupid here."

"Go dad! Go dad!" Tyler's voice cut through the afternoon heat. "You can do it, dad!"

Jimmy ran into position for the throw-in restart and called for the ball. He was unmarked closest to the line, but the full back threw it at another teammate. He called again for the pass but was bypassed as the blue team moved up the field.

He accelerated and felt an extra gear kick in. He ran alongside the wide player crying out for the easy pass but again he was ignored. Trying to go past the defender himself, the player was tackled and the Whites were on a three-against-one breakaway.

Jimmy was left stranded again, but this time was different. He turned and started chasing the attackers, gaining on them with every stride. All his aches and pains had disappeared and his legs felt strong and young.

The Whites player who stole the ball was trying to draw out the last defender and waited for just the right moment to slip a pass sideways so his striking partner had only the keeper to beat. It was inch perfect, right into the path of the onrushing player, but just as he was about to pull the trigger, a long leg slid all of 10 yards to block the shot.

If Jimmy had got the timing a second wrong it would have been a certain penalty, but the ball bobbled safely out for a corner. He'd run the entire length of the field faster than three 20-year-olds and he wasn't even out of breath. He stood up, pushed back his hair and looked for a man to mark for the cross.

There were perhaps just a couple of minutes left on the clock as the corner came over high to the back post. Jimmy had been marking one of the opposing centre backs at the front but cycled back as he saw the ball coming over and leaped twice as high as anyone else to cushion the high ball on his chest and bring it down just behind the penalty spot. Without allowing the ball to touch the ground, he dinked it over the scrum of players into an open space on the right.

He saw the lone centre forward on the halfway line, hoisted the pass to him and ran to collect the return pass that never came. Instead of the obvious, the forward switched to the left wing, trying a difficult pass the wing back was never going to reach.

Without breaking his stride, Jimmy crossed from right field to left, reaching the ball just before the defender and stopping it dead, leaving his off balance opponent floundering. There were still two defenders in front of him and he had no support from his own team.

Standing just outside the penalty box on the left of the field, Jimmy slowed everything down in his mind until it felt to him like slow motion. Everyone else was running around frantically, but Jimmy was the calm in the storm.

He flicked the ball up and played keep-me-up two times before nonchalantly crossing it to a point in front of the penalty spot. He kicked the ball a little higher than necessary, just allowing himself time to dash around the defenders and meet his own cross with his head and fire the ball like a bullet into the top right hand corner.

Jimmy trotted back, still not out of breath, and nobody congratulated him. The whistle went and still there was nothing.

But this time it wasn't because of any cold shoulder. They were simply stunned. Nobody had ever seen anything like it.

The stadium was completely silent.

Then the trance was broken by a small boy, his two younger sisters and their mother, all going absolutely bonkers on the terraces.

CHAPTER THIRTY-FOUR

It was only much later that night, after a family celebration at their favourite Italian on the way home, that Zoe asked the question that had been bugging her ever since the game. They were laying in bed; the children were finally asleep after making Jimmy run through his goal over and over again and Zoe was snuggled against his chest.

Jimmy couldn't move without crying out in pain but he was as happy as he could remember.

"Okay sugar, so you have to tell me now." She looked up at him with the big brown eyes he'd lost himself in all those years ago.

"Tell you what?"

"What the hell happened out there today? Did you take something when you went back to the changing rooms? Did you find some time machine or something?"

"I don't know what you mean." The truth was that Jimmy wasn't really sure himself. Not yet.

"Oh! Come on, Jimmy. One minute you're looking so wiped out you could hardly stand up and the next you're galloping around like a teenager. I mean, it was awesome and all, but there has to be some kind of explanation."

"You wouldn't believe me if I told you, Zo."

"Try me." She paused and added: "It wasn't drugs, was it?" She really hoped it wasn't drugs.

He shook his head.

"Booze then?"

"Yeah, I downed a couple of vodkas in the changing room. That was it."

"Don't be sarcastic, Jimmy. I just wanna know. You were amazing. I know you used to be good. I remember standing on the touchline watching in the freezing cold every Sunday morning when we were in London. But you looked like someone else out there, someone a lot younger."

Jimmy shifted up the bed so he was sitting upright and Zoe moved with him. The curtains were open and they could just see the moon through the open window.

"That's because I was someone else out there…someone a lot younger." His eyes were begging to be believed.

"You're taking hormones? Youth pills?"

"Nothing like that." Jimmy was nervous about sharing the epiphany he'd felt on the field at the Galaxy. It made no sense to him let alone anybody else but it was the only explanation.

"It was the boots."

CHAPTER THIRTY-FIVE

The more Jimmy tried to convince Zoe the more he was convinced his boots were channeling Duncan Edwards. The problem was that the more he tried to convince her, the more she thought he was losing his mind.

All his talk about the Busby Babes didn't help. "They weren't a bunch of hot cheerleaders. They were really good footballers who happened to be young." Jimmy was getting exasperated. "And Duncan was the best of them all. He was only 21 when he died but he'd already won everything with Man United and played for England 18 times."

"And now you think you're him because you found his old boots?" Zoe was a school psychologist and she sometimes dropped into a habit of talking to him as if he was one of her students. "Does that sound really plausible to you, Jimmy? Just take a second and think about what you're saying."

"I understand that it makes no sense. I'm trying to persuade you that I'm playing like this legendary footballer who died in 1958 because I'm wearing his crappy boots. Of course I sound like a lunatic." Jimmy grabbed Zoe's shoulders with both hands. "But I'm also telling you that as crazy as it sounds, it's the truth!"

She still wasn't having it. "Babe, you don't always need to find an excuse to put yourself down when you do something well. It's like your dad would never let you take credit for anything and now he's gone. Now you're giving yourself the chance to shine."

Zoe smiled sweetly at Jimmy and he tried to keep his temper. "It's all you, Jimmy. It's not some ghost who died in a plane crash. It's all you. You need to be proud of what you did today and not try and explain it away as some kind of weird magic."

She hugged Jimmy close and kissed him hard with her soft lips. Pulling back, she whispered in his ear: "This is who you are, Jimmy. You know what I think you found out here today? Yourself. You finally learned to believe in yourself. You don't need to struggle any longer. I'm so happy for you."

He really didn't want to talk about it after that. Perhaps it was enough that Zoe and the children had seen him do something special. It was certainly better than all the messing up he'd been doing recently.

Jimmy didn't expect anything more to come of it. A couple of the kids had come up and congratulated him after the game but that was about it. What had he done anyway? Made one tackle, scored a fancy goal. That was about it. Maybe he'd helped them forget how much of a loser he was in the drills but barely.

Murray hadn't said anything to him when he left. He was surrounded by the younger players and Jimmy gave up trying to say goodbye. The kids were hungry and excited and he didn't want to keep them waiting any longer.

He kept the shirt as a souvenir. *Enough now*, he thought as he walked off the field arm in arm with Zoe, with the kids running in front of them. It was time to buckle down and put this nonsense behind him.

He'd wiped a few smiles off the faces of those snotty teenagers and shown his family he still had a few moves. Any tricks he had up his sleeve on the field from then on would be reserved for the FOBD.

Perhaps his wife was right. He'd shown everyone today that he, Jimmy Keen, could play, not some shadow from the past. It was as simple as that.

But lying awake after Zoe had gone to sleep, Jimmy couldn't get the idea out of his mind that he'd found those old boots for a reason. A sharp pain was still burrowing into his right knee and both legs ached relentlessly. He'd looked like 100 walking from the bathroom to bed. This wasn't the body of the man who played those last 10 minutes of the Galaxy scrimmage.

That was a young man at his very peak with a strength, a vision and a raw, explosive talent Jimmy never had, not when he was 21, not ever. Once upon a time Jimmy had been good, definitely better than average…but not superhuman.

Jimmy had learned his lesson trying to explain it to Zoe. Nobody was ever going to believe that Duncan Edwards' old boots were the reason he was suddenly able to hold back time.

From now on, Jimmy thought, his hands behind his head, sleep still some way off, he'd keep the secret of the boots to himself. But he would try and find out some more about Duncan Edwards, the boy/man whose giant shoes he'd stepped into.

CHAPTER THIRTY-SIX

Wally's hearing was failing and at first he couldn't hear what Jimmy was asking.

"I just wanted to know a bit more about Duncan Edwards and what he was like." Jimmy tried to speak slowly into the telephone so the old man could follow.

"Great footballer, the best there ever was." Wally hesitated. "You know he used to live next door in your old house?"

"Yes, I remember. What about you? Do you remember much about him?"

"He lived next door." Wally's early stage dementia was more obvious on the phone. "Great footballer."

Jimmy took a deep breath. He'd been trying the old man's landline for a few days. Wally didn't trust mobile phones. "Can you tell me some stuff about him? You know, what kind of player he was? That sort of thing."

"I'll tell you something funny, Jim. He was a terrific Morris dancer. I think it was his mum's influence. He was so good when he was 14 he was selected to compete for the school in the National Morris and Sword Dancing Festival on the same day as his trial for the England Schools team. Thankfully he went to the trial. I think Man United already had an eye on him even then."

Warming to the subject, Wally continued: "Wolves were also after Duncan and Stan Cullis, the manager then, was furious when United stole the local boy from under his nose. The boy was a fine carpenter, too. Did an apprenticeship just down the street for a few years. His dad insisted on it in case the football career didn't pan out. It was the same for the great Tom Finney. He was a plumber. Can you imagine?"

"That's really interesting, Wally," said Jimmy, "but what about the football? What kind of player was he?"

"He was better than Bobby Charlton, better than Bobby Moore, better than all of them. He was the complete player; he had it all. I saw him making his debut for England in a 7-2 win against Scotland. He was only 18 but he already looked like the most experienced player there."

This was what Jimmy was after. "Tell me more about him on the pitch."

Wally went into a coughing fit and took a few minutes to get a glass of water. "Aargh! Never did like the stuff. Give me a bottle of stout any time." He coughed one more time and continued: "Duncan was strong as an ox; he was what you'd call a defensive midfielder these days, except he'd score goals as well.

"He had a cracking shot, could play with both feet and he was incredible in the air. He'd jump twice as high as anybody else. Fantastic tackler, never seen anyone else like it, and his passing was like a dream. I'm trying to think if he had a weakness, but there really wasn't one. He could play anywhere; I think he started out at left back.

"And he was a natural born captain. Everybody just loved the lad. He'd come back here for visits and he'd be exactly the same. Chunky, we used to call him; he'd even sign his letters, Chunky Edwards."

Wally went quiet and Jimmy started to worry he'd stopped breathing.

"Are you okay, Wally." He said it twice before the old man replied. This time he sounded more wistful. "I was just thinking about poor Gladstone, Duncan's father. A lovely man. He used to walk a mile-and-a-half every day from the Priory through the Tipton council estate to the Bean's Industries factory, where he worked as a labourer. The curtains would twitch as he passed through the estate and the parents would tell their kids, 'That's big Duncan's dad.'

His voice was now so soft Jimmy could hardly hear him. "After Munich they never saw Gladstone again. He gave up his factory work, struggling to cope with the loss of his son, and got a job cleaning up the leaves at the cemetery in Holly Hall where Duncan was buried. He never did get over what happened."

Wally started coughing again and the retches became more prolonged. Jimmy said he should call for help. "I'm fine, just fine, son, not a problem. Maybe I'll pour a little snifter and sit quietly for a while. Don't worry. Give my love to Zoe and those wonderful kids of yours and tell them to hurry back soon to see old Wally."

"All right, Wally, but call me if you need anything." Jimmy was still worried. "You shouldn't be coughing like that."

"It's just my age."

"Yeah, and the 20 fags a day."

"That's our little secret," he cackled. "Don't tell Zoe.

"And Jim. One more thing." Wally was wheezing and had trouble getting the words out, but he was determined to finish. "Like I told you before, Duncan adored your dad. Just adored him. Your dad lived around the corner from him growing up. Even when he was with United Duncan'd come over and your old man would go head to head with him in the back garden.

"He'd never come back to Dudley without seeing your dad."

CHAPTER THIRTY-SEVEN

After his first day on the construction site in Crystal Cove, Jimmy had discovered a whole new set of aching muscles.

He'd persuaded Zoe to swallow her pride and call her developer friend, the one he'd stood up the previous Sunday. Although the guy had found another foreman he'd agreed as a favour to give Jimmy some labouring work and, if it all worked out, he'd consider him for something better.

"I had to call one of my regular guys last night and tell him he wasn't needed," the white-haired, polo-shirted developer told Jimmy when he arrived on time at 6am. "Zoe's a great girl. I went to school with her and she said there'd been some big mix up last week. I hate to say no to her so I'm hoping it'll all work out. Why don't you give the stonework guys a hand?"

Eight hours of heavy lifting later, Jimmy staggered to a co-worker's truck and they lined up in the procession of vehicles waiting to be allowed out of the heavily gated community. All he'd eaten was a salad and a diet coke Zoe had packed in his lunch box and he was hungry and caked in stone dust when he was dropped off up the road from the flat at 4.30pm just as Tyler arrived back on his bike.

Jimmy pulled off his boots and called out for Zoe to put the kettle on.

"I'm inside, at the dinner table." He heard Zoe's voice from the back of the apartment and walked through to find her sitting with Neil Murray, who was cradling a mug of tea.

The Scotsman stood up, holding out his hand. "I'm sorry we didn't get to talk on the field the other day. I asked around for you and was told you'd already gone."

"Well, I, er, had my family with me." Jimmy felt awkward in his shabby work clothes, a pair of ripped old jeans and a white t-shirt. "I see you've met my wife, Zoe."

"Yes," said Murray. "We've had a nice little chat. She tells me you've just started a new job."

"Kind of. Yes, I guess I have." Jimmy was wondering why Murray was there. He assumed he was there to let him down gently. "Thanks so much for the opportunity, Neil. I knew I was too old to really stand a chance but it was good of you to let me have a run out."

"Don't thank me, Jimmy."

"What do you mean?"

"I should be thanking you." Murray put his hand out again and this time he held onto Jimmy's hand. "I want you to sign for the Los Angeles Galaxy."

Jimmy tried to remove his hand but the older man held it in a vice. "That's really cool of you, Neil, but I think I'm a bit old in the tooth for the youth team."

"I don't want you for that." Murray stared him straight in the eye. "I want you in the first team."

Jimmy's jaw dropped and he stood there in a gormless silence.

"What do you say, Jimmy? You wanna give it a go?"

Still, Jimmy couldn't find the words.

"It's just a three month contract. We'll see how it goes and take it from there, no pressure." Murray had a piece of paper in his hand.

"Say something, Jimmy." Zoe threw her hands around his neck.

"Tell him yes."

CHAPTER THIRTY-EIGHT

Jimmy peered across at the alarm beeping next to his bed. It showed 6:00. He pressed the snooze button and closed his eyes. Zoe reached over and pulled his body closer to hers. "You don't need to play today, baby. You should conserve your energy for the real thing on Monday."

She pushed even closer, just in case he'd missed the signal that it would definitely be worth his while to stay in bed and Jimmy was sorely tempted. But he'd made a pact with himself the night before. He had to test the boots. He needed to be sure before turning up at the Galaxy's Carson training ground.

Levering himself out of the warm covers, he limped into the bathroom. The face staring at him in the mirror showed every one of his 47 years. He splashed some water, hoping for a miracle, but he opened his eyes and followed the fault lines cracking his smile. He looked as old and tired as he felt. He looked like his father.

Martyn was waiting outside in the alley for him a few minutes later. They followed the sunrise down the coast in Martyn's Porsche Panamera and Jimmy pretended to sleep as they climbed up to the Top of the World Park at Vista Park. Jimmy was still trying to understand everything that was going on. *Zoe's right about one thing*, he thought. *I'm just not used to good things happening to me.*

He'd signed the contract. He'd even cashed the first check.

But he still didn't quite believe it.

Several of the guys were already at the bench when they arrived soon after 6.30. Jimmy signed his name on the scrap of paper keeping track of who arrived and when so they could split into two games if too many players turned up for one.

Familiar faces ambled over in a steady stream from the parking lot, all carrying bags filled with shirts and various creams, tonics and braces to keep the years at bay. Paul had his usual coffee and bacon and egg sandwich from Starbucks; Martyn's knees were bandaged up with ice packs; Thor had more rollers and stretch bands than 24-Hour Fitness; and Simon's head was pressed hard against the stone gazebo to force his once-broken back into place.

Ibuprofen was handed out like contraband, three pills at a time, enough to allay the pain until it was time for Sunday brunch alcohol to play tag with the medication.

Jimmy hadn't bothered bringing his newer boots. He took the old pair out of his bag; the worn leather smelled more mildewy than the modern plastic ones, which reeked of rotting bodies and refuse dumps after a couple of games.

He was afraid to put them on, worrying that he'd imagined the magic.

What if the whole thing was a fluke?

But pushing his left foot into the shoe, Jimmy felt a rush of blood racing up his entire body. It was like a youth transfusion.

He had to stop himself from shouting out with joy, so transformed did he feel.

Jimmy's usual routine involved some ponderous stretches and a slow jog around the field, but he didn't want to risk any of that now. Both boots were laced on tight, his feet encased under concrete toes, but they felt like carpet slippers.

Every muscle was raring to go; it took all his willpower to keep his own body in check and he started kicking the ball around with a couple of the others deliberately reining in the power of his passing. He was exulted with the sheer joy of playing soccer.

If he still had any doubts that the boots were the font of his newfound skills, they were already banished. Nobody had mentioned Jimmy's LA Galaxy try-out and he was happy to leave it that way.

The players gradually migrated from the bench to the pitch and Jimmy helped put out the cones, able to bend over for the first time without wincing. They'd reached 25 players and the debate was over whether they should play one game of 12 versus 13 or split up into two matches.

Jimmy assumed that was what they were to discuss when Bill and Mark called for everybody to gather in the middle of the park. It was still only 7.15am but the sun was high in the sky and the temperature was rising with every kick.

"We just have a quick announcement before we start," said Bill as the players gathered around in a circle. "It won't surprise anybody that Dylan, one of our younger players, has won a place on the LA Galaxy youth team. So congrats Dylan."

The youngster smiled and politely acknowledged the applause, his footballing dreams still very much intact.

As the players went back to their stretching and theories on the day's Premier League matches, Bill put up a hand. "There is something else that is more surprising, considering the age of the person concerned. I don't know if any of you know this but one of our own FOBD regulars also had a trial this week with the Galaxy.

"I know we call this place the Field of Broken Dreams but Jimmy Keen has shown us that perhaps our dreams aren't so broken after all."

Jimmy shuffled, uncomfortable in the spotlight.

"We don't want to embarrass Jimmy, but we felt we should mark the achievement and show our appreciation and support."

The group was silent, the air completely still, as Bill continued: "Some of us have been meeting here every Sunday for 10 years now and I think we all believe we have something very special. We have a band of brothers."

He hesitated and carried on: "For one of us to have made it to the pros at the age of, well…let's say he's older than 21…is something we can all be proud of."

The players burst into an impromptu round of applause and broke ranks to shake Jimmy by the hand and pat him on the back.

"So Jimmy," said Mark, putting an arm around his shoulders, "did you hear back yet? Are you going to leave us for the big time?"

"Yes and no." Jimmy tried to shrink back into the crowd. "I did hear back and I'll be training with the Galaxy on Monday… but I'll still be coming to FOBD every Sunday whatever happens.

"At least here I'm not the oldest on the pitch by 20 years."

Formalities over, they decided on a single game. Every pass had to work through a bundle of players on the cramped pinball field. But that didn't stop Jimmy. He scored four spectacular, some would say impossible, goals and made another four for his teammates before half-time.

It was all because of Duncan Edwards' boots, Jimmy was sure of it. But just to be sure he changed back into the spider boots for the second 45 minutes and barely got another kick.

CHAPTER THIRTY-NINE

The greeting when Jimmy walked into the LA Galaxy
dressing room was as antiseptic as the smell. Everyone was
sitting on benches by their clothes pegs in various states of
undress. The players were older and their faces were more
familiar than the kids at the try-out but they looked just as
suspicious.

Neil Murray had met Jimmy for breakfast at the Denny's
diner just outside the stadium and introduced him to the
manager, Giorgio Rossi, a tough, no-nonsense Italian-American,
who'd played in Serie A for Napoli and had only retired a
couple of years earlier. While Jimmy wondered if he should
order bacon and eggs before training, Rossi got right to the
point.

"This is not my idea - you're only ten years older than me -
but Neil here vouches for you so I said I'd give it a try. You
come to training, you give it your best and we'll see what
happens. No promises."

He stuck out a hand. Rossi was wearing a sharp, navy suit
and his hair was perfectly mussed into place. Jimmy felt like a
tramp in an old grey Adidas tracksuit and a kitbag he brought
with him from England.

"I'll do my best, Mr Rossi."

"Call me boss."

"Sorry, Mr Rossi, I mean, boss."

"Okay, good. Just as long as we understand each other." He looked across at Murray. "We're down about five players because of injury and I'm being told I can't buy anybody else. Neil tells me that you and some kid from the trial are supposed to fill the gap until we can get our proper players back. I'll be honest, I'm not being given any choice with this, but I won't have it turned into some great big media circus because you're old enough to be a grandpa."

"All I'm asking is you give Jimmy a chance." Murray was paying the check before Jimmy even got the chance to order. "Although we do have a few members of the media coming for a wee chat with Jimmy later."

Rossi stood up and wagged a finger at Murray, looking daggers at the older man. "No circus…no circus!" he said and walked out without saying anything more to Jimmy.

Murray drove Jimmy to the stadium. After walking him down to the dressing room, he pointed at the door. "You're on your own now, son. Don't let me down."

With that, he walked back upstairs, leaving Jimmy to face the first team squad for the first time.

There were a couple of nods and some curious stares but most of the team ignored Jimmy as he stumbled uncertainly around looking more like a painter and decorator than a footballer. He even had a couple of white paint splashes on his pants. He finally found a peg bearing a number 6 shirt with his name on the back. Keen. *At least it wasn't Eager*, he thought, sitting down on the bench in between Otto Weissman, the giant German centre back, and the US National team full back, Robbie Norton. Both ignored him.

Jimmy had brought both pairs of boots; the Mundials and the old pair. He'd hoped to put his lucky ones on without the others noticing but that was impossible in the busy changing room and he worried they'd look ridiculous with the brand new kit.

There were a couple of players still in their tracksuits who clearly weren't getting ready to play and Jimmy felt one of them, in particular, staring at him. Recognising him as Francesco Torres, the veteran big money signing from Real Madrid that summer, Jimmy nodded and smiled.

"Don't mind Francesco. He's just pissed because he twanged his hamstring." The burly black midfielder Mike Terry, a US National team mainstay for years and long term Galaxy skipper, stuck out a hand. "You must be Jimmy. I'm Mike."

"I know who you are." Jimmy stood up. "Good to meet you."

Terry put his arm around Jimmy and steered him away from the others. "Francesco's worried you're gonna come in here and show him up."

"I wish!" Jimmy looked back to where he'd left the old boots on the bench by his bag. He wanted to go and put them away but Terry still had him by the arm.

"Let me introduce you to the rest of the lads. They're really not that bad. Well, most of them, anyway. I'm sure an experienced guy like you has seen it all."

"I'm not really that experienced, just old. I've never played pro before."

Jimmy could see the flicker of surprise in Terry's eye but it was quickly covered up. "No worries, perhaps you've been saving it all up." Terry laughed, but not unkindly. "We need all the help we can get right now."

They did the circuit around the room and when they returned to Jimmy's peg, his boots were gone. He looked up to see Torres turning them over in his hands.

"You bring your father's boots, señor?" He spoke in strongly accented Spanish. "Maybe you can't afford some new ones."

Jimmy went over and put his hand out for the boots. Torres threw them at him to catch. "Don't get too comfortable around here," he said. "I'll be back playing very soon and you can crawl back into whatever century you came from."

Jimmy stuffed the boots deep in his bag and put on the Copa Mundials. He'd come back and change them before they played a scrimmage. That way nobody need notice.

Only they did drills all day and didn't return to the dressing room until the training was over at 4.00. Rossi made it a triple session as punishment for the 4-0 drubbing they'd suffered at the weekend to Real Salt Lake. They didn't play a game; they weren't even allowed balls. It was all running.

The day was a disaster for Jimmy. He came in last every run and some of his drills were so bad Rossi sent him to the sidelines to watch. He played like he was 47. Even Terry didn't know what to say to him as he walked off the field soaked with sweat.

Jimmy hadn't seen anything of Neil Murray all day, but as he neared the tunnel he saw the Scotsman rushing towards him.

"How did it go, Jimmy?" he asked. "Don't forget, I'm relying on you."

Jimmy shrugged. Even that was an effort.

"Just before you get changed I'd like you to meet a few people." Murray grabbed his arm and led him towards the corporate suites. "I've set up a few interviews."

Jimmy tried to pull away but Murray's grip tightened.

"No need to be like that." Murray was insistent. "They're fascinated how you've been able to pull this off at your age. Perhaps you can tell them the secret to your eternal youth."

CHAPTER FORTY

Jimmy was blinded by flashbulbs the moment he opened the door to the club's conference room. There were at least half a dozen TV crews as well as photographers and reporters.

And they all came running at him at once.

"Whoa! Steady on, folks." Murray stepped in front of Jimmy and ushered over a track-suited security guard. "Let's keep this civilised, everyone will get an opportunity to talk to Mr. Keen."

Jimmy felt a cold clammy sweat down his back and wasn't sure if it was from training or his terror at being in front of so many cameras. He pushed his lank, damp hair back with both hands and took a deep breath to try and steady himself. He didn't have a mirror but he knew he looked terrible and probably smelled even worse.

A brunette who looked about 17 to Jimmy introduced herself as the club's media relations manager and led him over to the front of the room where a chair had been set up next to a phalanx of TV cameras.

"My name's Michelle, I'm going to keep everybody to a couple of questions," she said. "I know this is your first day."

"But what are they going to ask me?" Jimmy was genuinely bemused. "I haven't even played yet so I really don't know anything."

She brushed a stray piece of grass from his shoulder. "I don't mean to be disrespectful, Mr Keen, but I think they'll be asking you about your age. You're 43, right?"

"Actually I'm 47."

The PR girl nodded thoughtfully. "Yes, they're definitely going to be asking about your age. I'll try and keep them brief."

Jimmy could see the cameramen squabbling over who was going to be first, but Michelle pointed at an older woman and she moved in to sit in a chair facing him.

The woman, her hair dyed a hard yellow, shook Jimmy's hand. He recognised her from the evening news.

"Hi, I'm Sherri Walker. Thank you for talking to me, Jimmy. May I call you Jimmy?"

Jimmy nodded. He felt even shabbier sitting across from the meticulously dressed reporter.

"Congratulations on signing for the Galaxy, your family must be very proud."

"Yes." There was no way out. "I guess they are."

"Am I right in thinking you have three children, Jimmy? A boy and two daughters?" She moved a little closer and slanted her head slightly to one side.

"I do, yes." Jimmy was trying to answer while keeping his stomach pulled in.

The cameraman, a bald guy in a denim shirt, looked up from his lens and swiped a hand across his throat. "Cut for one minute. Jimmy, could you just get your hair out of your face please? We can't see you."

"Oh yes, sorry." Jimmy did what he was told and the cameraman settled his eyes back on the viewer.

"So Jimmy," continued Sherri, "you're a family man and you are now the big hope to help the Galaxy turn their season around."

"I certainly do love my family, but I'm not sure I..."

"The extraordinary thing about all of this, Jimmy, is that you are old enough to be the father to many of your teammates." Sherri turned around and looked straight at the camera. "Jimmy Keen is 47 and he's the oldest person to ever play in Major League Soccer."

"Technically, I haven't actually played..."

The interviewer interrupted him again with another question. "You are closer to retirement age than to your teens, what makes you think you can compete out there with some of the best players in the world at your age?"

"I just love playing football and I don't think age matters when you love something. I'm just going to do my best and we'll see how it goes." Jimmy let his stomach muscles relax, but he felt his face going red.

He looked across the room hoping to see Murray and when he turned back Sherri was gone and another reporter was sitting in her place.

"Hi Mr Keen. I'm Selma Garcia, sports reporter for Channel 4. Can I start by asking what it feels like to be just starting your soccer career at an age most people start thinking about their pension? What's your secret?"

For two more hours, he answered questions from every network about his age. When he finally slumped in the back of an Uber to take him home just after 7pm, the driver insisted on handing him that morning's copy of the Los Angeles Times.

"Hey man, aren't you this guy?"

Jimmy flipped open the sports pages to see a giant photo of his police mugshot from the drink driving arrest illustrating a story about him joining the Galaxy.

It was headlined: "The Oldest Winger in Town."

CHAPTER FORTY-ONE

Jimmy ran out onto the field and tried to remember every second; the sea of expectant faces, the echoing voice on the tannoy announcing the team, the heady smell of grass and anticipation filling the chilly Californian October evening.

He'd waited until the very last minute to put on his old boots, hoping the other players wouldn't notice. The first teamers were going through their rituals - a last pee, a snatched prayer, a gobbled down banana - and paid him little attention anyway. Only a couple had been friendly during training. Most had assumed Jimmy would be on his way once the publicity about his age had died down.

He hadn't dared wear the old boots before. Consequently the training sessions had been an unmitigated disaster. He played like who he was — a middle-aged man trying to relive his youth. Jimmy was all over the TV and stories about his late blooming had spun around the world, which hadn't helped his standing with the squad, who nicknamed him "grandpa." Fortunately, the training sessions had all been closed to the media so the public hadn't seen how poorly he was doing.

His touch had been terrible and he was last at everything; falling asleep immediately after dinner every night. Rossi hadn't spoken to him since the Denny's breakfast.

Jimmy pulled the laces tight, stood up and straightened his shirt and limbered up a little. Across the room, Francesco

Torres, still injured and dressed in a sharp blue suit and tie, was watching him intently. He pointed two fingers at his eyes and thrust them in Jimmy's direction.

"I got my eyes on you, old man," he said. "You and your ugly ass boots."

Other than the fact they played the same position, Jimmy couldn't imagine why Torres, once one of the best players in the world and still a formidable character, had it in for him. He smiled self-consciously and joined the huddle of substitutes who were heading out to kick a few balls around before the Friday evening fixture against Seattle Sounders, the Western Conference leaders.

Jimmy was left to juggle the ball himself; the other subs wouldn't pass to him. The euphoria at being on the pitch had quickly subsided with the realisation that he was on his own. Then he heard a tiny voice from the sideline and saw Grace standing up, waving desperately in his direction: "Dad! Dad!"

Jimmy looked over and waved. Grace, somehow looking more vulnerable since her operation, Tyler and Charley all stood up as well and were caught on the Jumbotron, triggering a ripple of applause around the stadium. Sitting next to the family in the front row was Martyn, Paul, Stuart, Bill, Sean, James and Mark. They had a banner unfurled over the wall "FIELD OF BROKEN DREAMS." Behind them, Jimmy picked out Andrew, Ken, Dylan, John, Randy, Dom, Luis, Nils, Carl, Enrique and a bunch more FOBD regulars.

A whistle blew and the assistant coaches were waving them off. The game was about to start. Jimmy took his place with the other substitutes.

The first half went in a whirl for Jimmy. He'd never been so close to the action and yet felt so detached. Rossi's voice was in his ear the whole time, screaming at his players to go back or go forward, to mark or get free. He was in a constant state of angst.

The air went out of the stadium on the beat of 45 minutes when the Sounders finally scored the goal they'd been threatening for most of the game. While the Galaxy were passing around, often sideways or backwards to the great consternation of the coach, Seattle was going route one, muscling their opponents out of every challenge. The goal was predictably simple; a long kick from the keeper, a flick from the centre forward and a tap in from his strike partner.

Rossi rushed back down the tunnel as soon as the whistle blew. "I want you back here right now — all of you!" he shouted over his shoulder.

Jimmy was one of the first in the dressing room and watched the first team slump on the benches. The other coaches were there but there was no sign of Rossi.

When they were all sitting down, the coach burst in through the back door, slamming it behind him.

"Perhaps I am missing something," he started. "Perhaps this game is not so important, no?"

Nobody dared speak. Most knew better, they'd been here before.

"Let me see, do we need to win this game to go through to the play-offs?"

Silence.

"Somebody answer me." Rossi's voice was rising and as it did so, his Italian accent became more pronounced.

"Yes, boss." Several of the players mumbled.

"Yes, what?"

"We need to win boss."

"That's funny because I think maybe my players are tired and looking forward to a vacation. You all have your trips booked with your girlfriends? You ready for some time off?"

"No boss."

"So why you all play like you don't care?" Rossi's voice was rising with every sentence. "You let them beat you to every ball, you pass like you're scared of their goalkeeper. You don't want to bother him? Not one shot on target. Not one shot, period! You play like a bunch of pussies."

The red-faced coach kicked out at the water cooler and it crashed to the floor, sending a tidal wave across the players' feet.

"You want vacation? You get vacation. But if you lose this game you might as well stay on vacation the rest of your life. I don't need you here. I don't need pussies. I replace all of you."

"We're trying boss." Mike Terry tried to placate Rossi. "But they're pressing really hard. We can't keep hold of the ball. We…"

Rossi put his hand up. "No! No excuses. We run harder, we work harder. We play football. Simple."

"But boss, if we draw we still…"

"NO! Rossi threw his clipboard towards Terry, hitting the wall a few feet from his head. No excuses. We win or you're gone. I don't care about tie."

With that, the coach stormed back out, leaving the shell-shocked players in stunned silence once more.

"Right then lads," Terry broke the spell. "You heard the man. Let's go win this."

The players and most of the subs formed a circle and put one hand each in the centre. "GO TEAM!"

They sounded like they meant it but Jimmy was left on the edge. He'd never felt so far away from the Field of Broken Dreams.

CHAPTER FORTY-TWO

The longer the game went on the more frustrated Jimmy became. With the old boots on, he felt twitchy, ready to go. The desire to play was so strong it was almost impossible for him to watch.

Rossi had already used two subs, one of them the bearded Hispanic player who was the only other one to make it through the try-out with Jimmy. He'd been friendlier in training - Jimmy had mistaken the fact that he struggled with his English for an antagonism towards him - but he'd not been able to affect the game. The Galaxy was still one down with 15 minutes to go and the end of their season beckoning.

Jimmy knew he wasn't going to get called upon; he was destined for the vacation of no return.

Then John Whelan, the Galaxy's Irish-born centre-forward, went down in a crumpled heap just outside the Sounders' penalty box. He'd been poleaxed by an elbow as he jumped for a cross and his nose was smeared with blood. The trainer waved different numbers of fingers in front of his eyes but dazed Whelan was out of it.

The referee gesticulated towards the bench and Jimmy saw Rossi's confused face scanning the subs. There was a keeper, two fullbacks and a centre back. They weren't going to get the equaliser.

And there was Jimmy.

Whelan was led slowly off the pitch, his face swaddled in bloody napkins, and still Rossi was hesitating. The referee was looking at his watch and his assistant was asking Rossi what number to put on his substitution board. Finally, he saw him mouth Jimmy's number 6.

Rossi pointed over at Jimmy. "Get warmed up, in a hurry." He didn't look happy. "You're on."

Jimmy stood up and tore off his tracksuit. There were no nerves now. He'd been waiting his entire life for this…perhaps several lifetimes. He slipped on his shin pads and ran down to the edge of the field to stretch.

Rossi came up to him. "I want you to hold the ball up front. That's all, don't try anything stupid. Just get the ball and dish it off to one of the others."

The referee had lost patience and was signalling for the free kick to be taken. The Hispanic youngster, Hector Gutierrez, was demanding the ball and appeared to be in heated conversation with Robbie Norton, the full back and the usual free kick taker.

The whistle went again. The referee was intent on restarting the game and wouldn't look over to allow Jimmy on.

Gutierrez pushed Norton away and took four steps back. There were five Sounders defenders in a green wall lined up behind the ref's foam barrier 10 yards away.

Jimmy watched as he limbered up. The youngster looked up once towards the goal and trotted towards the ball, hitting it with his instep and keeping his head down as it looped over the keeper's head into the top right hand corner of the goal. Gutierrez looked up just as the ball hit the back of the net, triggering pandemonium in the crowd.

Gutierrez set off on a celebration run to the corner, mobbed by the other players, even the disgruntled Norton. Rossi, leaping with delight, ran halfway down the touchline - and outside his technical area - to hug the kid who was playing youth soccer in the barrios of Santa Ana just a few weeks earlier.

As he walked back, Jimmy saw Rossi point to the substitute centre back, former UCLA star Roger Davies. "You're on," he shouted over the roar of the supporters.

Confused, Jimmy held his ground as Rossi tried to brush past. "What's going on? I thought I was up."

"Need to defend now. Save the draw."

"I thought you wanted to win." Jimmy was desperate to play. He was certain he could get the winner.

"Tie is enough for play-offs. Now you sit down please. It's probably for good, we don't want to embarrass you." Rossi put his arm around Davies' shoulders to give him some instructions.

"It may be time for your vacation," the coach said as Jimmy sulked slowly back to his seat.

For the second time since the court case, Jimmy thought that he could really, really do with a beer.

CHAPTER FORTY-THREE

The Sunday morning alarm showed 6:00 and Jimmy burrowed deeper into his pillow. He dropped his phone trying to turn it off and woke Zoe up with his cursing. "I can't even see to turn the damn thing off. It's ridiculous, what's happened to my eyes?"

"You're an old, grumpy man, that's what's happened to your eyes." Zoe kept her own eyes determinedly shut. "And I keep telling you that you need glasses…shouldn't you be getting up for soccer?"

"I'm not going." Jimmy pulled the covers over his head like a naughty boy.

"Why not? You always go." Zoe was awake now. "You love it."

"I'm just over it. I need a break."

Zoe sat up. "Is this about the Galaxy game, babe? I told you, you can't let them get to you. You've hardly said a word to me or the kids ever since."

"Let's just go back to sleep, we can talk about it later."

"But you never miss FOBD. It's your thing."

"Maybe it was my thing. I'm too old for this lark, who am I trying to kid?"

Zoe pulled back the covers from Jimmy. "You're not kidding anybody, we're all really proud of what you're doing. The kids are excited, too."

The alarm went off again and Jimmy covered it with a pillow. "Not after the other day. The coach is never going to play me; he made that crystal clear. It's just embarrassing. The kids were disappointed and all the guys were there to see me on the field. After the stuff on TV and in the papers last week, the whole damned world was disappointed. All this nonsense about magic boots. I must be out of my mind."

Zoe was suddenly furious. "It's not nonsense. You have a contract, you're a professional footballer, that's a fact. And I keep telling you Jimmy, it's all about you, not some ghost from the past. I can't tell you how amazing it is for me to finally see you believing in yourself and in what you can achieve."

"But it's only a three-month contract. I may not even last two weeks." Jimmy knew he was whining. He couldn't help it.

"They will play you, Jimmy. Give them time. Neil told me to reassure you he'd fix it. Now will you please get out of this funk? It's making all of us miserable." Zoe lay back down and faced away from Jimmy.

He sat quietly for a minute staring at the clock. 6:15. It was too late to go. "I'm sorry, babe," he said quietly. "I'm being daft. I'll buck out of it today, but I don't feel like playing."

Just at that moment, he heard a quick horn blast from the driveway outside.

"Too bad," said Zoe, her eyes closed again. "I need another couple of hours sleep and the only way I'm going to do that is get rid of you. I made a call last night and got you a ride."

Jimmy got out of bed and went to the window. Bill and Martyn were standing on the doorstep, about to ring the bell.

"Get a move on, Jim," Martyn shouted up at him. "We wanna make the first game."

"Or if you like, you can come later and be sub!" added Bill.

While they were cracking up, Jimmy kissed Zoe on the forehead and ran down to find his boots. Perhaps it was about time he gave them a run-out, after all.

CHAPTER FORTY-FOUR

If Jimmy still had any doubts that Rossi regarded him as a publicity stunt for the under-achieving club, his first proper conversation with the Italian coach confirmed just how unhappy the "boss" was with the arrangement.

He'd called Jimmy into his office after Tuesday's morning training session.

"If it were up to me you wouldn't be here," he started. "I'm sorry to be blunt but this is true."

"Okay." Jimmy wasn't sure how to react. It wasn't any great surprise.

"You don't show me anything in training," he shrugged. "You're older than I am. I honestly don't understand why Neil is so desperate for you to play, but I'm just the coach. Nobody tells me anything."

Jimmy fidgeted in his chair and pulled his shoulders back to stop slouching. He'd worn the old boots in training that week and had definitely done better, but they hadn't played any games, not even short-sided ones. To really show what the boots could do, he needed a game situation. "All I want is the chance to let you see how I play in a match. I promise you, I won't let you down…er, boss."

"Hmm." Rossi wasn't convinced. "Anyway, I tell you that you must stay with the squad. That's what I'm ordered by your

Mr. Murray. He tells me, Jimmy stays. I don't know why Jimmy stays but that's what's happening."

"Thank you." Jimmy waited to see if Rossi had anything else to say but the coach started shuffling papers. "I appreciate the heads up."

"You can go now. Thank you." Rossi didn't look up, but as Jimmy got to the door, the coach added: "If you ask me, they want you to stay because of all the publicity about you being old and having family and everything. Then they must have you play as well or look stupid. I said you can stay but can't guarantee you will play. That's my decision. It's my team. They want you to play, maybe they have to fire me."

Four days later, Jimmy found himself in a familiar position on the back row of the LA Galaxy's substitutes' bench, only this time he was in Portland and not Carson. Having squeaked into the MLS play-offs in 6th place, the Galaxy had drawn the 3rd-placed Portland Timbers.

Gutierrez was named in the first eleven, replacing Robbie Norton. Torres, the new, big money star, was still sitting on the bench dressed for a nightclub rather than watching a football match. He was three or four seats across from Jimmy.

Despite it being a poor season for the Galaxy, the MLS play-off system meant it was still possible to turn the tables on the more consistently successful sides and win the championship and that was the theme of Rossi's pre-match talk.

"Yesterday is yesterday," he told the team. "We start with new brush, new paper. From now on we play only masterpieces."

He sounded much more optimistic and the players seemed encouraged, thought Jimmy. But as Jimmy stayed behind a little longer in the dressing room to put on his old boots he overheard the coach moaning to Murray.

"The squad is so thin it could break any time. I have all injuries and no replacements." They were in a room Rossi was using as his office but the door was open. "And all you bring me is a kid and an old man."

"The kid saved your butt last week." Murray wasn't backing down.

"He may turn out okay, but you promised me you'd sign me some real replacements to help us." Jimmy could hear the emotional Italian slamming his hand down on the desk.

"I have told you 100 times Giorgio. We have no more cash to spend. You got three designated players, they're all crocked. You got your big shot from Real Madrid, the player at the top of your list, and he's hardly played a minute because he turns up with a dud hamstring. What do you want me to do?"

"I don't want you to make me play an old man." Rossi's decibel level was creeping back up.

"It's the best I can do right now. He's got us more good publicity this week than we've had in months. Disney's talking about doing a movie." Murray's voice was quieter, as if he didn't want anyone else to hear.

"I don't care about movies or newspapers. I want a real footballer." Rossi was almost screaming. "I can't play some 47-year-old over-the-hill has-been or never-was."

Murray's voice was so quiet Jimmy couldn't hear and he didn't want to be caught eavesdropping. The Scotsman was mumbling something about him but he heard a chair scrape back and decided to leave before he heard anything even more demoralising.

This match started off much better for the Galaxy, even though the away stand was sparsely populated. It was a long journey up the West Coast and few gave the depleted Galaxy much hope. Nevertheless, Terry began pulling the strings in midfield and Whelan was back up front looking lively. Gutierrez, the kid signed with Jimmy, had also brought a new energy and commitment to the play.

The Galaxy scored first in the 22nd minute with Whelan pouncing on a loose ball five yards out after a poor clearance from a corner. Former Duke University standout wing back Glynn Barber doubled the lead five minutes later when his cross from the right hand side sailed over the stranded keeper's head and into the empty net.

Rossi was so relaxed he even sat down in his seat for a couple of minutes. The Galaxy could have easily scored twice more with 75 percent possession. Jimmy looked over to where

Zoe was sitting with the kids in the same section as the other wives. They'd come up separately from Jimmy and the team and were up in the fourth or fifth row. He looked down and was stunned to see the Field of Broken Dreams banner draped over the front row wall and he could see a few of the lads laughing with their beers. Paul caught his eye and he gave the thumbs up.

Jimmy had told them not to bother coming, not on his account anyway, as he didn't expect to play. Rossi had made that much clear. There were five possible games left in the season, each more important than the last. And that was if they kept winning all the way to the Championship game. After what he'd heard from the coach, there was no way he was going to be trusted enough to show what he could do.

CHAPTER FORTY-FIVE

This half-time talk was very different from the last. Rossi was going around the changing room, praising the players one-by-one. He was especially glowing about Gutierrez, calling him the new "engine" of the team.

"Just keep doing what you're doing guys," he told them. "Don't let them back in."

But five minutes into the second half that's exactly what happened. A miscommunication at a set piece left a Timbers striker unmarked to head an easy goal and the momentum switched. The Galaxy was suddenly chasing the game and Rossi's anxiety levels rose accordingly.

A poor clearance went straight to Peter McParlane, Portland's US international number 10 and he fired it straight back into the right side of the goal past Venezuelan Galaxy keeper Santo Rivera's outstretched glove. It was 2-2.

Rossi tried a double switch, a defender and a defensive midfielder to try and shore up the team, but they'd totally lost their shape and their confidence. In contrast, the Portland Timbers were flying in search of the winner.

Two balls were cleared off the Galaxy goal line and Rivera pulled off a couple of point blank saves, but it was only a matter of time. On the 81st minute, McParlane scored a simple tap-in after an elaborate Timbers passing move on the edge of the box. The Galaxy was within 9 minutes of a season-ending loss.

Driven on by Rossi, both big Galaxy centre backs, Davies and Weissman, went up for a corner, but the German headed the ball right into the Portland keeper's hands. He immediately hurled it diagonally across the halfway line into the path of the rampant McParlane, who was surging through the centre unmarked. Three touches and a calm, uncontested strike into the corner. It was 4-2.

Jimmy saw Rossi gesture angrily towards Norton to warm up. Moments later Murray was rushing across to the bench. The Scotsman, red-faced, had a finger in the Italian's face. Whatever he said was brief and incendiary. Murray left without waiting for a response, heading back up the steps to the director's box.

Rossi suddenly looked deflated. He told Norton to sit back down and shouted over at Jimmy. "Keen. You're on. Now!"

Jimmy was ready, more because he didn't want to draw attention to his 1950s footwear than any expectation of getting on the pitch. There was no time to stretch or warm-up.

He was replacing Whelan, the centre forward, but there was no pep talk now. "Do what you want," said Rossi. "Remember to smile for the TV cameras."

As Whelan reached the touchline, looking confused, Jimmy shook his hand. "Well played, chief."

He bounded on with a giant leap in the air. He'd never done it before, nor had he called anybody chief, but it all felt quite natural as he raced to the centre spot to restart the game with just 5 minutes regulation time to go.

Gutierrez, playing right wing back, had run up to stand next to him, ignoring the screams of his coach. "Senor," he said. "Just do what you did last time." He tapped the ball sideways and Jimmy set off up the pitch. He could hear the crowd shouting and his teammates yelling for him to pass but as he ran faster everything around him seemed to slow down. He skipped over the first tackle and then made as if to pass to the wing but cut back the other way leaving two more Portland players in his wake.

Three defenders surrounded him, cutting off his route to goal and steering him to the side. Instead of being pushed out, Jimmy put down his head and stabbed at the ball with the most delicate of chips. It skied up over the defence and he allowed it to bounce once before collecting the ball and rolling it left past the onrushing keeper.

His final touch was slightly heavy and he'd gone too wide of the goal. He was virtually on the end line. There wasn't room enough to steer the ball into the empty net. He could either double back or try and reach Gutierrez, who was rushing towards the back post behind two big defenders.

There was no way a normal cross was going to get over the heads of the retreating centre backs, but Jimmy knew instinctively what to do. He stopped dead, putting his left foot on top of the ball to ensure it was still. Then from a standing start he sliced it with the outside of his left boot so finely a sharper edge would have sliced it in two.

The ball, spinning wildly right to left, hopped onto the crossbar, the power of the spin enabling it to hug the entire length of the woodwork until, its force spent, it dropped down onto Gutierrez's head and into the goal.

The stadium went absolutely silent. Then exploded. Jimmy grabbed the ball and raced back to the centre circle. It was 4-3 with one minute left.

The referee's assistant signalled there would be three minutes of overtime. The Portland Timbers players were taking their time with the kick. They were still trying to digest what Jimmy had just done and whether it was a fluke. Their coach was frantically urging them from his technical area to slow everything down.

The ball went straight to the Timbers full back from the kick-off. Jimmy had already visualised what he was going to do next. The defender was trying to slow the game down. He wasn't going to go forward; he was going to pass sideways to his central defenders.

Jimmy made up his mind and went, ignoring the ball. Head down, he ran full speed towards the right centre back, reaching him with a clattering smash the exact moment he received the ball from the left side defender. The centre-back crumpled to the floor clutching his jarred leg and screaming for a foul.

But the ball was squarely at Jimmy's right foot. The tackle was perfectly fair — hard as nails but completely within the rules.

Playing at the FOBD, Jimmy made a point to include all his teammates, even allowing the odd opponent to win a challenge so as not to show off. He capped his goal tally each Sunday at four and played the rest of the games as a provider. But there was no time for such niceties now.

There was just one other Timbers defender in Jimmy's path and, having seen what happened to his teammate, he made a half-hearted attempt at a tackle that Jimmy muscled through imperiously.

Then he made as if to shoot with his left foot to the goalkeeper's right but side-footed the ball with his right instep to the left. The bemused keeper could only stand helplessly as the ball dribbled over the line across the opposite side of the goal.

4-4.

The referee blew his whistle and pointed back to the centre. There was just two minutes remaining. Rossi was standing gobsmacked on the sideline, unable to move. The crowd was just as bemused, excited and horrified at the same time.

The Portland coach, on the other hand, was screaming at his team to keep the ball. They tried a different tactic, punting the ball upfield into the corner from the kick-off and dashing after it in the hope of keeping it penned in and away from Jimmy.

Terry and Weissman were passing back and forth to each other in the tight space but they couldn't get away from the swarming Timbers players to get the ball free. Two Portland strikers were also blocking their path back to the keeper, Rivera.

Jimmy looked up. There was just 30 seconds left of extra time.

Dropping back, he found a space and demanded a pass from his captain, Terry, who squeezed it in between two covering players. Heading back infield towards the centre of his own defence, Jimmy looked back up at the stadium scoreboard. Five-seconds left.

His eyes dropped to the opponent's goal. The keeper was virtually on his line. He couldn't lob the ball over him. He'd have to go for power.

Jimmy took one more touch so he was midway between his own penalty box and the halfway line. Then he put his head down, his eyes focused on the ball and nothing else, and put the laces through it with every ounce of power he had in his right boot.

The ball kept a low trajectory at first, just a foot or so off the ground, and barely went any higher. It was like a bullet gathering more and more speed. Every single person in the stadium, players and spectators alike, were locked in on it.

The last one to realize what was happening seemed to be the opposing keeper. He moved too late to his right, thinking he had time to make the block. But the shot, still rising just perceptibly, blew right by him before he had time to lift a hand and crashed into the back of the net, ripping it wide open with a ball-shaped hole, and kept going up until it hit a metal stanchion high up at the back of the stadium.

The whistle went for the end of the game.

5-4

The LA Galaxy was through to the next round.

CHAPTER FORTY-SIX

Jimmy had to give it to Rossi; he was adaptable. The Italian coach made a beeline for him as soon as the whistle blew and smothered him with a hug that almost left both men on the floor.

"Magnifico! Magnifico!" He grabbed Jimmy's face and planted a smacker on his cheek. "I knew there was something about you, vecchio mio! Che figata!" There was a wild look in the disheveled coach's eyes, like a religious epiphany. "That was….a miracle!"

Players from both sides came over, but were unsure how to behave; Jimmy's teammates embarrassed at how they'd treated the newcomer and Portland still unable to comprehend how victory had been snatched from them so dramatically.

The crowd, 90 percent of them Timber fans, had no such qualms. They were all on their feet applauding Jimmy's exploits, aware they'd seen something uniquely special.

Thirty minutes later, most of them were still there, deep in conversation over what they'd just witnessed.

Jimmy tried to walk across the pitch to where his family and friends were sitting but he was overrun by the media, taking photographs and begging for interviews. Murray materialised from nowhere and shepherded him back towards the tunnel with the help of two burly stadium guards.

Gutierrez ran across. "Thanks for the assist, señor." They both laughed and Jimmy felt the tension ease a little, but all he could think was to get back into the dressing room and change his boots so he wasn't asked about them. He was terrified he'd be quizzed over his unusual footwear on live television.

Mike Terry, the captain, had been the most friendly in Jimmy's first, difficult week. "That," he said, grabbing Jimmy in a headlock, "was the most incredible thing I have ever seen. You were like a tank out there. Unstoppable."

Jimmy felt a hand in his back and turned to see Murray pushing him forward through the throng. "Come on, son. Let's get you out of here."

Jimmy gratefully ducked a couple more TV reporters and dashed into the quiet safety of the tunnel.

Standing there, decked out in Armani, was Torres. He wasn't smiling and didn't say anything at first. He certainly didn't look happy. He just pointed both fingers to his eyes again and jutted them out at Jimmy. "Don't forget, I'm watching you, old man," he whispered as Jimmy walked past. "I'm watching you."

Opening the changing room door, Jimmy was greeted by a burst of applause and soaked by a blast of champagne from a bottle shaken up by Terry. "It may have taken a little too long and for that we all apologise, but tonight, Jimmy Keen, henceforth to be known as 'The Tank,' we all want to welcome you to the Los Angeles Galaxy and thank you for saving our miserable asses!"

With that, another four players aimed champagne bottles at Jimmy and he was finally allowed back to his peg where he was able to quickly slip off the old boots and put them in his bag.

At that very moment, all the youthful energy and fire he'd felt during the game and in the immediate aftermath drained away and he slumped exhausted onto the bench.

"Pretty overwhelming, eh?" Glynn Barber, the full back, sat down next to him. "Felt like that after my first game."

"Yeah." Jimmy could barely get a word out. His feet were killing him. They felt like he'd danced the female lead in Swan Lake.

"Me and Mike and some of the lads are going out tonight in Portland. We're not flying back until lunchtime tomorrow so we were going to have a few beers and check out the clubs, if you know what I mean." He smiled conspiratorially at Jimmy.

A dirty sock was hurled in his direction; it seemed Jimmy was, indeed, now accepted. But he didn't hang around and, after getting a short text, "Outside," from Zoe, he slipped quietly out of the ground and into a taxi where she was waiting for him with the kids. They had just enough time for a celebratory MacDonald's and then they raced for the last Saturday night flight back to LAX.

Jimmy and the FOBD boys had a game of their own early the next morning.

CHAPTER FORTY-SEVEN

Jimmy knew something was up the minute Martyn turned left at the T-junction at the top of the hill and started driving towards Vista Park. Paul was sitting in the passenger seat - they'd taken it in turns to carpool ever since Jimmy's driving ban - and he pointed to the end of the road ahead.

Usually at 6.30 on a Sunday morning the place was pretty deserted other than the odd local walking the dog or a mountain biker heading for the dusty trails branching down from the peak.

But the dead end street was packed with vehicles, including several vans with satellite dishes on the roof.

"Oh man," said Jimmy, slipping down in the back seat. "This isn't good."

"What do you want to do, superstar?" said Martyn. It was obvious the interlopers were there to see Jimmy.

"What can we do?" Jimmy shrugged. "Let's go in as normal and if it gets too crazy I'll call Zoe and see if she'll come and pick me up."

They drove up slowly to the entrance, where about 20 people were standing around looking bored and drinking coffee. They weren't dressed for football.

"Morning, gents." Martyn inched into the car park and Jimmy ducked further down in the back. A couple of the photographers craned their neck trying to see inside but went back to their coffee and pastries when they saw Paul in the passenger seat. He was a Londoner and a fine footballer, but his family was Punjabi so was clearly not the Galaxy's "Super-Sub," as the late night TV sports news had anointed Jimmy.

They parked furthest from the media pack and closest to the park bench meeting place in the hope that Jimmy could evade his pursuers, but as soon as he got out of the car, a shout went up and the TV crews and photographers ran towards them in a giant scrum, shouting his name.

"Jimmy! Jimmy! Can we ask you a few questions about last night?"

The first reporter to catch up with them said breathlessly: "Everyone's talking about the game. It's gone viral on YouTube. There's already more than a million views." He stopped to catch his breath. "How did you do that at your age?"

A cameraman from another network was already pushing the reporter out of the way as they all jostled for position. Jimmy quickly sent a text to Zoe: *help. press everywhere, come + save me!!!*

Murray had told Jimmy he was setting up a press conference for Monday and he tried to tell the media that, but it was clear nobody was leaving empty-handed.

Andrew, Ken and Dylan emerged through the media ranks. "So are you going to make us famous, Jimmy?" Ken found it all hugely amusing.

"Hey guys, do you want the real facts on Jimmy?" said Dylan, who was by then also playing for one of the Galaxy's youth teams. "He's really 64!"

Jimmy hadn't brought his old boots. His plan had been to play really low key so he wouldn't need them. He figured the less people saw them the less questions he'd get asked. Now he risked playing like crap in front of the world's press.

"How about I answer a couple of questions, you get some shots, and then you leave us alone to play our little game? Would that work?"

There were some nods of agreement and the four TV crews pushed forward to get clear shots of Jimmy as everyone jockeyed for position around him. The studied boredom and the lazy coffees were gone now, replaced by a manic desperation not to get left out.

"So what's your secret, Jimmy?" One of the female reporters, who Jimmy recognized as a network sports anchor, was holding her ground and blocking Jimmy's path halfway between the bench and the parking lot.

"Three cans of Red Bull, a double espresso and a cheese and ham omelette an hour before the match." He said it with a straight face and the woman reporter was taken so much by surprise all she could manage was, "Really?"

"No, I'm sorry," said Jimmy. "I was kidding. It was actually ham and mushroom."

The dad jokes were going down well with his FOBD teammates but not so well with the media.

"But surely at 47-years-old you're not able to play professional sport with that kind of diet?" said a male reporter who identified himself as being with the Los Angeles Times. "You must have some really crazy fitness regime."

"I don't," said Jimmy. More FOBD regulars were arriving and peering over at the spectacle around him. "I'm sorry, I was joking about the energy drinks and stuff but I really don't do anything special to prepare for a game. I've been playing with these guys on a Sunday at the Field of Broken Dreams and I've been training just recently with the Galaxy, but the truth is I just love playing soccer."

"But Jimmy," shouted another female reporter from the back, "you broke the net!"

"I'm guessing it must have been a faulty net then." Jimmy shrugged. "I mean, I caught it pretty good but it was a kinda lucky shot. I just gave it all I had because there was no time left and it went in."

"But the ball was still going up when it hit the net." The reporter was persistent.

"I'm just glad it went in." Jimmy tried to move on. "Now if you don't mind, we'd like to get started."

"One more question." One of the older TV sports correspondents muscled in front of the female anchor. "One of your own teammates, Francesco Torres, said after the game last night that you got lucky. What do you say to that?"

"Maybe Francesco was right. Perhaps it was all a fluke." Jimmy said, looking down at his watch. It was already 7.15, the time the game was supposed to start. "I guess we'll find out in the conference semi-finals."

Jimmy put his hand up and headed to the bench to put on the boots Zoe had bought him. But nobody was leaving. One camera crew was filming Sean, Brad and Pete warm up and another was setting up on the halfway line, presumably so they could shoot the game.

"This is hopeless," Jimmy said to Bill and Martyn as they walked over to the first field that lined the fence on the far side. He still had his phone in his hand and was checking it every few seconds. "Count me out when you sort out the teams. I'm going to do a runner."

The media was trailing behind, hauling all their gear with them, the impromptu deal to leave forgotten.

As Jimmy walked onto the pitch, he felt the phone buzzing in his hand and looked down to see a text from Zoe: *here*

"I'm gonna take a leak," Jimmy said loudly, winking at Mark, who was sorting out the sides so there was a fair game.

Jimmy ran over to the fence, darting through a gap to the trail below, and then skirted back around the park to the parking lot where Zoe was waiting in the minivan with Tyler, Grace and Charley in the back.

"Thanks babe, you're a lifesaver," he said, jumping into the passenger seat. "Can we go home now?"

"We could I suppose." Zoe looked frazzled.

"What's up?"

"The street's full of photographers." Zoe was unsettled by all the sudden attention. The family hadn't arrived home until after 1.00 am. "They've been there since just after you left this morning. They even followed us for a couple of blocks until they saw you weren't in the van. It's going to be as bad as this if we go back now."

Jimmy looked at the kids in the back. "Well, it has been a wild and crazy couple of days, I've got an idea I think you're going to like."

"What's that?" Zoe didn't look so sure.

"Let's all go to Disneyland!"

CHAPTER FORTY-EIGHT

He felt the rip during a four-on-one rondo at the Galaxy training ground adjoining the StubHub Stadium in Carson. In the drill earlier that morning, Jimmy had been wearing his regular Copa Mundials and he'd been run ragged trying to get the ball back from the other four players. They all had to keep inside the lines of a small box chalked into the turf.

Frustrated by his helplessness, Jimmy laced up the old boots for the post lunch session and easily intercepted the ball any time he was the one against four. "Once you get in your 40s, you'll find you get stronger in the afternoons," he told his teammates. "It takes a while for the progesterone to kick in." He didn't know what he was talking about but nobody was arguing. Being 47 was not something they wanted to think about.

"You need to get some new boots, Tank," said Walker, the young full back. "Your Addams Family shoes are falling apart."

Jimmy hadn't dared look. But he glanced down now to see the studded sole had pulled away from the leather on the side of the ball of his right foot.

"Those things are nasty," said Gutierrez. "They're older than you are, man."

"Just my lucky boots." Jimmy ran back into the changing room to get his other pair, cursing his luck. He felt Torres' eyes burning into his back. There was something about the ex-galáctico that made him nervous. He was off the injured list and making it very clear to Rossi that he was expecting to be back in the line-up for the first leg of the Conference semi-final versus the Colorado Rapids that Wednesday night.

Standing alone by his peg, Jimmy was able to examine the boot more carefully. The coarse, thick leather was stained white where it met the sole, probably from a combination of sweat and the wet turf they'd played on immediately after its morning sprinkle. The boot had stiffened through decades stuck in his dad's attic and the tear looked irreparable. Looking again at the steel toecaps, nobbly studs and the worn, crinkled black leather, Jimmy marvelled at how comfortable they felt.

"Maybe you must throw them away now?"

The heavily accented voice startled Jimmy and he turned to see Torres had followed him inside.

"Why you wear those old things, Keen? They your magic shoes, quizás? Your, how you say, baby blanket?" The Spaniard smiled, again surprising Jimmy. He'd only seen the striker sneer. "They bring you luck, no?"

"I guess they do." Jimmy laughed nervously. "They're just a pair of old boots I found and I kind of like playing in them because they're different." He didn't want to say too much but he couldn't pretend it was normal wearing them. The other players had ribbed him but Torres was the only one who'd taken a special interest.

"You can have a new pair every game as Galaxy player." Torres was frowning. "Why you don't want new boots? I don't understand."

"I guess my feet are just messed up from years of doing construction. These boots feel good to me. I just find them more comfortable."

"Show me. Let me see them." Torres reached out and grabbed the damaged boot, tearing it a little more. "My great grandfather had a pair like this. He let me wear them when I was a kid." He looked up at Jimmy, his eyes sparkling. "Much too big, no!" He burst out laughing. "I wish I have them now. At the end of the season I go back to Valencia and find them. Ask my father. Maybe score impossible goals."

He handed the boot back to Jimmy. "You look after your magic boots, senor," he said over his shoulder as he headed back towards the training field.

Jimmy tucked them a little further into his kit bag and ran out after Torres and the rondos where he spent much of the rest of the afternoon chasing the ball as the man in the middle. The Spaniard, in particular, seemed to delight in his discomfort.

CHAPTER FORTY-NINE

The team sheet went up at 3:00 pm on Wednesday afternoon, four hours before kick-off and Jimmy looked at it long and hard and then went back and looked at it again. It didn't make any difference. He still wasn't in the starting line-up.

Terry and Whelan came up behind Jimmy, who was having trouble moving away. "Sorry Tank, I was going to have a word with you before the team went up." The skipper put an arm around his shoulder. "The boss loves you now, he really does, but he's worried Saturday was kind of a fluke and Francesco has been pressuring him about playing. He did cost a bucketload of money and he was Rossi's pick."

Just then Torres strode up the corridor, checked the board, and marched back out, a slight smile on his face.

"Not sure how three goals can be a fluke, but hey, Francesco is a great player." Jimmy didn't trust himself to say more. "I'm a little disappointed, I must say."

The three men went into the break room together and the news was already breaking on TV.

"After literally saving the LA Galaxy from a season-ending loss, 47-year-old 'SuperSub' Jimmy Keen has been relegated back to the bench for the Conference Semi-Final first leg match tonight," the ESPN anchor was saying. "Over to our Soccer

Correspondent David Williams at the Stub-Hub Centre for the full story…"

Jimmy saw Rossi heading into the room and quickly backing out when their eyes met. "He won't say anything." Whelan had seen the coach's sudden retreat. "He can't handle confrontation…not unless he's screaming at you."

"I was only going to ask him why he decided to bench me," said Jimmy. "I get it. He can do whatever he thinks is best, but it would be nice to get an explanation."

"Forget it," chipped in Terry. "He'll ignore you right up to the moment he calls you into the game. Believe me, I've been there. If you're smart, you'll just prepare for the game like before and grab your chance when it comes."

Jimmy took his captain's advice. He didn't even bring up the team selection when he saw Murray later as he was changing for the game. The two men shrugged. "You'll get on, son, don't worry. I'll make sure of it," said Murray, "but I can't tell him who to pick. There'd be hell to pay from here to Madrid."

Jimmy waited for Murray to leave before putting on the old boots. He'd stuck some gaffer tape around the tear and blackened it with marker pen to blend it in. It didn't look pretty but Jimmy felt pretty sure it would hold up until he could find somewhere to try a repair. Everyone had been so caught up with the goals in the last match that nobody had paid any attention to his footwear, but Jimmy knew people were going to start asking questions at some point. He still hadn't worked out what he was going to tell them.

He heard the clatter of studs on the concrete floor and looked up to see Torres smiling down at him. "You won't be needing those today, senor. We have a real goalscorer back today, no?"

Torres leaned down and patted Jimmy on the back. "Let the professionals take it from here, old man."

He carried on towards the tunnel and turned around just as he was walking out. "I tell you what, old timer, if I score the winner tonight, I'll buy you the best pair of boots that money can buy. Then you can throw the disgusting booties away and look like a real player. Sound good?"

Jimmy smiled and followed Torres out onto the pitch for warm-ups. He passed right by Rossi, who showed no sign of recognition.

Running onto the field he leaped into the air and had to make a real effort not to jump too high. Jimmy felt so strong and fit as he ran through some stretching exercises with the others; he could already visualise exactly how he would score. He knew he could win the game single-handed.

But when the players were called back into the tunnel he had to separate from the first team and take a seat on the bench. He'd seen Zoe and the kids sitting in the second row near the halfway line but he'd been so intent on the warm-ups he hadn't paid much attention to the sold-out crowd.

Sitting waiting for the game to start, he noticed a giant banner covering the ads running around the inner wall. It read: *Jimmy Keen and the Field of Broken Dreams. Time to Believe.*

Behind the long banner and for several rows behind were dozens of FOBD regulars, all standing and chanting: "Galaxy, FOBD, Galaxy, FOBD." They were all standing up. It seemed like everyone was there; Martyn, Stuart, Bill, Paul, Randy, Sean, Hue, Simon, the Petes, Thor, Andrew, Ken, Mark, Dylan, Enrique, Nermin, Martine, Mike, Nils, Marco, Jorge, Papa, Jovan, the Johns, Luis, Brad, Reza, Burdy, Bjorn, Adam, JC, Kevin, Tony, Lloyd, Dave, and many others.

Jimmy looked across and saw Zoe, Charley, Tyler and Grace getting to their feet, joining the chant, and clapping their hands.

Then gradually, section by section, the rest of the crowd started joining in until the entire stadium was chanting, "Ga-La-Xy, F-O-B-D, Ga-La-Xy, F-O-B-D."

Jimmy stood up to acknowledge what was going on and was greeted by a huge eruption of applause. He waved, embarrassed, and sat back down.

"Man," said Brian Scott, the substitute keeper who was sitting next to him. "Some players are here for years and barely get a reaction. You play for five minutes and the crowd loves you."

Seeing his family and friends cheered Jimmy up. He'd told Zoe he wasn't in the team and no doubt the others had seen it on the news, but they'd turned up anyway. He was itching to show everybody what he could do.

There was a quieter reaction to the team as they were called out by the announcer, although the returning Torres commanded a standing ovation.

The opposition was the Colorado Rapids, who'd pulled off their own miracle by rising from the bottom of the division earlier in the season to finish first. They were an athletic, pressing team with a Scottish coach, Archie Hanlin. He had a tough Glaswegian reputation and he demanded that same no nonsense outlook from his players.

The match started with the Galaxy back on their heels. Without the space to get comfortable on the ball, they were hurrying passes and making too many mistakes. With just 5 minutes gone, Rivera dived at full length to turn away a shot from the Rapids' big Mexican international striker, Ramon.

On the very next attack, the Rapids went ahead after a long ball was accidentally sliced into the centre by Walker from the right wing and right into Ramon's path. He cut in and shot the ball back towards the front post. This time, Rivera was a moment too slow and the ball slipped under his body.

The crowd was hushed as Torres restarted the game. He'd been demanding the ball up front but the two kick-offs were his only touches.

The pattern remained the same for most of the first half with the harried Galaxy players unable to settle into their usual game and Torres becoming an increasingly isolated and irritated figure. But then finally, in the 44th minute, Terry pushed the ball quickly out to the former Real Madrid star just inside his own half and he galloped through an empty slot on his left hand side of the pitch. Reaching the box with three Rapids players in hot pursuit, it looked like he was running head-on into a clash with Eric Yeng, Colorado's Chinese centre-back and captain. Torres made as if to shoot from the edge of the box, sending Yeng the wrong way, and switched the ball to his other foot to skip back into the middle and perform the most delightful chip over the onrushing keeper's flailing arms.

The goal seemed to energise Torres and he was suddenly back to his old Champions League best, tormenting the Rapids defence. After half-time he struck three times in quick succession to make the game safe for the Galaxy. He seemed able to score at will once his tail was up. His fourth, a penalty, was typically brilliant.

He'd been pulled down in a one-on-one with the Rapids keeper, who was sent to the changing rooms, and left nobody in any doubt who was going to take the kick. Putting the ball on the spot, he took an unusually long run-up, looking for all the world like he intended to crash the penalty as hard as he could into the net. But just as he was about to strike, with the substitute goalie already diving to his right, Torres stopped, stood still, watched the keeper helpless on the floor, and softly side-footed his shot into the right hand side of the open goal.

It was a moment of sheer bravado and the crowd went wild. Jimmy's exploits from the last game were forgotten now. This was all Torres.

A couple of minutes before the end of the match, with the score still 4-1, the striker made a meal of what appeared to be a mild push and beckoned to be substituted. "He wants the standing ovation," said Scott. "That guy lives for all that stuff."

Jimmy nodded in agreement just as Rossi waved over at him.

"Keen, you're on for Francesco."

Jimmy jumped up to take off his tracksuit but his toe caught in the metal bleacher and stripped off the gaffer tape, leaving the boot sole flapping.

"Dammit!" He had his Copas with him. He'd planned to put them on straight after the game to avoid any raised eyebrows about the old boots. Now he quickly took them out of his bag and fumbled with the laces.

"Keen!" Rossi was shouting. "Now!"

Fortunately, Torres was taking his time to walk off, soaking up the adulation. By the time he reached the sideline, Jimmy was ready to go on. Rossi didn't give him any instructions; there was only a few minutes of regulation left plus three minutes of overtime as a result of the sending off.

Jimmy didn't feel the same leap in his legs; he made a half-hearted attempt at a jump as he ran to take his place up front.

The short sprint halfway across the pitch left him out of breath and he felt a niggling ache in his left knee.

Terry was waiting over the ball to take the free-kick. As Jimmy ran past he said: "Far post, Tank. I'll put it on a plate for you."

Jimmy didn't have the energy to say anything back. He was still trying to catch his breath when he took his place on the edge of the penalty box.

Terry's hand went up and he swung the ball hard and in-swinging exactly where he said it would be.

Jimmy burst his lungs lunging towards the far post and he made it just behind the last covering defender. But when he coiled to jump nothing happened; his knees locked, he barely left the ground and went crashing into the post. The ball whipped harmlessly about 2 foot over his head and into touch.

Jogging back slowly to face the goal kick he could see the FOBD guys waving scarves and shouting his name, but they were the only ones. The rest of the stadium had gone strangely flat and many sections were emptying out into the parking lot.

The ball came out to the Rapids left midfielder and he lofted it into the Galaxy's penalty area. Rivera punched it out and the ball landed at Jimmy's feet. He controlled it comfortably, lifted his head and saw Whelan on his own screaming for the ball in acres of space just past the halfway line.

Jimmy felt like he made contact well enough, but he hooked the ball on the inside of his boot and it went straight to a yellow-shirted Rapids player, who had a direct run on goal. Three strides and he blasted the ball on the floor low into the right hand corner of the goal, leaving Rivera no chance.

It was 4-2. Colorado had no chance of catching up but the away goal could yet prove decisive. If the stadium was quiet before, it was silent now. Even the FOBD cheerleaders were sitting down.

The whistle went a couple of minutes later without Jimmy touching the ball again. All the excitement from earlier had dissipated and he trudged off with a discreet wave to Zoe and the kids just as Torres was coming back on in sweats to take a last bow.

CHAPTER FIFTY

Three shoemakers had already told Jimmy they couldn't help him and 'Cobblers' in one of East Los Angeles' seedier neighbourhoods was pretty much his last chance. But the guy at the front of the store didn't speak English and couldn't work out why he was being shown a fifty-plus year old boot that clearly should have been thrown away decades earlier.

"Can you sew the sole back on?" Jimmy made the appropriate sewing motions and then held the boot together but it didn't do any good.

The only word the disheveled shopkeeper could manage was, "Why?"

"To play football…soccer?"

"Ahh futbol." Finally there was a hint of understanding.

Encouraged, Jimmy put the other boot on the counter. "Can you mend both of them? Make them like new?"

The shop was littered with pairs of old shoes in varying states of disrepair. They weren't as old as Jimmy's but they were far from new. The man held up a hand, suggesting he understood, and disappeared in the back.

He was there so long Jimmy thought for a moment he'd been abandoned but then he came back out clutching a pair of reasonably old soccer boots. The leather was so worn and hard the toes curled up and there was a white tidal mark all around them as if they'd been stored in a bucket of water. But the shoemaker clearly thought they were a much more preferable alternative to his own, older pair.

"For futbol," he said, holding the boots up and offering them to Jimmy.

"No, it must be these," replied Jimmy, pushing Duncan Edwards' boots towards the man. "I need these fixed."

Again, there appeared to be a flicker of understanding. The man rubbed at his grey stubbled chin and picked up Jimmy's boots.

He held them still for perhaps a minute, long enough for Jimmy to feel uncomfortable, and then turned them over several times in his hands and lifted them to his ear. He looked like he was concentrating really hard and then suddenly dropped them lower and clutched them close to his chest, hugging them with his eyes clamped tight shut.

Jimmy was looking around the shop, unsure what to do with himself, when he felt the man's eyes on him. He was pointing to his own mouth. "Voice," he said. "Voice."

Now it was Jimmy who couldn't understand. He copied the man's gestures. "Voice?" he asked.

"Yes, voice." The man was really excited now. He was transformed, desperate to convey what he was trying to say. "I hear....voice."

"You hear a voice?"

"Yes, yes." The man was holding Jimmy's arm, his sunken eyes alive. "I hear voice talk to me."

"So you will mend them." Jimmy tried out the sewing action again.

"Yes, I will work. Manyana. Come here." He looked at his watch and pointed at the time. "Same time."

It was the Friday and Jimmy had to catch a plane the following morning for the second leg of the conference semi-final in Denver on Sunday. If the boots were repaired when the shoemaker said they would be, he'd have just enough time to pick them up and make the flight. But it was a big if.

Jimmy decided he couldn't risk it. "I'm sorry, no time," he said pointing to his watch.

But the man wouldn't let go of the boots, turning away with them so Jimmy couldn't reach them. "Manyana," he said. "Same time." He put both hands on his heart, without letting go of the boots. "Manyana," he smiled.

Jimmy didn't have a lot of options. One of the boots was impossible to play in. He'd considered wearing the other one with one of his Copas but knew he'd look ridiculous.

"Okay," he said. "But it can't be late."

The man smiled and nodded enthusiastically. But Jimmy had no way of knowing he'd understood. He'd have to hope the boots were ready - or he was screwed.

CHAPTER FIFTY-ONE

When Jimmy arrived with Zoe at the shoemaker's the following morning, the boots were sitting on the counter.

His wife was the only person he'd told about the history of the boots but after that one time, they hadn't talked about them again. Zoe made it clear she thought Jimmy's success was because he'd finally started to believe in himself and not in some fairy story.

"It's only a slight detour," he told her. "We'll have plenty of time to get to the airport." In fact, time was already tight for them to make it to Santa Monica Airport for Jimmy to meet up with the rest of the squad.

"Let's just pick them up after you get back from Colorado." Zoe was a nervous driver and was becoming increasingly uncomfortable in the heavy traffic in East LA. "He probably hasn't finished them anyway. You only brought them in yesterday."

"He said he'd get them done." Jimmy was trying his best to remain calm but he was panicking. "I need those boots," he added, quietly.

"You don't need any boots," Zoe answered softly. "It's all you, baby. I promise you. Boots don't do what you did the other night, people do."

But Jimmy wasn't going to Denver without his boots and they arrived at 'Cobblers' with enough time to make the flight, just as long as they didn't have to wait.

"Oh my!" Zoe was shocked to see the boots on the counter.

"Man," said Jimmy, his heart leaping. "Do you think they're the same ones?"

It looked like they'd just been polished. The boots were a rich, supple black and smelled to Jimmy of a long ago childhood winter. The solid metal toes had been pressed down to make them way less obvious. The worn down shine was gone, replaced by a soft matte black.

Jimmy picked up the boots and turned them over. The soles were sewn so perfectly it was impossible to see they'd ever been split; the old, worn-down screw-in studs had been replaced with new ones and the underside was scrubbed white. On the top, the shoemaker had cleaned up the two white stripes on each boot. They'd been polished so thoroughly there wasn't a mark on them.

"Ah, senor!" The shoemaker came hurrying out and embraced Jimmy. "I work all night. Beautiful, yes?"

"Yes, beautiful," said Jimmy, and he had to ask, "They are the same boots, right?"

"Futbol, futbol. Yes, the same."

There were a couple of telltale marks no amount of polishing could hide and Jimmy saw quite clearly they were still there. He thought for a moment he'd try them on to check if that familiar strength washed over him, but they were already running behind and Zoe was worrying.

"Bueno, bueno." Jimmy's grasp of Spanish ended there but it seemed to get the right reaction and they embraced again. This time the man — he introduced himself as Emilio - hugged Zoe, as well.

"How much do I owe you?" Jimmy got out his wallet and pointed to the notes.

"No, no, no!" Emilio waved his hands around to show Jimmy he didn't want any money and then put them both over his heart.

"I love…to do."

When Jimmy tried to force a $50 into his hands, Emilio refused point blank.

"My honour, my honour." There were several more embraces and Jimmy and Zoe left with the new/old boots.

"You're going to be great." Zoe hugged Jimmy outside the entrance. She was following with the kids on Sunday morning.

I am now, thought Jimmy. *Nobody's going to stop me…or Duncan.*

CHAPTER FIFTY-TWO

This time, Jimmy didn't need to look at the team sheet; he knew he wouldn't be on it. Rossi hadn't mentioned the error that allowed the Rapids to get a goal back in the first leg but he hadn't spoken a word to Jimmy since.

Before he'd got the old boots fixed, Jimmy had tried his best to remain low-key during the daily drills but the gulf in ability between when he had them on and when he didn't was so huge it was difficult for him to hide. Fortunately, with the season funnelling down to just a few more games, the training sessions in Carson were mercifully short. With a squad still decimated by injuries, the coach didn't want to risk any more problems.

Arriving at the stadium in Denver, the high altitude meant Jimmy was gasping for breath even more often than usual. The sky was blue but it was cold and there was talk of a storm on the way. As a kid, he used to smoke a cigarette at half time and he remembered going out for the second half feeling a little like this.

Jimmy waved at Zoe and the family from the subs bench. They were cuddling together for warmth and had a blanket swathed around them. He sneaked a look down at his black, polished boots. They felt like Uggs and, for the first time, he wasn't self-conscious wearing them.

Slipping the boots on in the changing room he'd been nervous in case the shoemaker had somehow robbed them of their power. But it was like switching on an electric light; the energy pulsed up through his legs as he tightened the laces and he felt invincible. Swaggering through the tunnel for the warm-ups he was actively trying to calm himself down so he didn't bust the net with every practice shot. He tapped the ball to the keeper and saw him wince and look at his gloved hands in surprise.

Sitting down to watch the start of the game, Jimmy couldn't stop fidgeting. He wanted the match to fast forward but the Galaxy build-up play was slow and laborious. Rossi was determined to hang onto the 2-goal lead and he'd instructed Torres, his furthest forward player, to remain deep.

He could see the Spaniard getting frustrated in his limited holding role. After his four goals in the first match he clearly thought he had the beating of the Colorado defence but rarely got far enough upfield to test it. Twice he went down under scything tackles from the centre backs who were sticking to him like glue. The other Galaxy players weren't getting much change, either, but were manfully sticking to their task of shutting down the game.

Thirty minutes in and neither team had managed a shot on target. It wasn't pretty but, for the Galaxy at least, it was effective.

The game had started in hazy sunshine but an icy wind whipped up from the Rockies and, in minutes, the sky had turned a dirty grey. By the time the teams went in at half time at

0-0, flurries of snow were beginning to whiten the billiard green pitch.

Jimmy wasn't really feeling the cold but following the training staff into the tunnel he could see Zoe and the kids buried deeper under their blanket in the stands.

The Galaxy hadn't managed a shot but then neither had the Rapids. "Just keep doing what you're doing," Rossi preached to them. "No fancy stuff. Just run, run, run."

"If you can get the ball to Francesco, he'll hold it up." The coach looked across at his sour-faced striker. "That okay with you, Francesco? We keep possession as much as possible. I don't care if you pass the ball sideways or back a million times, just don't give it away."

The players jogged out of the tunnel 10 minutes or so later to find themselves in the middle of a snowstorm. The referees had checked the playing surface and decided that, as the snow wasn't settling as yet, the game could go on. Jimmy glanced across at Torres; the weather had put him in an even fouler mood. He was haranguing the kit man for a pair of gloves and glanced over at Jimmy, who was waiting to get to his seat. "You clean your boots, Keen? You be careful, you lose your mojo!"

Torres ran off to take his position and Jimmy steeled himself for a long 45 minutes on the bench. He couldn't even see his family in the stands, the whiteout was so intense.

The Rapids clearly had a very different team talk and they went right on the offence, pulling back a goal almost immediately from a corner. Torres was moaning at his teammates now. With two Colorado players shadowing him wherever he went, there was no space for him to hold up the ball, let alone do anything creative.

The game became a war of attrition, with the Rapids launching an arsenal of shots on the Galaxy goal. The keeper, Rivera, was giving the performance of his life but something was eventually going to have to give. Every time the Galaxy tried to clear, the ball was breaking to their opponents. Torres was harried off the ball every time he tried to offer an outlet, his temper rising with every challenge.

The flashpoint came the moment after he was bundled onto the floor deep in his own half. As he fell near the right touchline, Torres lashed out a boot, catching the Rapids right midfielder in the shins. The victim fell like he'd been shot. Almost anywhere else on the pitch, especially in such murky conditions, the Galaxy striker would have gotten away with it. But he had lashed out right in front of the assistant referee who immediately waved his flag to alert the attention of the centre ref, whose mic had long given up for dead.

It only required the briefest of conversations for the red card to come out of the pocket and Torres was limping miserably off to the dressing room.

Rossi ignored Jimmy and called for Whelan to go on in Torres place. The big forward lumbered out into the snow leaving Jimmy bitter that Zoe and the kids were waiting in vain in the freezing cold to see him play.

The weather had deteriorated and the snow turned to hail as the temperature plummeted further, but visibility had slightly improved and the officials had clearly decided to try and complete the one-sided match.

Whelan didn't fare any better than Torres in providing respite for his overworked defence. He lasted only 15 minutes before pulling up short with a recurring groin strain and waving over towards the bench for a replacement.

Rossi had already subbed in one defender for his more creative midfield player, but Jimmy could still see him struggling with the decision. By the time he made up his mind the ref's assistant was pushing him for a number for his electronic board.

"Keen!"

Jimmy was ready to go. He stripped down to a short-sleeve shirt, cast off his sweat pants and edged down to the pitch.

"Keen! Here!"

The coach beckoned Jimmy closer. "I don't want any fancy stuff from you either, Keen. I need for you to keep the ball. I don't want you to score goals, no. Do anything you want but keep the ball for the next 10 minutes. You understand?"

Jimmy nodded that he understood and the referee gave him permission to join the game. He gave a giant leap from the touchline and bounded over to where the referee was waiting to restart with a drop ball.

The moment the ball touched the ground, Jimmy tapped it around the Rapids player, collected it and headed for the corner flag. Boos rained down from the stands. "Time waster," shouted one of the politer fans. "There's still 10 minutes left."

Three players ran to tackle him and Jimmy swerved around each one, leaving two of them on their backs. He stood near the opposition corner flag and waited for another defender to approach. The rest of his own team were waiting behind the halfway line for him to lose the ball. He could see Rossi going wild in the coach's area.

When the first player got close enough, Jimmy waited just long enough to spot a gap between his legs. He called "nutmeg" and planted the ball plumb through the gap and ran like lightning to trap it behind the red-faced player, who turned and lunged, only for Jimmy to knock the ball just far enough to elude the flailing leg.

Jimmy brought his head up to see the entire Rapids team converging on him in the corner. Unconcerned, he played keep-up with the ball three times as they ran closer and then blasted the ball skywards so far it was just a tiny speck in the black/grey sky. Watching the ball the entire time, he jogged casually towards the goal, breaking into a five-yard sprint just as the ball expanded out of orbit to cushion on his left boot. The goalkeeper, as confused as his outfield teammates, was way out of position still scanning the skies, and Jimmy took careful aim.

The ball landed exactly where he'd intended in the middle of the crossbar, rebounding a few more feet across the pitch where Jimmy trapped it again and ran slowly towards the opposite corner to where he'd been before.

His own team was still in their half and the Colorado players were still over by the other corner. Even the referee was way out on the other side of the pitch.

Jimmy was standing alone with the ball pretending to smoke a cigarette. He didn't know why he did that, but it felt natural enough and the freezing air worked well enough as mock smoke.

"Tank! Tank!" Jimmy saw Terry running through the hail. "Pass, here let me help."

Jimmy stroked a short pass to his captain and found a space for the return, but four Rapids players were surrounding Terry, blocking any exit pass. Terry tried to chip the ball over the wall but it caught the head of the tallest player and he knocked it down to one of the others.

With Jimmy apparently stranded in the opposition half, the four headed towards the Galaxy end, inter-passing as they went. With Terry also out of place they spearheaded a gap big enough for Ramon to get one-on-one with Rivera. He ratcheted back his right boot just a fraction to pull the trigger when the ball was swept away by Jimmy, diving with a perfectly timed tackle.

Ramon swung and missed, flopping to the ground crying out for a penalty, but Jimmy hadn't touched him and the referee waved his arms to play on.

Although Zoe and the kids were sitting watching at the Galaxy end, Jimmy ran over with the ball to be closest to them and then set off on a swerving diagonal run to the opposite corner, speeding up when any Colorado player came close.

From there he ran across the opposition goal, tapping the ball around the keeper and collecting it, ignoring the gaping open goal, to head for the other corner flag. Any time a Rapids player came close, he set off again for open space until the referee, as bewildered and exhausted at trying to keep up as the players, finally blew his whistle to end the match and send the LA Galaxy into the Western Conference Final.

The freeze had coated the grass in frost but Jimmy felt like he was only just warming up as he went over to applaud the traveling fans, who gave him a standing ovation in return.

Running off past his bemused coach he slowed down and shouted across to him: "Well, you told me not to score!"

CHAPTER FIFTY-THREE

The excitement lasted as long as Jimmy kept his boots on. He ran across to Zoe and the kids and jumped over the terracing like it wasn't there, hugging them all in a jumble of overcoats, beanies and screaming, red-faced exuberance.

"That was awesome, dad," shouted Tyler. "How did you do that?" Charley and Grace were holding onto his neck, unwilling to let go as people all around were slapping him on the shoulder and congratulating him. Zoe stood aside, beaming. She didn't know much about football but she knew her husband had just done something very special.

"I don't even feel tired," Jimmy whispered in her ear. The numbers of people crowding down on them was becoming uncontrollable. Jimmy clambered back over the wall onto the pitch and jogged to the dressing room. He was catching a flight back to LA with the team later that evening and his family were following on the next morning when the storm was due to have blown over.

Rossi had banned any champagne celebration, insisting the job was far from done, but Jimmy's teammates were in a celebratory mood. Last to walk in, he was greeted with a round of applause, led by captain Mike Terry. The only person not joining in, Jimmy couldn't help but notice, was Torres, sitting head in hands by his peg.

Embarrassed, Jimmy walked quickly to his locker, shaking hands along the way. Any animosity he'd felt during all those rondo box sessions was gone now. They were two matches away from the MLS Cup Final.

It wasn't until Jimmy was sitting down that the Spaniard lifted his head. The cocksure striker looked utterly spent; all his bravado was gone. "I don't know how you do it, my friend." He didn't look very friendly.

"In training you look like an old cow ready to be put out to pasture and then you go out on that pitch like a young calf. It's impossible," he said again, shaking his head and putting it back in his hands.

Looking down so all Jimmy could see was the top of his head, he added quietly: "But I'm going to find out, I promise you that."

Terry shoved him playfully on the shoulder. "C'mon Francesco, we're through, there's nothing to sulk about. We live to fight another day."

"Maybe you do." Torres kept his head down.

"It's a one-match ban. You'll be back to get all the glory in the second leg. You gotta admit Jimmy's one-man show was pretty entertaining. It was magic."

"It was an illusion, yes," he said, lifting his head. "Jimmy Keen the illusionist. He gets top billing now, no need for Torres. Nobody asks how is Francesco after working so hard and getting red card for nothing, all my goals that got us here are forgotten. All people talk about is Jimmy Keen this and Jimmy Keen that. Who is Jimmy Keen anyway? Who is Jimmy Keen?" He asked the second question to himself. Terry had given up, gleefully giving his teammate the finger before heading back to the others.

"Don't listen to him, Jim," he said. "I don't care if you're 15 or 50, that was one of the most incredible things I've ever seen."

Glad to finally be left alone, Jimmy quickly pulled off his boots and put them in his bag; he didn't need Torres picking up on them again. He wanted to call Zoe and make sure she was safely back at the hotel before heading off to the airport. Walking back out of the changing room to get a better signal he was almost knocked off his feet by a ferocious gust of icy wind. There was no green to be seen; the pitch was blanketed by a thick layer of snow and it was freezing, much colder than California. For the first time it occurred to him that this wasn't perhaps the best weather to fly in.

CHAPTER FIFTY-FOUR

The calm voice on the loudspeaker was in startling contrast to the maelstrom Jimmy could see outside his cabin window. "Good evening, ladies and gentlemen, my name is James Thain and I will be captaining this evening's flight back to Los Angeles. Sitting alongside me is my co-pilot Captain Ken Rayment. Some of you may be a little alarmed by the storm, but I just want to reassure you all that Captain Rayment and I are based out of Denver and this is pretty routine for us so there's no need to worry. We're just doing a few last minute checks and we'll have you on your way in no time. Please relax and enjoy the journey."

The flight was a charter with just the players, the coaching staff, a few members of the admin team and several L.A.-based sports journalists along for the ride. In all, there were 44 people on board.

Rossi was impatient to return to Los Angeles and had pushed for the flight to go ahead as planned, even as some scheduled flights were being cancelled. He was sitting in the front cabin, his huge headphones resolutely over his ears, his eyes clamped shut. The players, so boisterous earlier, were quiet now, listening to music and playing video games. Some were feigning sleep.

Jimmy felt a growing sense of unease. He'd never worried about flying but when he tried to drink from his water bottle he had trouble lifting it to his mouth without shaking. After two tries he gave up, not wanting anybody to see him. *It's just like a match*, he thought, i*t'll all be fine once we're on our way.*

He fiddled with his phone, trying to find something to divert his mind away from the giant elephant crushing his chest, making it almost impossible to breath. This was what happened to Duncan Edwards.

A game, a snowstorm, a plane crash. And then nothing.

On February 6, 1958, British European Airways Flight 609 crashed on its third attempt to take off from a slush-covered runway at Munich-Riem Airport in West Germany. Duncan and his Manchester United teammates were on their way home after a European Cup tie against Red Star Belgrade when they made a refuelling stop in a heavy snowstorm. Twenty-three of the 44 people on board would never finish the journey, among them Duncan, the club's mercurial captain, who finally succumbed in hospital some days later.

But I'm not Duncan Edwards. I'm Jimmy Keen. I'm just borrowing his boots. As much as Jimmy tried to rationalise his thoughts he kept coming back to the irrationality of all that had happened to him since finding the old boots in his parents' attic. Was it all leading to this? History replaying itself in the cruelest way possible? The plane shook and slowly rumbled into life.

He felt a sense of relief as the plane's engines roared and they started off down the runway. Somehow the ground crew had managed to clear a path through the snow piled up either side. The plane shuddered and Jimmy gripped the armrest, waiting for the nose to rise but the lift never came.

"What's happening?" Jimmy didn't recognise the voice behind him but he heard the panic. The lights had suddenly gone out emphasising the flashing lights shooting past outside along the runway. The engine roar died, replaced by the squealing of tires and several cries of alarm.

The calming voice of Captain Thain was back on the loudspeaker. "My apologies for the slight hiccup," he said. "We're going to head back for one more check before taking off. It's just a precautionary measure, nothing to worry about. We noticed something a little unusual with the port supercharger gauge and decided to get it checked out before going ahead with the flight. I'm terribly sorry for the inconvenience."

The intercom went off as the lights switched back on and Jimmy looked back at his teammates. Nobody had their eyes closed now.

Jimmy wasn't sure if he was imagining it or perhaps it was the stark lighting, but the stewardesses, offering water and snacks during the delay, looked shaken too. One said she was pretty sure they'd all be spending the night in Denver as the conditions were worsening. Jimmy got his phone out of his pocket and sent a quick text to Zoe telling her not to worry. He looked out of his window to see big trucks pushing piles of slush into the darkness.

Another hour passed and Jimmy couldn't stop shaking. He closed his eyes so nobody would speak to him but he wasn't sleeping. He kept trying to think of his exploits on the pitch a few hours earlier to take his mind off his anxiety but it was useless. The last straw came as Captain Thain came back on the speaker.

"We've been cleared for take-off," he said, "so if everybody would please make sure your seat belts are fastened, we'll be about five more minutes and then we'll be off. Once again, sorry for the delays. Cabin crew, please ready for take-off."

"I've got to get off." Jimmy said it quietly to himself at first and then repeated it louder and louder. "I'm sorry, I can't do this." He unstrapped and stood up, grabbing his rucksack. "I need to see my family."

Squeezing into the aisle, Jimmy set off a chain reaction with pretty much everyone else standing up.

"Me, too."

"I'm getting off."

"Thank God!"

By the time everyone had filed off the plane there were just two people left in their seats. Rossi, scowling, still had his headphones on. He'd given up trying to persuade the players to stay. Torres was sitting at the back of the plane, apparently fast asleep. The most relieved people looked to be the two young stewardesses. One tried to wake up the striker but couldn't get any response.

Jimmy only felt the shaking recede as he entered the warmth of the airport terminal. He looked down at his phone to see a text from Zoe.

Who's Duncan?

Confused, he checked his own text he'd sent from the plane. It read: *All flights cancelled, flying tomorrow. Duncan*

CHAPTER FIFTY-FIVE

Rossi was like a bear with a sore head all week in training. They'd been stuck two more days in Denver after the airport was totally shut down by one of the worst storms to hit the region in 20 years. Jimmy knew the coach blamed him for the mutiny on the flight but there was little he could do about it. Torres was suspended for the first leg of the Western Conference Final because of his red card and Jimmy was the toast of the nation's media.

The story of the 47-year-old soccer star wasn't just a sports phenomenon; the club's PR department was besieged with interview demands from mainstream media organisations around the world.

"What do I tell them that I haven't said already?" Jimmy asked as he was led down the hall to a press conference being thrown in the Galaxy's main convention room.

"Just smile and tell kids to eat their vegetables." Murray, the general manager, walked a few paces ahead. He'd promised Rossi he'd get the player back to training in 30 minutes.

"He's not getting any special treatment just because he's old," Rossi shouted after them as Jimmy was plucked from a 2v2 game. Jimmy felt Torres' eyes burning into the back of his head.

He could hear what sounded like Wembley in full voice as he came out from the elevator into the hall and it got louder as they neared the convention room's double doors. Murray pulled open the handle and Jimmy felt like he'd been hit by a freight train; a blaze of flashing lights and a scream of competing voices shouting his name.

Look this way. Jimmy, Jimmy, Jimmy, Jimeee!

Jimmy was ushered to a plush leather chair behind a phalanx of microphones. The room was huge and it was packed. Murray sat next to him and leaned across. "Thank you for coming everybody. I know a lot of you wanted to speak to this man, Jimmy Keen. As you can imagine, it's a busy week in training. We missed a couple of days being holed up in Denver and the first leg of the final is just two days away so we decided to do it in one go so Jimmy wouldn't be tied up too long. So who's going to get us started?" He paused before adding, "Jimmy just has one request; he doesn't want to talk about his age."

Taken by surprise, Jimmy looked quizzically at Murray.

"Just kidding folks. Ask away." Murray smiled. "I want to know how he does it at 47 as much as you do."

A mass of hands shot up in the air and Michelle, the club's PR woman, pointed to a man in the front dressed in a suit with slicked back hair and a bright orange, tanned face.

"Hi Jimmy, Rod Frost from Fox. Congratulations on your incredible exploits in Denver the other night. Are you aware that the YouTube video of your substitute appearance has now logged more than 10 million views?"

Jimmy shook his head. "No."

Frost continued. "With Francesco Torres banned for the first leg, you'll be in the starting eleven for the first time. How do you think your legs will hold up? Is there a chance that the last couple of cameos from the bench were just once-in-a-lifetime freaks?"

"Yes, my legs will be fine and no."

Murray looked daggers at Jimmy and mumbled under his breath. "Play the game son. Give 'em something."

"Put it this way," added Jimmy. "I've been working toward this my whole life." He could sense the cameras zooming in. "Some people get their break in their late teens or their 20s." He paused. "Some of us have to wait a little longer."

A ripple of laughter spread through the room and Jimmy felt a little less intimidated.

"But can you make a full 90 minutes?" Frost followed up.

"Look, I've worked plenty of 18 hour days on construction sites. I'm not going to start complaining about running around a football pitch for an hour-and-a-half. If the manager includes me in the team I'll do my very best to ensure he doesn't regret it." Jimmy looked at Murray and got a half-smile in return.

"Jimmy, I'm Tracy Harrison from ESPN. Good to meet you."

Jimmy nodded his head in thanks. He'd seen her on TV. "Good to meet you, too."

"We've been hearing rumours that some English Premier League clubs have been making enquiries about you after your incredible performances in the last couple of games," said the brunette presenter. "Our sources say that Manchester United and West Ham United are sending scouts to monitor the conference final. What do you think about that?"

"I think somebody's pulling your leg," said Jimmy. "Now if you were to tell me a really big club was coming in for me, a club like West Bromwich Albion, then I'd be interested."

There were blank faces all around. "So you'd rather play for West Bromwich?" Harrison looked confused.

"I would, as it happens," said Jimmy. "But it's not going to happen, is it? Nobody's going to pay good money for a player my age. This is all about the Galaxy and getting through to the MLS Cup Final. That's all I'm concerned about right now."

"What does your family feel about all this attention?" Harrison asked.

"Obviously it's all a bit of a shock to me as much as it is for them. I never expected this to happen. But my wife Zoe and my kids have been great. They're my biggest fans, I guess. It's been a tough year for my family because my daughter, Grace, got sick, but she's doing much better now and she'll be at the match on Saturday with my other kids, Tyler and Charley. I don't really think they can believe it either."

From a couple of rows back, a more casually dressed older man stood up. "Jeff Edmunds, NBC Sports. Can you tell our viewers something about your background; where you came from; what teams you played for in the past; that kind of thing?"

"Sure." Jimmy hesitated. "Before I came out here I played for the Plaistow Irons in London."

"Are they a Championship team? I don't recognise the name from the EPL." Edmunds had his phone in his hand. He looked like he was googling the Irons.

"East London Conference League," said Jimmy. "They are a Sunday morning side. Before that I played for the Shenfield Strollers, another Sunday team, but that was, like, 20 years ago. I don't think they're still going. As a kid, I played for the Leyton Orient. They're in League Two now, but I got hurt and they let me go. That was 30 years ago though…"

The TV reporter was momentarily lost for words and stumbled for a follow-up question. "Great, that's great," he said. "How about in the United States? What teams did you play for before being discovered by the LA Galaxy?"

"I've really only played for one team and that's more of a pick-up side in Laguna Beach, California. We call it the Field of Broken Dreams."

"I'm not aware of this place. Is that the name of the stadium?" Edmunds was looking more and more confused.

"No, it's what we call ourselves. We play every Sunday morning on this crappy field in Laguna; there's a bunch of expats from all over and some Americans. Most of us have seen better days and our best football's behind us. That's why we call it the FOBD."

"FOBD?"

"Field of Broken Dreams."

"Yes, of course." The NBC reporter sat down, defeated.

"Only I suppose not all the dreams are broken, are they? I seem to be living out mine right now."

Jimmy answered a dozen or so more questions, all of them about his age, before Murray asked for one final question before they wrapped up.

From the back of the room, a middle-aged man in a sports blazer shot up his right hand and walked towards Jimmy, an oversized, old-fashioned tape recorder in the other hand. "John Glynn of the National Enquirer," he said and the atmosphere in the room changed.

"Great to see you here, Mr Keen. I'm a Seattle Sounders fan myself but I have a lot of respect for what you've done at your age," he said. Jimmy smiled, unbothered, but the rest of the room was on edge. There was a reason the Enquirer was there and it probably wasn't good.

"Perhaps I'll see you at the game then," said Jimmy. "You have a great team there."

"A great offence," said Glynn, "but I'm not so sure if we're strong enough at the back, especially with you and Torres."

"You're very kind, but I think it's going to be a tough match-up." Thank God I finally got a question about football, thought Jimmy.

"Okay then, if that's it I'd better get Jimmy back to the rest of the team." Murray grabbed his charge by the arm and tried to lift him out of his seat.

"I just had one little question for Jimmy." Glynn was holding his ground.

"Of course, mate, no problem." Murray tried to manhandle Jimmy out of the room but he felt bad avoiding the friendly reporter's question. "Just this last one."

"I have to ask for your comment, Jimmy, on our cover story tomorrow that reveals how you've cheated by wearing illegal boots. We tell our readers exactly how you manage to leap so high and run so damned fast at your age. Enquiring minds want to know how you do it and we can tell them - it's your cleats."

Jimmy felt his body collapse from within and shut up shop. Suddenly his mouth stopped working. He managed to mumble "no comment" as he was jumbled out of the door by Murray and a couple of the PR staff.

As the door closed behind him, Jimmy heard Glynn asking one more time: "My editor has asked me to get a look at your footwear close up. We know that's the reason, Jimmy. You've got magic boots."

CHAPTER FIFTY-SIX

Jimmy couldn't get all those laughing faces in the media out of his head as they walked back towards the dressing rooms after the press conference.

They were laughing at the Enquirer reporter's theory about Jimmy's footballing exploits but it was like they were all laughing at him. He'd been found out and the whole world was about to discover he was a fraud.

Murray looked relieved. "Magic boots," he said. "Whatever will those tabloids come up with next? I've never heard of anything so daft, eh Jimmy? If you have a pair of those I'll get one myself. The things they do to sell papers."

Jimmy kept quiet. Now he was imagining the headlines. *How could they know?* He was wracking his brain. The only person he'd told was Zoe.

Rossi barely acknowledged him as he joined the first team training group. "You didn't miss anything, Tank," whispered Terry. "We've been working on holding up the ball and that's hardly something you have trouble with! How did your big press conference go? I heard it was packed."

"Good," mumbled Jimmy. "It went fine." Now he was worrying about what his teammates would say once they learned the truth, especially Torres. He'd always had a thing about Jimmy's boots. "I just wish they'd leave me alone to play."

"Comes with the territory, Tank. Everybody's going to want a piece of you now. Nobody's ever done anything like this before."

"There was Stanley Matthews."

"Stanley who?" Terry had no clue who Jimmy was talking about.

"Stanley Matthews. He played in the English league until he was 50."

"Well, I've never heard of him."

"It was a long time ago." Jimmy just wanted training to end so he could go home and lock himself away from the world. He had less than 24 hours left as a professional footballer. When the National Enquirer printed their story in the morning he'd be ruined.

"Think fast!" Gutierrez pinged the ball at him and it cannoned off Jimmy's Copas. He tried not to use the old boots during practice but that meant he had to deal with moments like this when his reactions were the speed of a middle-aged man, not a soccer phenomenon.

"Focus!" shouted Rossi. "You're not a big shot here, Keen."

I don't want to be a big shot, thought Jimmy, but he kept quiet. Training was almost over for the day and Zoe was picking him up with the kids. He had to spend the following night in the hotel with the team preparing for Saturday's home first leg.

Jimmy was quiet all the way home. Fortunately, the kids were full of stories about school. He pretended to listen but his thoughts were dominated by the story about his "magic boots."

It wasn't until late that night, sitting with Zoe on the couch, that he told her what happened.

"Is that really what's been worrying you?" Zoe didn't seem too concerned. "I thought you were nervous about the game. You haven't said a thing all night."

"That's because it's all over. Somehow they know about the boots."

"Know what? That you're wearing some old guy's boots? Nobody's going to care about that; it's sweet."

Jimmy wasn't comforted. "But the writer from the National Enquirer said my boots were the reason I was jumping so high and had so much energy. He said they were magic. How could he know?"

"There's nothing to know, Jimmy. How many times do I have to tell you? It's all you, Jimmy Keen, not Duncan whatshisname." She kissed his cheek and pulled him closer. "Just stop worrying and relax. You've got a big game coming up."

They fell silent and Jimmy realised he was wasting his time; she didn't get it. But then Zoe turned to face him, suddenly interested. "I've just had a thought. If you really do believe those crummy old boots make you perform like a 20-year-old, how about you go out into the garage and put them on and I'll meet you in the bedroom!"

Just then, Jimmy's mobile rang. He didn't recognise the number but answered it anyway. The caller didn't need to identify himself; Jimmy knew the instant he heard the voice.

"Mr Keen, hi. This is John Glynn from the National Enquirer. We didn't get to finish our conversation today and I very much wanted to get your comment on our story about your boots."

"I think I said no comment." Jimmy wanted to put the phone down but another part of him wanted to know how they'd discovered his secret.

"How about I explain the allegations to you and then you can decide whether you want to say anything about it? Then at least I can feel comfortable that I've given you every opportunity to respond." Glynn was polite and matter-of-fact.

"I guess that can't hurt." Jimmy muttered. "But how did you find out?"

"I'm afraid I can't reveal my sources, Mr Keen, but I do want you to know it has nothing to do with me being a Sounders fan. I'm super impressed with all you've achieved; I've watched your games over and over on YouTube and they're just fantastic. They give all us old guys some hope."

"Well, er, thanks, I guess."

"So here's what we're reporting." Glynn sounded like he was rustling some papers. He was clearly on speaker phone. "As

I mentioned earlier, we've been told by several excellent sources that the explanation for your incredible energy and, particularly, for the amazing distance in your leaps, is because of your boots. My apologies if this is upsetting for you, Mr Keen, but we're branding you a cheat. In fact, full transparency, the headline in tomorrow's issue will read, 'Boot Out Soccer's Cruel Grandpa Cheat!'

"But I'm not a grandpa." Jimmy couldn't help himself.

"I realize that and I apologise, but we're using the word descriptively here," Glynn didn't sound sorry but was happy to explain. "It suggests you are, if you'll excuse me saying, quite old and you could, indeed, be a grandpa unlike, say, your teammates."

"But why am I cruel? And how do you know the boots are magic?" Jimmy could only think that somehow Duncan Edwards' family had found out and were upset about him wearing the Busby Babe's boots.

"Again, I'm afraid I can't reveal my sources, but I can tell you that those boots you've been wearing are banned in California. They're from a protected species."

Jimmy knew Duncan Edwards was revered in Dudley, but he'd never considered the boots as being sacrosanct. *Perhaps they want them for a museum*, he thought.

"We have statements from PETA - People for the Ethical Treatment of Animals - and from Adidas." Glynn said. "The story is 100 percent accurate but it would be great to add your comments before we go to print."

"But what have Adidas got to do with it? Or PETA?" Now Jimmy was really confused. *Did Duncan have pets?*

"It's your Copa Mundials." Glynn was beginning to sound a little exasperated. "You know, your soccer cleats."

"Yes," said Jimmy, slowly. "I do have a pair of those."

"And do you know they have been banned by the state of California?"

"What are banned?"

"Your boots."

Jimmy was totally lost now. It was confusing enough channeling the spirit of a dead footballer without being accused of wearing illegal boots and kicking animals. "But why are my Copa Mundials banned?"

"Because they're made of kangaroo leather, of course," said Glynn. "That's how you manage to jump so high. It's the only logical explanation."

Jimmy hung up a few seconds later with a huge grin on his face.

"So your secret's safe then?" Zoe snuggled under the sheets. She watched Jimmy as he edged back towards the door.

"It is."

"You'll stop pacing and get to bed then?"

But instead of getting into bed, Jimmy darted out of the door and shouted over his shoulder as he dashed downstairs.

"Hold that thought," he said. "I'm just going out to the garage for me boots…"

CHAPTER FIFTY-SEVEN

Match day always brought a few butterflies, even when Jimmy was playing for the Plaistow Irons, but this was very different. This was the MLS Western Conference Final and unlike the other Galaxy games he'd been involved in there was no doubts over whether or not he'd get off the subs' bench. He was in the starting line-up.

The only feeling he could compare it to was FA Cup Final day as a kid in Dudley. The excitement was something you could feel; it touched everything you did or said as the morning wore on and the kick-off loomed larger. On other days, football was an important part of the day but just a part nonetheless. On FA Cup Final day it was everything. He saw it on the faces of the surfers at the beach when a big swell hit; the suppressed adrenaline that made the hushed preparations almost as thrilling as the main event. You almost wished kick-off never came because it meant the end was that little bit nearer and normal life would resume.

Jimmy had gone to bed at ten, woken up at midnight and hadn't gone back to sleep, lying in wide-eyed panic. But his thoughts were less about whether he was going to play well and more about how to adapt his game so he didn't dominate so much that he raised suspicions. The kangaroo story got some laughs — and plenty of ribbing in the dressing room — but more searching questions were bound to be asked if he started scoring and couldn't stop. What if he scored 10 goals…or 20? In the middle of the night in his unfamiliar bed in a strange hotel room, Jimmy's mind ran riot. In the morning, the solution seemed pretty simple; he'd play the final just like he played on Sundays at the Field of Broken Dreams. He'd involve his teammates as much as possible and keep his goalscoring down to four or five. He would, he decided at about 6.30am, try his best to enjoy himself.

Zoe and the kids called on FaceTime after breakfast to wish Jimmy well and they had some news. "Uncle Carl and Auntie Sarah are coming over with Jade and Emma," said Charley. "Uncle Carl said they were going to make it for the next match in case you lost and didn't make it to the big final."

"Typical," said Jimmy. "My own family never did believe in me."

"They're excited for you, Jimmy," said Zoe. "They would have been over for today's game but Wally had to sort out his passport."

"What do you mean, Wally?"

"Uncle Wally's coming, too, dad," said Tyler. "He's never been out of England before."

"He's probably not been outside Dudley," said Jimmy. "Bloody hell, we'd better win at home today then."

"They were hoping to get over for today's match and surprise you but then Wally said he wanted to come and things got complicated. You can imagine what Carl said." Zoe raised her eyebrows. She loved Carl but they'd never quite clicked. "He had to change all the plane tickets. Wally was quite determined."

Jimmy felt himself becoming emotional in spite of himself. "It'll be great to see the old man. He's been pretty sick since dad died, hasn't he?"

Zoe had always been Wally's favourite and they spoke on the phone at least once a week. "He's been in and out of hospital but the moment I mentioned Carl and Sarah had bought their plane tickets he said he was coming, too. He said he didn't want to miss it for your dad."

Jimmy couldn't talk for several seconds and swallowed hard, moving away from the camera on his laptop so the kids couldn't see him. He'd been fighting off thoughts about his dad all night. What would he have made of all this? Jimmy really didn't know. "It'll be great to see him," was the best Jimmy could manage in a tight voice.

"Are you okay, dad?" Grace was always the worrier.

Jimmy shook it off. "Yeah, I'm great. Excited. It's just a bit overwhelming, that's all. I'll watch out for you guys in the crowd and give you a big wave."

Zoe ushered the children off to get ready and managed a moment with Jimmy before hanging up. "I'm so proud of you, babe. You made your dreams come true. You never gave up and now look at you. It's incredible."

Jimmy wiped back another tear. He was feeling really emotional and couldn't work out if it was the nerves or lack of sleep. "I don't know how it's happened really. It really is like a dream."

"It's all you, Jimmy. For the first time in our lives we have no debts, the kids are happy and healthy and you have a job, the best job in the world. You can say it's because of this Duncan guy or the boots or whatever helps you best but all I know is that you made it happen for yourself and you deserve all the good things that are happening to you."

A knock on his hotel room door stopped Jimmy from blubbering. "I love you, Zo," he said quietly. "I gotta go. They're calling me for the team meeting. I'll see you on the other side."

CHAPTER FIFTY-EIGHT

The next time Jimmy saw his family was when his name was called out over the tannoy as the Galaxy players were announced to the jam-packed StubHub stadium. He'd waved across at Zoe and the kids moments before and they'd suddenly disappeared amidst a sea of waving arms as the entire crowd stood to welcome him. The response to Jimmy was by far the biggest of the team and he wiped off yet another tear with the heel of his hand as he pretended to push back his hair. He still hadn't managed to assuage the ghost of his father.

Mike Terry had won the coin toss and chosen to kick-off. Watching the Sounders line up, Jimmy knew right away what he was going to do. The last time the two teams had played the Galaxy had swamped their opponents in the middle of the park, pushing the Sounders' key players wide and dominating the midfield. This time, Seattle was sending a message that they weren't going to allow that to happen again. With the exception of two wing backs, the other eight outfield players had taken up central positions. Four players, the centre-forward, the centre-midfielder, the centre back and the goalkeeper, stood one in a virtual line, one in front of another.

John Whelan, Jimmy's strike partner, placed the ball on the centre spot and stood waiting for the whistle.

"Do you mind if I take it?" Jimmy asked, but it wasn't really a question.

Whelan turned around, surprised, but moved to the side, expecting Jimmy to pass the ball to him. But Jimmy was walking backwards slowly until he was about halfway between the centre line and the apex of the centre circle.

The referee checked with his sideline team and put the whistle to his lips. The moment he did so, Jimmy jumped into the air in what was now his trademark bound and ran full pelt towards the ball. As he struck it with every ounce of power he had with his right foot, he yelled a single word that seemed to reverberate around the ground.

"Nutmeg."

The velocity with which the ball was struck made it hard to follow with the human eye. The entire stadium was straining forward. They were just able to see it pass through the legs of the centre-forward; it was so fast he felt only the faintest whiff of wind. Moving just an inch off the ground, although the watching thousands wouldn't have known it's metrics, the ball powered through the legs of the unwitting midfielder and, before he knew what was coming, through the legs of the centre-back.

Apparently defying the laws of physics, the ball gathered force the further it travelled. If the goalkeeper saw the ball at the last moment he gave no sign of it. He still had his arms crossed, waiting to see what the old man playing for the Galaxy was going to do. He'd already taken a few steps back when he saw Jimmy take a run-up as a vague precaution in case he attempted a shot, although the idea of him being caught unaware from so far out was to him, simply laughable. *Let the old boy shoot,* he thought. *At his age he'll be lucky for it to dribble into the penalty box.*

The keeper's legs were barely apart; his hamstrings were always a little tight at the start of a game and he'd stretched his hands to the floor a couple of times to loosen them up. It was the crowd that first alerted him that something was up. All but the traveling Seattle fans in the corner were up on their feet cheering and yelling. His right back turned and pointed towards the goal and there, nestled in the centre of the net, was the match ball.

The referee had spent a couple of seconds trying to find out what had happened to the ball, spoken to the goal-linesman — who went and got the ball and checked the markings, just to be sure — and finally blew his whistle.

It was 1-0 to the Galaxy.

"How on earth did you do that?" Whelan asked as they waited for the Sounders to re-start.

"Lucky shot," said Jimmy, "but I'd close your legs if I were you."

"What did you shout?" added Gutierrez, who had jumped on Jimmy's back celebrating the goal.

"Nutmeg," said Jimmy.

"Nut-job?"

"No, I said nutmeg. Where I'm from you're supposed to warn an opponent before you put the ball through his legs. It's just what you do."

He'd intended to ease his way into the game with a few deft touches but the crowd, on its feet to celebrate the goal, refused to sit down. They were chanting his name, urging him on. *So much for the stealth approach*, he thought, dropping back to mark the Sounders' franchise player, a striker who'd played in the English Premier League for Tottenham Hotspurs and Fulham.

Jimmy's biggest problem was containing himself. He felt like he could score at will; that nobody could touch him but if he wasn't careful he'd end up drawing too much attention to himself and irritate his teammates.

He waited until the striker tried to cut in from the wing and then cherry-picked the ball from him. He could visualise his path to goal but resisted the impulse to gallop ahead, instead passing a short ball to Marco Fuentes, a tough-tackling, unspectacular midfielder. He ran into space for the return. Fuentes stabbed the ball back to him and three Seattle players rushed him at once, goaded on by their coach who was yelling from the sidelines at the top of his voice to triple team him.

Jimmy glanced up to see the wing back, Gutierrez, dashing full speed down the left side of the field unmarked. The problem was that he had no support; Whelan had been caught flat-footed by the sudden swing in play and Jimmy had been dragged deep shadowing his striking counterpart. He was standing still with the ball with no momentum of his own. The easiest, logical ball would have been to his own keeper and the opportunity to restart the move, but Jimmy waved off the call to pass back. Using the inside of his right foot, he brushed the ball like a tennis shot, hardly touching it but imparting the maximum amount of spin. To Jimmy, it felt like the whole pitch had slowed down and the only things still moving at normal pace were Gutierrez and the ball, both heading irresistibly towards one another. The ball took a giant arc around the back of the Seattle defence and met the Galaxy wing back ten yards out from the goal. All he had to do was stick out a foot and the ball cannoned into the net.

2-0

The third Galaxy goal had nothing directly to do with Jimmy, except that the Sounders now had so many players marking him that there was acres of space for everyone else. A thumping goal kick found Whelan on his own two-thirds down the field and he ran on to score with ease.

Jimmy decided to play out the rest of the first 45 minutes putting out fires rather than starting them. He was everywhere, preventing the other team from getting any kind of grip on the game. As soon as the team in green strung together more than a couple of passes he was there to block their path forward, using his strength, speed or positional knowledge to steal the ball and pass it on to a colleague.

Half time took Jimmy by surprise. He hadn't stopped running but felt as fit and strong as he had at kick-off. He even sprinted across to where Zoe and the kids were sitting and blew them a kiss.

As he turned to run towards the tunnel, he heard a familiar voice. "Are you playing in the morning?"

Jimmy looked up to see Martyn waving from the front centre row with his wife Debbie and their twin girls. He was surrounded by other FOBD regulars with their families. They seemed to fill the entire section.

"Need some help?" shouted Sean.

"I'll put a word in," Jimmy shouted back. He felt pretty sure he could have won the final playing with his Sunday morning mates at his side, so confident was he that he could carry the team. "See you in the morning!"

He waved, realising he was the last player left on the field. As he ran towards the dressing rooms he heard the chant start off where he'd just left:

"FOBD,

Galaxy,

Jimmy Keen

For MVP."

By the time he reached the tunnel, the whole crowd had joined in.

CHAPTER FIFTY-NINE

Seattle had clearly decided on a new strategy when they came out for the second 45 minutes. Every Sounders player had one tactic uppermost in his mind — keep the ball away from Jimmy Keen.

Rossi said little in his team talk other than to reposition Jimmy in the centre of midfield and tell his players to pass the ball through him. He wanted to protect the 3-0 lead for the second leg rather than go out looking for more goals.

"Good play, Keen. Keep it going," Rossi said as they walked back out. It was the nearest he'd come to a bona fide compliment but he still eyed Jimmy suspiciously. "I'm still trying to figure you out," he added

Francesco Torres remained aloof from the team and wasn't even sitting on the bench. He was dressed in a sharp navy Armani suit and tie and was sitting in the director's suite with his Italian agent.

The "FOBD" chant started up again as the Sounders kicked off the second half by passing right back to their goalkeeper. Jimmy could see the keeper checking him out and punting the ball the opposite side of the pitch and from then on every time he ran towards the ball, a Sounders player would try and switch the passage of play as far away from him as a 120 yards long x 75 yards wide patch of grass would allow.

For the first 15 minutes of the half, Jimmy couldn't get a touch. His legs felt as strong as before but even they couldn't outrun the speed the ball was being pinged about. On the 19th minute, Seattle's centre-forward made a diagonal run that lost his marker and left him alone with just the goalie to beat 20 yards out. He settled himself for the shot and Jimmy reckoned that even though he was running across from the opposite touchline he just had enough time to reach the striker and snatch the ball with a last ditch, perfectly timed tackle. But instead of shooting, the forward passed back across goal and Jimmy swept away his legs instead of the ball. The Galaxy's defenders cleared the ball but it was a clear penalty.

Jimmy disentangled himself from the striker and hopped up, none the worse for wear but embarrassed about the foul. Then he noticed that the goalkeeper, Santo Rivera, was still on the ground clutching his hand. Rivera was generally believed to be among the top ten goalkeepers in the world, even at the age of 35. He had a long and distinguished career with Barcelona and then Bayer Leverkusen before being tempted to LA with some pre-retirement cash and if he'd lost a step, it was barely discernible. He was certainly the best keeper in the MLS by a considerable distance. He shook his head at Jimmy. "Feels like my fingers are broken," he said. "I know how it feels; it's happened before. I'm done."

The physio was quickly over and on his radio to Rossi, who was gesturing for Scott, the back-up keeper, to get warmed up.

The youngster was fresh out of college and caught unprepared. He wasn't wearing his boots and was scrabbling in his bag for his orange jersey. With Rossi haranguing him and the Seattle coach haranguing Rossi for time-wasting, the harried back-up keeper had no time to warm-up and scurried across the field towards the goalmouth where players from both teams were waiting with the ref. About halfway, while running with one glove under his arm and trying to pull the other one on with his teeth, he suddenly stopped short, grabbing at the back of his left thigh. He looked like he'd been shot. "My hammy," he cried out, squirming on the ground. "It's gone again." He'd only recently returned to training after tearing a hamstring.

The physio had been walking back to the bench with Rivera and now sprinted over to the back-up. It didn't take him more than a couple of seconds before he was back on his headset to Rossi: "There's no way he can play; he can't even walk."

Rossi threw his hands up in the air and had to be restrained by his assistants from attacking the Seattle bench after the coach again suggested this was all a delaying tactic. "I have no keeper!" he roared to nobody in particular.

Jimmy had never played in goal other than taking his turn at the Field of Broken Dreams. But he knew he could save this penalty. He didn't know how; he just knew. He sprinted over to where Rossi was in deep conversation with his number two trying to work out what to do.

"Not now, Keen. We're busy," he said as Jimmy tried to get his attention.

"I'll go in goal."

"What did you say?" Rossi asked irritably.

"I said I'll go in goal. I can save the pen."

"What makes you think you can do that?" Rossi was dismissive, going back to his clipboard.

"I guarantee it." The words were out of Jimmy's mouth before he could stop himself. "And I'll keep them out the rest of the match."

"We haven't got a lot of options, gaffer," said Rossi's English assistant, Paul "Hendo" Henderson. "Might as well give it a go."

The coach humphed his approval and pointed to Rivera. "Get a shirt from him. Turn it inside out," he said. "Norton," he shouted at substitute defender Robbie Norton, "you're on in place of the old man."

Jimmy changed his shirt and ran back over to take his place for the penalty, ignoring the quizzical looks from players on both teams. The referee was eager to press on and set the ball on the spot before checking with Jimmy that he was ready.

The long wait didn't appear to have bothered the penalty taker. He stood nonchalantly at the edge of the box waiting for the whistle. The ref blew and the striker began his run-up, took a stutter step and fired what looked to be a hard, clean, perfectly struck shot low in the left corner. As soon as he hit the ball he knew it was going in and swooped around to celebrate, but there was no roar from the crowd, just a numbed silence.

The striker looked back over his shoulder to see Jimmy standing on the line on the left hand side of the goal with the ball nestled at his feet. He hadn't dived and he hadn't moved before the whistle, but the exact moment the ball left the striker's foot Jimmy had taken two huge strides to his left and trapped the ball, cushioning it on his instep. Then he launched it into the afternoon sky to the feet of Glynn Barber, who was already on the counter attack for the Galaxy.

The attack fizzled out and for the next 20 minutes the Sounders threw everything they had at the Galaxy. Without Jimmy breaking up their play, they were running rings around their tired opponents but with every shot and every header they made, Jimmy was one step ahead. He turned sure-fire headers over the bar and around the posts, plucked balls off the feet of onrushing strikers and stopped several shots from point-blank range.

With just two minutes of overtime remaining, the Sounders won a free-kick by the right touchline about 10 feet out. The Galaxy's supporters had been shellshocked into silence by the unrelenting attacks and the stadium fell hushed as Seattle's playmaker waited for his goalkeeper to make his way upfield for one last, do-or-die attempt to pull a goal back and give them a chance when they play the second leg at home in Seattle. The Sounders keeper was 6ft. 7 Ins. tall and scored a headed goal from a corner in the previous round to help decide the match in the final minute. Only when he'd taken up his position on the penalty box did the free-kick come swinging in high above the Galaxy defence.

It looked like an easy, uncontested header as the keeper jumped way above his markers but just as he was taking aim, Jimmy leaped a good six feet higher to take the ball at it's highest point before it started dropping. With his neck starting all the way back so Jimmy was staring at the sky he snapped it forward just as he reached the ascendant ball, sending it high into the night sky above the lights towards the Sounders' goal. The entire crowd craned its neck in unison watching the ball fall out of the floodlights and bounce three times into the empty net.

4-0

There was just enough time for the restart before the referee blew the whistle to end the game.

CHAPTER SIXTY

Jimmy no longer felt the need to prove himself to his teammates and slipped into a comfortable pattern in training that helped preserve his boots and his energy levels. Wearing the old boots may have enabled him to run around like a teenager, but he felt like a 100 years old as soon as he took them off. The longer he played with them on, the tougher it was on his body afterwards.

His routine was to wear them on the first training session, make an impact, and then put on the Copas during the second, warm-down and take it easy, apparently out of choice but in reality, out of necessity. It became a locker room joke that Jimmy would save himself for match-day. Nobody suspected that he didn't have any choice in the matter.

They had just five days between the first and second leg of the Western Conference Final and Rossi had insisted they all travel up to Seattle the day after the 4-0 home victory to get acclimatised to the rain. It had been pouring all week and the forecasters had predicted another storm for game day that Sunday.

There was an incessant drizzle as the Galaxy players trained on a college field just outside the city. Jimmy zipped up his sweat top to the neck and jogged on the spot to stay warm. It wasn't so different from the many miserable Sundays Jimmy had spent running around a windblown pitch at Hackney

Marshes or Wanstead Flats in East London. If the boots had been waterproof once, the leather had long ago deteriorated to allow a steady stream through the various gaps in the stitching. Everything was wet. The cobbler's attentions had helped but there was only so much he could do to repair half a century of neglect. Just for once, Jimmy was actually looking forward to swapping into his new Adidas boots.

Torres usually practiced in another group from Jimmy, but he'd made a point at the beginning of the session of ensuring they would work out together. With his one-match red card ban served, he was back available for selection, but he wasn't his usual cocksure self.

Rossi was determined his team wouldn't lose for lack of fitness and drove Hendo to push the players harder and harder until several were close to exhaustion.

"The gaffer only wants to do one session today instead of the usual two," said Hendo after gathering the players around. "So if you want to take a quick breather, we'll get back to it in a few minutes and do some five-a-sides. Then you can do 30 minutes in the gym and head back to the hotel."

Worried his soggy boots would decompose on his feet, Jimmy sprinted back to the dressing rooms to change into the newer ones. He didn't have his usual locker, but quickly stuffed the soaked boots deep into his holdall before any of the others could see him. Closing his bag, he pulled on the Copa Mundials and sprinted back into the rain just as Hendo was making the final picks for the 5-a-sides. Rossi was watching in silence from the sideline, swathed in several layers of Patagonia.

There was rarely much contact in these games. Although they were competitive enough to wager on the results, the players didn't want to get injured. But right from the whistle, Torres was on Jimmy's back. Hendo had split the two strikers into opposing teams and it seemed the Spaniard had a point to make.

Jimmy was doing all he could to remain anonymous but Torres was hacking at his heels every time he touched the ball.

Jimmy was trying to slow the game down so his poor touch was less obvious. He fell onto his knees a couple of times, losing his footing on the slippery turf and calling foul to hide his embarrassment.

"What's wrong old man? I thought you could do everything." Torres was constantly in his ear, riding him, seeking confrontation. "You'll have to be faster than that if you want my job."

"I don't want your job." Jimmy shielded the ball, looking for a pass but Torres was crowding him and kicking at his ankles. Norton ran across to give him an option and Jimmy turned, took a step and, to his own surprise, managed to guide the ball away from Torres' outstretched boot.

Jimmy went for the return pass, limping into space, intent on controlling the ball if it came back to him. He had to concentrate; his 47-year-old reflexes would go awry otherwise.

He knew enough to be in the right place and the ball was duly pinged back to him by Norton.

The moment Jimmy touched the ball he felt a screaming pain in his calves and collapsed to the ground on top of Torres, who slid in with both studs showing, taking out both the ball and Jimmy.

"Aargh! What are you doing?" Jimmy lay writhing on the ground. His right leg, the muscles slightly flabby with age despite the recent flurry of activity, was on fire. There was a trickle of blood from where the first stud hit and the skin was already showing four or five blueing imprints from the others. Jimmy was afraid to move; he wasn't even sure he could.

The physio raced over, bag in hand. "Are you okay, Jimmy?"

Lying on the floor, giving in to the rain on his face, the sweat from his exertions and the soaking grass, Jimmy did a mental checklist, bending his knee, ankle and toes trying to work out if anything was broken. He decided he'd be okay, but Torres' boot print on his leg would be a lasting reminder that not everybody was so happy about his twilight career as a professional footballer.

They didn't bother to restart the game and the players jogged to the dressing room, leaving Jimmy to limp back slowly on his own. Torres didn't apologise; he was the first to leave and was already showered by the time Jimmy had hobbled back into the warmth.

He sat down and took another look at the ugly blue and purple leopard print on his right calf. Torres walked past, ignoring Jimmy, his bag slung over one shoulder. There was nowhere for him to go; the training field was in the middle of nowhere, but he went and took his usual seat in the front row of the coach to wait.

Jimmy was way more laborious. He was last in the shower and gingerly pulled his dry team sweats over the purple war zone on his leg, wincing in pain as the material stuck to one, still bloody, stud mark. They all threw their wet clothes in to be washed and the kit man, Joe, was waiting patiently for Jimmy so he could finish loading up the coach.

"Sorry, Joe. This is killing me." Jimmy pointed to the bruises. "One of my co-workers got a bit too carried away."

"I heard Torres took you out." The old man drawled. "Looks to me like he's worried for his job. Little birdie told me you're in the starting line-up for Sunday."

"Really?" Jimmy had assumed Torres would be playing. "What about Francesco?"

"On the bench. That's what I'm hearing." The overweight, balding kit man waddled out of the room dragging a bin liner full of wet uniforms. "And so you should be playing." He looked over his shoulder and winked at Jimmy. "Gives us old guys something to work towards."

Jimmy smiled and looked outside. He was the last to leave. He picked up his Copas and went to put them in his bag. Some of the other guys left their boots for the apprentices to clean but, for obvious reasons, Jimmy preferred to keep his close. Lifting his holdall it felt lighter than usual but the thought didn't really register. Jimmy rummaged around for the plastic bag he'd brought for his wet gear; he'd spent enough time playing in England to learn that much. He couldn't find the bag, but remembered he'd already used it for his old boots.

It was only then that he realised that his old boots weren't there.

He felt the panic rise from the bottom of his stomach and he managed to push it back down, thinking he mustn't have looked hard enough. They were in his bag. They had to be.

But they weren't.

The coach driver was honking now and he heard Terry's voice outside. "C'mon Jimmy. The guys want to get back to the hotel before we all drop dead with pneumonia."

Jimmy ignored him. He was going through his bag for the fourth time. He threw open his empty locker and then went around blindly opening the others. The coach honked again. He went back to his bag and looked again. They weren't there. He slapped himself in the face just in case this was a nightmare. The slap hurt and so did his right leg as he brushed it on the side of the bench.

Terry was in the doorway. "Jimmy, we've gotta go. The boss is getting pissed."

He watched as Jimmy picked up the unzipped bag and waited for him. Jimmy wanted to go back one more time and throw out the contents of his holdall just in case he'd missed something, just in case the boots, his magic boots, were hidden in the lining or wrapped up in an old jersey. He was hoping for a miracle but Terry wasn't going to let him wait any longer and Jimmy couldn't explain to his club captain why he could hardly breath and his legs felt like jelly and he knew for certain now that millions of soccer fans around the world and his own family, friends and teammates would soon discover that he was a cheat and a fraud and had about as much skill as any other old has-been trying to relive past memories being outrun and outplayed every Sunday morning over the park by younger, faster and better youngsters who could run rings around him.

With Duncan Edwards' boots, Jimmy could live out the dreams of every old player who thought that life had passed them by.

Without them he was nothing.

CHAPTER SIXTY-ONE

Jimmy spent the 45-minute journey back to the hotel in Seattle staring at the back of Francesco Torres' head. The Spaniard must have taken his boots; Jimmy couldn't think of any other explanation. He'd been the only one to pay attention to the boots and Jimmy knew Torres had his suspicions about them.

By the time they reached the hotel, Jimmy had decided there was no other choice; he'd have to confront Torres. But he'd been forced to sit in the only open seat at the back and watched helplessly as his nemesis got first off the coach and walked briskly into the foyer. He was carrying two bags. *He'd never want my old, stinking boots to touch his fancy gear*, thought Jimmy.

When he finally got into the hotel, Jimmy caught sight of Torres on the second floor landing. The building had a giant atrium with exposed glass elevators up to rooms which all had views of the water and Jimmy dashed to catch the nearest elevator, keeping his sights on Torres the whole time.

Stopping at the second floor, Jimmy sprinted after Torres, calling out for him to wait. His teammate either ignored Jimmy or didn't hear. He had his card key in one hand and swiped it in the lock before hurrying inside with his bags.

Jimmy caught up moments later and banged on the door. Nothing. He banged again.

"Torres, I know you're in there. It's Jimmy. I want a word."
He banged louder this time.

As he went to slam his hand on the door a fourth time it
suddenly opened and Torres, changed and wearing a white
tracksuit, almost got hit by Jimmy's flailing fist.

"What do you want?" Torres did not look happy.

"My boots." Jimmy wasn't backing down, not this time.
"I've lost my old boots and I think you may have them."

"Who told you that?" Torres was trying to close the door.

"Nobody." Jimmy hesitated, embarrassed. "But they're gone
and you were the only person who noticed them before. I don't
know what else could have happened to them."

"Probably someone threw them in the trash. Those old boots
are disgusting." Torres turned his nose up. "Why would I take
your trash?"

"I don't know, I…"

"You want to check my bags, treat me like cheap thief?"
Torres stood back and acted as if to invite Jimmy in.

"No, I, er, well, yes. Can I?" Jimmy suddenly felt really
small.

The imperious striker stood back to allow Jimmy in and
pointed to the two bags he carried from the coach. "You check,
then you apologise."

Jimmy had to know. He went over, picked up the larger
Galaxy bag and put it on the bed. He unzipped it and opened the
sides so he could see inside. Spare socks, shorts and training

tops were folded neatly side-by-side. There was a brush and some expensive-looking bathroom soaps and shampoos, some headphones, a tablet and there was a pair of boots, but they were orange. In fact, one was orange and the other was green. They certainly never belonged to Duncan Edwards.

With a growing sense of dread, Jimmy zipped the bag back up like an awkward airport security screener and reached down for the smaller bag, hoping to solve the mystery right there. It smelt strange, a little funky, like his boots. He'd already decided he'd take the boots and walk out without any explanation. He'd let the matter rest rather than stir anything up that could be hard to explain. He didn't want a fight, he just wanted his boots back.

Only they weren't there. Inside the smaller bag was a thick deli bag full of sliced chicken.

"Protein." Torres reached his hand out for the bag. "Satisfied?"

Jimmy handed over the chicken and backed out sheepishly, apologising as Torres took out a slice and put it in his mouth. "You should try this, Keen. It's good for your stamina." But he didn't offer Jimmy any.

Heading back to his own room, Jimmy decided to try and call Zoe. She was the only other person who knew. Perhaps she would know how he could save himself. But when he went to dial his wife's number, Jimmy saw she'd already called him. Five times.

There were a couple of messages but Jimmy called back without checking them.

"Oh, thank God, Jimmy, where have you been?" Zoe wasn't happy. "I even tried Murray and he said you should have got back from training a while ago."

"I'm sorry, Zo, I've got a bit of a situation." Jimmy sat down on his bed, ready to tell his story.

"Well, we've got a situation here, too." She didn't wait for Jimmy to explain. "Carl and Sarah are here with Wally but there's no way he can fly. He can hardly breathe."

"What's wrong with him?" Jimmy's problems suddenly felt less urgent.

"He's apparently been hiding some big heart thing from everybody. Didn't tell his doctor he was coming and only told Carl when he was practically suffocating on the flight. He still wouldn't get help from the crew, the stubborn old goat. He's on the sofa as white as a sheet and his breathing sounds like a Harley Davidson. I keep telling him that there's no way he's going to be able to fly to Seattle but he won't hear of it. Says he came to see you play and he's not going home until he has."

For a second, Jimmy had forgotten he'd lost his boots. The thought of Wally watching him falling over his feet sent him into a new panic. "Perhaps you'd better all stay home then," he said. "Better be safe than sorry. It'll be on TV."

"Don't be crazy, Jimmy. We're talking about Wally here. He's not going to miss watching you play now, not after all these years." Zoe sounded impatient, ready to get off the phone. "The best we can do is stop Wally flying again, at least for now. Carl's rented a mini-van. We've cancelled the flights and we're driving up in the morning. Should work perfectly with a little luck. We can do it in a couple of days if we share the driving."

"I guess that'll work." Jimmy didn't sound convinced. "Just be safe."

"Don't worry, baby. You just concentrate on your football and then show your family what you can really do. We're so proud of you."

CHAPTER SIXTY-TWO

There wasn't a lot more that Jimmy could do. He searched his bag a dozen times and even asked his other teammates if they'd seen his missing boots, but all to no avail. There were two training sessions the following day and he could hardly walk afterwards; he'd spent so much energy trying to keep up so as not to appear totally spent.

Torres had been less confrontational, content to let Jimmy struggle, and didn't even seem too bothered when the reporters swarmed Jimmy at a media session held at the Sounders' CenturyLink Field after the second session.

"What position will you be playing this time Jimmy, striker or goalie?" asked the Seattle Times sports editor.

"I'll be playing wherever Mr Rossi asks me to." Jimmy wasn't much good at these at the best of the times and this wasn't that.

An ESPN correspondent stuck a microphone in Jimmy's face. "You seemed to be having some difficulties in training just now. Do you have an injury or perhaps a problem with your fitness?"

"I'm just a little tired," said Jimmy. "As you can imagine, it's been a crazy few weeks for me so I'm trying to conserve all my energy for Sunday. I'll be raring to go by then, I promise." He tried to smile but the grimace froze on his face. "The important thing is that the team gets the results; it's not really about individual players."

He fielded about a dozen more questions before the scrum broke up and the reporters wandered off to talk to the other players. Rossi was penned in by the goalmouth being asked about his starting line-up for the second leg.

"Have you decided to play Torres or Keen, Mr Rossi?" The Los Angeles Times soccer correspondent had asked Jimmy the same question moments earlier.

"You'll have to wait and see. It's too early to discuss this today. They are both scoring goals and both very good players. We obviously all know about Francesco and Keen has, well, he's improved very much. It's a tough decision, I can say this." The coach refused to be drawn.

"You must be very confident with a 4-0 advantage in your pocket," said NBC's sports producer. "Is this an opportunity to rest some players for the final?"

"They can rest after the season. Nobody rests now." Rossi was getting impatient to return to the safety of the dressing room.

"What about Jimmy Keen? His legs have more mileage in them than the rest of the team. Did you think about keeping him on the bench to start?

Rossi was already trying to muscle through the reporters. "Keen gets treated like everybody else," he said.

Jimmy had slowed down to listen as he walked past and felt a shove so hard he almost fell over as Torres brushed by him. The Spaniard reached out a hand to save Jimmy from tumbling over. "Have you found your antique boots," he said. "Perhaps that means you don't play so well?"

"Perhaps that means you're a thief. Perhaps you're scared you're going to be outplayed by an old man." Jimmy jabbed a finger into Torres' chest. "If I find out you took my boots I'll make you pay, my friend. Don't worry about that."

Jimmy pushed Torres with both hands. Red-faced, he moved menacingly towards his teammate until the mist cleared a little and he saw the cameras turning towards them. Forcing a smile, Jimmy patted Torres on the arm. Moving closer, he whispered: "Enjoy watching from the bench on Sunday!" Then he pulled back, saying loudly: "Sorry Francesco, my fault. Guess I'm getting nervous for the big game."

Jimmy left before he could be asked any more questions and headed over to his locker to check his phone. Zoe had promised to keep him posted on the progress of their road trip and he hadn't heard from her all day. It was getting to him.

He knew his family was on its way. Wally had recovered and they all set off the previous morning from Orange County in a rented minivan. The idea was that Zoe would share the driving with Carl and Sarah and they would plow on for two days straight up the I-5 and get into Seattle that night.

Zoe had been sending regular text bulletins the first day and halfway through the night but they'd stopped that morning before Jimmy went to training and there hadn't been any messages since.

Jimmy tried Zoe's phone but there was no reply and Carl's English mobile just rang out. The kids' phones all went straight to voicemail. He assumed that maybe they'd stopped for a nap somewhere on route. It was an exhausting drive.

He decided to head back to the hotel, draw a hot bath to prevent his aching legs stiffening up altogether, and wait to hear from them.

CHAPTER SIXTY-THREE

Jimmy awoke with a start in the cold, dank bath and blinked around the hotel room trying to work out where he was. It was dark and shards of rain were crashing on the floor-to-ceiling windows. His mind crept back into focus. Then he reached for his phone.

There was just one missed call from a number he didn't recognise. A cold fear had settled over Jimmy's heart and he prodded at the voicemail button on his phone. It was Carl, although it didn't sound like his brother. It sounded like all the air had gone from his voice, like he was breathing in reverse.

"Jimmy! Jimmy!" He didn't seem to understand he was on voicemail. "Jimmy, you need to call me now." Carl's voice was cold and hard and he said it again, softer now. "Jimmy, please call on this number when you get this…"

The call had come through about an hour earlier and Jimmy cursed himself for missing it. He pressed "Call Back" on his phone and sat on the side of his bed. It wasn't cold but he was shivering nonetheless. He had a very bad feeling.

The number rang out and Jimmy tried his other family numbers, but nobody was answering. He tried the number Carl left again and this time his brother's voice came right on the phone. "There's been an accident."

A dozen thoughts went through Jimmy's head at once. "Zoe…the kids?"

"The kids are fine, just a little shocked," said Carl. "They're with Sarah; they're all going to be fine."

"And Zoe?"

"Zoe's not so good, Jimmy."

"What do you mean, not so good? Do you mean…?"

"No, she's alive. But she's in a coma. There was some head injuries and they don't seem to know yet how bad. She was driving, she took the full force of it." Carl tailed off.

"I've got to be there."

"I know, Jimmy. I'm so sorry this has happened now, especially with the final and everything."

"Forget that, I don't care about that now." Jimmy was throwing some clothes in a bag as he talked. "Where are you?"

"We're at the PeaceHealth Sacred Heart Medical Centre in Eugene, Oregon." Carl was making a real effort to stay calm. "The accident happened just north of here on the I-5. There's nothing Zoe could have done; this truck slid out in the rain and slammed across the central reservation right into us. Zoe managed to turn the car so the kids weren't hurt in the back but she took the brunt of it. She's pretty banged up."

"What are the doctors saying?" Jimmy ignored the elevators and ran down the stairs.

"They don't know Jim. They say the first 24 hours are the most important. They don't know how much damage she suffered to her brain."

"Hold on, Carl." Jimmy was at the hotel reception. "I want to know the fastest way I can get to Eugene, Oregon," he said to the clerk. "I don't care how much it costs but can you sort it out for me right now?"

"Jim! Jimmy! I gotta go." Carl shouted into the phone, trying to get his brother's attention.

"I'll call you on route," said Jimmy. "Let me know everything that happens and get Tyler to call me, will you?"

"Okay Jim but I have to go now. They want to talk to me about Wally."

"Wally!" Jimmy had forgotten the old man was in the car. "Is he okay?"

"Not really. He had a heart attack. The shock caused it. We don't know if he's going to make it...I'd better go."

"Okay thanks Carl. Call me and let me know. I'll be there as fast as I can." The hotel already had a car waiting for Jimmy but it was going to be four-and-a-half hours on the road before he could get to Zoe.

CHAPTER SIXTY-FOUR

The car journey was a jumble of numbed emotions. Jimmy didn't breathe until they were two hours in and by the time they reached Eugene he'd imagined every possible scenario. The only one he dared not hope for was Zoe sitting up in bed, alive and well, asking him what took so long.

The driver pulled right up to the door of the ER and said he would be outside whenever Jimmy needed him. Now he was there Jimmy felt full of dread. A part of him didn't want to leave the leathery warmth of the Cadillac and discover what was really happening outside his imagination. The idea of losing Zoe was just too much to bear.

Walking through the swing doors to find a mass of humanity focused on their own particular emergencies and crises, Jimmy felt small and lost looking in vain for a familiar face. He looked down at his phone. There was one text from Murray, the Galaxy general manager, wondering where he was. Nothing from Carl.

A bunch of people crowded around the triage nurse and the guy taking insurance didn't know anything; he wouldn't even confirm Zoe was there. Jimmy had this nightmare before; trying to find his way through the night in a fog of bewilderment. Only when it happened to him before he woke up and everything was all right.

Nobody had a moment to help and a burly security guard prevented him from going through in to the wards. He'd have to wait in line, the nurse told him, she'd get to him as soon as she could.

Then across the room he saw Tyler, Grace and Charley standing by the drinks machine with Sarah, who was banging the side, presumably hoping violence would scare it into working. Jimmy shouted but his voice was drowned out by the chaos.

Charley was the first to see Jimmy as she turned her red eyes towards him and ran, deaf to Sarah's cries. For a few seconds at least, there was something Jimmy could do. All that mattered was reaching Charley and holding her in his arms. A few yards apart, Jimmy dropped to his knees and the little girl flung her arms around his neck with a single word.

"Daddy."

Grace was a moment behind and then Tyler, puberty forgotten, his arms circling his father and sisters, his tears joining theirs. All three had small scratches on their pale, shocked faces and there was a bruise under Tyler's eye but they appeared otherwise unharmed. Sarah stood slightly apart, one arm in a sling, not quite sure what to do with herself.

Jimmy eventually stood, wiping his eyes with his shoulder, and embraced Sarah. He asked the question and waited, standing upright, eyes down, for the answer he'd been dreading since leaving his Seattle hotel room. "How's she doing?"

"No change, Jimmy, she's still the same."

Jimmy breathed out, but only through his mouth; the rest of his body remained tensed against the worst. Holding the kids' hands he followed Sarah past the security guard and into the peace of the wards.

The difference between the two worlds was so dramatic that the silence was louder than the incessant din behind the double doors. White coats swished down the corridors and the wards hummed with a quiet efficiency. Everyone had a task, busy people purposeful in their movements with the occasional patient lying in their cots in the hallways.

It seemed to Jimmy, led by the hand into Zoe's ward by his children, that his wife was the only still person in the hospital. He'd watched her sleeping enough nights to know this wasn't a peaceful sleep; she wasn't dreaming of Venetian patios or bougainvillea pathways. A plastic mask covered her mouth and a thick tube disappeared down her throat but he knew she was fighting to get back to them. She was tougher than him; she was tougher than all of them. If it was physically possible, she would find a way.

Jimmy's eyes flickered down to Zoe's wedding finger, with a black clip crowding out her ring, checking her pulse, when it twitched almost imperceptibly and then lay crooked back on the white sheet. Sarah followed Jimmy's eyes. "It does that," she said.

The beeps and flashes on the screens by the bed meant nothing to Jimmy, although he knew a flat line wasn't good. The peaks and troughs on the graph weren't deep but they were the only real signs that Zoe was alive.

There was a light knock on the door and Carl came in, looking so much older than Jimmy had ever seen him. His jet black hair was usually swept rakishly back and he had a journalist's way of appearing untouched by the everyday stresses of life. Perhaps he'd seen too much, maybe he didn't care enough, but now, his uncombed hair revealing streaks of grey and his face marbled by worry and lack of sleep, he seemed very close to exhaustion.

Hugging Jimmy, he said: "Sorry Jim. I was in with Wally. We've been taking turns and Wally's been in and out. He's not making a lot of sense but at least he's talking."

"What about Zoe?" Jimmy pulled slowly away from his brother. "Is there any news at all?"

"The docs are saying that there's no change but that can be a good thing. They're worried there's some swelling in the brain. Apparently drugs can help it go down. She's not getting any worse and they put her into an induced coma to give her body some time to marshal all her strength to try and snap out of it." Carl spoke quietly, unemotionally. "It's not a lot but it's something to hang onto, I guess."

Jimmy's phone vibrated again. Murray had been trying to get hold of him for hours and left a slew of messages. Now Mike Terry was calling.

Jimmy switched off the phone. "Are you guys okay if I just have a couple of moments alone with mummy?" The question was directed at the kids and they didn't understand at first.

"You mean you want us to go?" Tyler asked.

"Just for a couple of minutes."

"Oh yeah, dad. Sorry we…."

"Don't say sorry, Ty. I just have some stuff I want to chat about with mum. Can you look after the girls for me for a few minutes?"

Tyler ushered out his sisters, holding their hands, followed by Carl and Sarah. All three adults hugged and Sarah kissed Jimmy on the cheek. "It's going to be okay Jimmy, I just know it."

Jimmy smiled but he didn't trust himself to speak. The door closed and he was alone with Zoe and his thoughts.

CHAPTER SIXTY-FIVE

For a long time, Jimmy just sat holding Zoe's hand and stroking her hair back from her forehead. He didn't trust himself to speak.

They'd been together for so long it was impossible for him to visualise a life without her. Looking back there seemed like an inevitability about their relationship, but a million stars had to align to make it possible.

Zoe was just 17 when they met. She was living with her parents in Kentish Town and already working at a London bank. She smoked and she drank and wore her hair crimped at impossible angles and seemed so much older and more grow-up than Jimmy, even though he was four years her senior and thought he knew everything. She understood some realities of life that he didn't and perhaps never would, but the knowledge came at a cost in a childhood that saw too much.

His upbringing had been whole and safe and hers was broken and dangerous; she came from the other side of the world and he came from just up the road; she was beautiful and determined and he was secure and unsure.

Almost every early milestone in their lives - their first date at a bowling alley (neither bowled), his marriage proposal (no down on one knee, no romance, she said no) and their wedding (he wanted a church service, she didn't) - were out of step. But everything in between was like a beautifully choreographed dance. By the time they had Tyler their contrasting vulnerabilities and insecurities had found their answers in one another. Grace and Charley had cemented those bonds and even as his unemployment, their subsequent debts and his occasional despair had scared and upset Zoe the solution was always going to be one they would seek together. Not once had they ever doubted the incredible luck and good fortune they had in finding their "one." They always had each other.

Only now, Jimmy was forced to accept, they might not.

He held Zoe's hand tighter, realising his inner dialogue wasn't helping. Carl told him before he left that the doctors suggested talking to her as much as possible in the hope that at some deeper level she would hear and fight even harder to regain consciousness.

The tears came before the words. Try as he might, Jimmy couldn't get out a sentence as the pent-up emotion of the past four or five hours - and perhaps much longer than that - burst the dam. Even when he regained his composure, his eyes refused to obey and he couldn't stop crying.

"Please Zoe, you have to come back to us," he said eventually. "There's so much we still have to do together. The kids need you, I need you. We all love you so much."

Jimmy thought he saw Zoe's eyes flicker but he might have been imagining it. He felt intimidated by the sterile ward with his wife's breathing interrupted by the intermittent bleep from the monitor providing the only light by the bed.

"Remember when you told me that this was only going to work if I was serious about it," Jimmy said softly. "You said to me, 'Are you in or out? If you're in you have to be in all the way or I'm out.'

"I think you were 17 when you said that, there were never any grey areas with you. It was all or nothing, simple as that." Jimmy smiled. "Well, I don't know if you can hear me, Zo, but I was 100 percent in then and I'm 100 percent now. Nothing has changed for me, but I'm going to ask you now to give me everything you have to fight your way out of this. Like you always said, there's no halfway when it comes to love."

He realised he sounded like a cheesy romance novel but nobody was listening other, maybe, than Zoe. Leaning over to kiss her cheek, it felt cold. "You need to fight like you've never fought before and drag yourself back to me," he whispered, staring at her closed eyes, wishing desperately that they would open.

Jimmy sat on the side of the bed and pulled his legs up so he lay alongside her, being careful not to disturb the plastic tubes. Cradling Zoe's head, he settled onto the edge of the pillow so his face was a few inches from hers, humming *Edelweiss* from *The Sound of Music* just as he'd done so many times to lull the kids off to sleep, and remained stock still in that position until Carl returned to check on them 45 minutes later.

A doctor was checking the ventilator and put a finger to her lips as Carl's eyes got used to the darkness in the room.

Carl looked at his brother for a few seconds, bathed in light from the corridor, and then turned back, closing the door behind him, to take care of the rest of the family.

CHAPTER SIXTY-SIX

Jimmy finally called Neil Murray at 6am the following morning - the Sunday of the second leg match against Seattle. By then there were more than a dozen increasingly panicked calls and texts from various members of the Galaxy team and coaching staff.

He wasn't going to call until Sarah showed him a story on her newsfeed about missing soccer player Jimmy Keen who had mysteriously disappeared from his hotel on the eve of the biggest game of his life. The story even went into his DUI conviction, suggesting that he may have gone off on a drinking binge triggered by the pressure.

Jimmy didn't care about the story, but Carl and Sarah persuaded him it was only right to let his teammates know what was happening.

"I can't play," Jimmy told Murray. "I need to be here with Zoe and the kids."

The Scotsman didn't try to persuade him. "I'm so sorry, Jimmy. We just had no idea what happened. We were worried."

A day earlier, this one match was Jimmy's everything. He thought of little else. He couldn't sleep worrying about what had become of his magic boots and he'd spent more time apart from his family in the past few weeks than he had his entire marriage and for what? None of it mattered without Zoe.

The phone conversation was brief. Jimmy's thoughts were focused on the intensive care ward a few feet away. At that moment he couldn't care less if the Galaxy held onto their four goal advantage that afternoon.

Carl took the kids back to a hotel nearby to rest and Jimmy managed perhaps two hours sleep in the chair next to Zoe's bed. He awoke to find a doctor examining her.

"Any change?" Jimmy stood up and stretched.

"The neurologist will be in shortly to carry out some checks but all the vitals are stable at the moment." The doctor looked little older than Tyler but he was pleasant enough. "We'll do everything we can, Mr Keen."

Jimmy's phone rang again. Murray had clearly put out the word about the accident and there had been a string of calls from the media that he'd ignored. This call was from Martyn from the Field of Broken Dreams and Jimmy picked up.

"Are you okay, Jimmy? Is there anything any of us can do?"

Jimmy quietly explained what happened. A big group from FOBD had travelled up together for the game and were in Seattle. "I'm so sorry I can't be there," he said, "but I can't play with Zoe here like this…"

"Don't be daft, you don't have to say sorry, we just want to help. Deb's here with me, we can come right there if you want us to look after the kids."

"Thanks but we're okay. I've got my brother and his wife here. Please go ahead and watch the game…and pray for Zoe for me. The doctors say they're going to bring her out of the coma later today so we won't know much more until then…"

The kids were with Sarah in Zoe's room so Jimmy went down to see Carl, who was in with Wally.

The old man had an oxygen mask over his face and opened his eyes when Jimmy walked in but he clearly didn't recognise him.

"How's he doing," Jimmy asked Carl, who was standing by the window.

"Not so good. The heart attack did some real damage this time. It took a while to get him breathing again."

"Is he talking?"

"Nothing that makes any sense. He's mentioned the old man a couple of times and he said your name but he doesn't know what's going on. The doctors are saying we should make some arrangements and tell his next of kin, but I don't think Wally has any family left."

"Just us, I suppose." Jimmy sat down on the solitary chair. "His neighbours were always his family. It doesn't seem right that it should all end over here so far away from home."

"At least we're all here with him." Carl moved closer to try and hear what Wally was saying. "I'm going to put the game on the telly later. You can put it on in Zoe's room as well if you like. Might as well see how they get on without their star striker."

But Jimmy wasn't listening. He was thinking that if he'd never found those crappy old boots in the attic he wouldn't be playing football and Zoe would never have been driving that minivan.

"It's all my fault," he said quietly. "None of this would have happened if I hadn't been prancing about with a football trying to make like I was 21 again."

"You were never that good at 21." Carl smiled wryly. "Come to think about it, you were never that good. I don't know what you've been doing in California - yoga, eating squash blossoms, smoking weed - whatever it is I want some."

"Yeah, but look where it's got me." Jimmy slumped down further in the chair, wishing he was back on a building site and his wife and children were safely back home.

"You're like a magician out there on the pitch. You've got the whole world watching you. It's been incredible what you've done." Carl was determined not to let Jimmy wallow in his grief. "Shit happens, Jim, it just does."

"Yeah and what can the big hero footballer do about it? Nothing, that's what. Maybe I have been blessed for some reason by the football gods, but this needs the real thing. It sucks when the closest you've come to religion is supporting your team. This isn't some stupid game; it's my wife we're talking about. Now's the time I need a miracle and there's nothing I can do but sit there singing show tunes." Jimmy paused. "What I wouldn't do for a drink right now."

"I've got a flask back at the hotel if that'd help?" Carl couldn't bear seeing his brother in so much pain.

"Not right now, I need to keep my mind clear," said Jimmy, without looking up, "but if Zoe doesn't make it…all bets are off."

CHAPTER SIXTY-SEVEN

It was 3.10pm when the nurse came in to say Jimmy had some visitors. Carl had taken the kids into Wally's room to watch the match. He thought it might help jerk Wally back into the present and take everyone else's minds off what was going on.

Jimmy decided to stay with Zoe. He was still having trouble reconciling the game with the bad luck that put Zoe and his family in the path of such danger. It was like he was being pulled down into a dark hole and he couldn't see any light. Everything he cared about was narrowing down to a single, all-engrossing thought; Zoe must survive. He'd even been short and distant with the kids; the burden of guilt was overwhelming him.

He ignored the nurse at first and continued staring at Zoe's face, willing her to wake up and when she tried to call him a second time he snapped back. "Tell them to come back later. I'm busy."

"Mr Keen, I think you'd better come. They're causing rather a disturbance."

Irritated, Jimmy pulled himself up, thinking it must be something to do with the kids. He hated leaving Zoe alone, fearing she'd wake up and nobody would be there for her even though he knew she was being administered enough drugs to keep her asleep for a week. "What's the problem?" he asked, following the nurse out of the door.

"It's not really a problem," she said, gesturing towards the reception area. "We're just not really sure what to do with them."

The room was full and it took Jimmy a moment to realize who they were. He saw Paul and Dimple first, then Martyn and Debbie, and Stuart, Bill, Sean and their wives. There were more than 20 people, maybe 30, and they were all from FOBD.

"I told everyone what you said," Martyn wrapped Jimmy in a bear hug, "about going to see the match. But they all decided it was more important to be here. We want you guys to know you're not alone in this."

One by one, the Sunday morning regulars, many with their wives or partners, waited their turn to embrace Jimmy before finding room to sit down. "We're just going to hang around for a while, if that's okay," said Paul. "Don't worry about us. It's going to work out, you'll see."

For the first time since the nightmare began, Jimmy felt a glimmer of hope and walked slowly back to Zoe's ward feeling just a little lighter. Passing Wally's room there was a cheer and Jimmy looked in to see Carl, Sarah and the children gathered around the TV in the corner. Torres had just scored a penalty. It was 1-0 to the Galaxy, making it 5-0 on aggregate. With or without Jimmy, it looked almost certain the team was on its way to the MLS Cup Final.

CHAPTER SIXTY-EIGHT

The small intensive care ward was so full of tubes and machines it was hard for everyone to squeeze in. The doctors had advised against it and the nurses had tried to enforce it but nobody was moving. Jimmy was standing on one side of the bed with Tyler, and Grace, Charley and Sarah were on the other side with Zoe's mother, Angela, who had flown in from Orange County. Carl and his two daughters were in the ward across the hall with Wally.

"Okay so we've stopped giving her the Propofol but we have to wait for Zoe to wake up in her own time," said the young attending physician. "Imagine it like switching on the light with a dimmer rather than a switch. We can't find any sign of brain damage but we can't be certain. She's probably going to be a little confused. Are you guys sure you wouldn't rather wait and I'll get you in when she comes around?"

Jimmy had gone over this several times already. "We're sure. We all want to be here, whatever happens." He hugged the kids closer to him, wishing more fervently than ever that he had a god to pray to. He hoped that Zoe's faith was enough for both of them.

Looking around the ward after a couple of hours, Jimmy could see they were all reaching their limits. Zoe hadn't shown any sign of life and he'd tried to persuade the kids to go back to the hotel with some of the FOBD guys but they were as obstinate as he was. They wanted to be there when their mum woke up.

When it actually happened, it almost caught them all by surprise. Charley saw Zoe's fingers moving just slightly, clawing at the bed sheet. There was a deep red scar across her forehead, just above the right eye, where her head hit the collapsed minivan roof and it wrinkled a moment or so before Zoe's eyes half-opened, squinting against the bright lights.

"Mum!" Charley and Grace cried out at the same time and Zoe looked startled. She reached her free hand to her mouth and grabbed at her plastic mask trying to say something. The doctor reached over to carefully remove the breathing tube and Zoe tried to speak. Her voice was so raspy it was impossible to hear at first, but she finally managed to get out a whisper.

"What was the score?"

Zoe remembered nothing about the crash or about being in a coma but the doctors told them that was perfectly normal. Most importantly, the swelling on her brain had receded and there didn't appear to be any lasting damage.

"I thought I remembered you scoring the winning goal and everybody was going crazy in the crowd," Zoe said later. Her voice was still hoarse but she looked remarkably well considering her ordeal.

"I didn't play," said Jimmy. "I was here the whole time."

"You were?" Zoe's face was flushed, making the scar an even deeper red. "I could have sworn you scored with this weird back flip shot over your head thingy. Even I knew that was pretty special. The kids were jumping up and down and everyone was chanting your name. It was incredible. I remember feeling so proud."

Jimmy looked into his wife's tired eyes. "I was afraid you weren't going to make it, Zo." He blinked back a tear. "I was so afraid." He put his head down and Zoe tousled his hair.

"I wasn't going anywhere," she whispered. "Too many things to do here. Who's gonna keep you and the kids in line? If I'm not around you're all going to be stuck in front of that TV all day and no homework's ever going to get done. Besides... I've still got to see you score that fancy goal to win the cup for the Galaxy."

Jimmy looked back in her eyes. "I don't think I'm going to play any more, babe. I'm too old, it's just stupid me acting like I'm some kind of superstar. I should leave it to the young lads like Torres..."

There was a knock on the door and Carl opened it enough to have a word, gasping with relief as he saw Zoe sitting up awake. "I'm sorry to interrupt Jimmy, but Wally's asking after you and he's not so out of it; he seems to know what's going on. He's pretty insistent."

Jimmy looked at Zoe and she nodded. "Go and see if there's anything you can do and send him my love," she said. "I'm not going anywhere."

CHAPTER SIXTY-NINE

Wally's eyes were closed when Jimmy walked in but they opened as soon as he sat down in the chair by the bed.

"You two be all right?" Carl stayed by the door. "I'm going to see if I can find a cup of what the people in this fine country like to call tea."

"We'll be fine, won't we Wally?" Jimmy had still expected to find the old man out of sorts and confused but he appeared remarkably lucid.

"In the pink, son. Feeling a lot better." Wally tried to pull himself up and Jimmy managed to stuff a pillow behind his head. "There's just been this thing that's been bothering me and I wanted to have a chat with you about it."

"Of course Wally, anything I can do."

"I wouldn't take you away from Zoe but Carl tells me she's doing a lot better so I could rest easy. She's a great gal that one. You did good."

Jimmy smiled, maybe for the first time in days. He did good, yes, and she was doing a lot better. "Now all we need to do is get you back on your feet and we can get out of here." Jimmy half expected Wally to jump out of bed and put on his jacket.

"I don't think that's going to happen, son. I'll more than likely be stopping here." Wally was very matter-of-fact but impatient to say more. "I hate to be rude but I have to say my piece. I'm not sure how long I've got like this."

Jimmy tried to argue but a glare from Wally silenced him, just as it used to when he was a kid.

"I've been watching you play, Jimmy. They show the games on TV at home now and you've been on the news a lot. That's our Jimmy, I tell everyone down at the social. They're right proud they are."

Jimmy blushed. He wasn't used to getting praise, certainly not when he was growing up. "It means a lot," he managed, worried he was about to start blubbering again.

"What I wanted to tell you, Jimmy, was that your old man would be proud of you, too. So proud." Wally coughed as he repeated himself and Jimmy had to get him a glass of water before he could continue.

"I know your dad wasn't always the easiest man to get on with, especially for you. He had such high hopes. He thought you were going to be the next Duncan Edwards. He told me once when you were little that he thought you could be better than Duncan."

"So why didn't he ever say anything to me?" Jimmy couldn't help being exasperated by Wally's stories about how his dad thought he was such a good player.

"It's complicated, boy. Those were different times and your father could be a difficult fella. I told you he was quite some ball player himself as a young man but his parents were strict, church people. They didn't believe in sport; they said it was the devil's doing. He'd sneak off and play without them knowing.

They weren't at the Dudley schoolboys games; they didn't even know he was playing. Then your dad got the injury and none of that really mattered any more. He'd help Duncan though. They'd spend hours in the garden and down by the allotments just kicking the ball back and forth talking about the game. Then after Duncan died you came along and in some ways it was very painful for him."

"What do you mean, Wally?" The room was really quiet; all the usual noises on the ward faded away as Jimmy slipped into the past. "Why was it painful?"

"Because you reminded him so much of Duncan. When you were a lad he was so excited; he'd tell me, 'He's going to be England captain, I'm certain of it.' It was like he could live his life and Duncan's through you. But then you got that offer to go down to London and you got injured and he knew then it was never going to happen. That's why it was so painful for him; you were a reminder of what he'd lost - of what you'd all lost - and he couldn't really deal with it. He'd rather pretend none of it had happened."

"But none of it was my fault." Jimmy felt the same old anger boiling over. "All I knew was that my dad loved football but never wanted to see me play and thought I was some kind of failure."

Wally propped himself up on one elbow, as clear-eyed as Jimmy had ever seen him. "That's what I'm trying to tell you, boy. It was never your fault so stop blaming yourself. Your father certainly did enough of that; blaming himself for not being a good enough father to you. He just couldn't say it out loud, not to you at any rate. He had his own struggle with depression after he got hurt, not that they had a name for it then. He'd tell me, 'The black dog's come for me again, Wally.' That's what he'd call it. But what I can tell you, and I know this for a fact, is that he'd be mighty proud of what you've been doing over here, at your age and all. Mighty proud."

The effort of talking so much suddenly seemed to have a detrimental effect on the old man and he slumped back on his side, his face still turned towards Jimmy, who had his head in his hands trying to process what Wally had told him.

"I noticed on TV that those boots you've been wearing look familiar," Wally said in a quieter voice. "Are they the old pair you found in the attic?"

"Yeah." Jimmy needed to tell somebody about them, someone other than Zoe, someone who would understand. "Can I tell you something about that, Wally?"

"Sure you can son." Wally's voice was still clear but his eyes had clouded.

"I can't really explain it, but when I put the boots on it's like I'm another person altogether. I can do anything I want with the ball. I can score, tackle, leap, whatever I want and I can run longer and faster than a 19-year-old. It's the only reason I'm playing like this at my age; it's because I'm wearing Duncan Edwards' boots."

The old man looked confused and Jimmy worried he was slipping back into dementia.

"When I'm wearing his boots, I actually feel like I am Duncan Edwards, like I'm channeling his spirit to play like he played. It feels incredible. Do you know what I mean?"

Wally's eyes were closed now and his head lolled over the side of the pillow. "I don't know what you mean, boy," he said softly.

"I mean that I play like Duncan Edwards because I'm wearing his boots."

"But that can't be right."

Jimmy was worried Wally would slip back into unconsciousness and looked around for someone to call. "Why can't that be right, Wally?" he said, trying to keep the old man engaged.

"Because they weren't Duncan's boots," said Wally. "They belonged to your dad."

CHAPTER SEVENTY

Wally fell asleep a few minutes later with Jimmy still holding his gnarled, liver-spotted hand.

Panicked, Jimmy felt for a pulse. Feeling nothing he leaned over the old man's face and there was still the faintest of breaths. To his surprise, Wally's eyes half-opened and he could see that he still knew who he was.

"I want you to make me a promise, son." Wally's voice was so weak Jimmy had to get him to repeat it. "Promise me something, Jimmy."

"Anything you want, Wally." Jimmy blinked back tears. He'd known this man his entire life. Wally was his last remaining link to his past; to his childhood, to Dudley…to his dad.

"Whatever happens to me, I want you to go play in that cup final," whispered Wally.

"No, I can't do that, not after this. I…."

"You have to promise me." Wally's voice was louder and more urgent. "You have to do this for me."

Jimmy still shook his head. He'd made up his mind. He was going to take his wife and his children home and stay right there with them. This dream, if that was what it was, had turned into a nightmare. He needed to wake up.

Wally had closed his eyes again but the old man wasn't done. "Just make sure you're out there. I know you'll do us all proud, just like you did when you was a nipper. It'll give me a great story to tell your dad when I see him up there. I can tell him I saw it with my own eyes - that you really did become the wonderful player he always thought you'd be, even better than the great Duncan Edwards.

"I'll be just fine here," he added. "Once you've won the final you can ship me old bones back to the Black Country and they can take care of the rest over there. Bill will take care of it with Mavis up the road. Don't worry about me. I've had a wonderful life. Wouldn't have played it any other way. Just do this one more thing for old Wally."

Jimmy stayed until the nurses arrived to do their checks and Carl took over so he could get back to Zoe.

Neil Murray arrived at the hospital later that morning. He tried to persuade Jimmy to return and train with the squad. The Galaxy had ended up on the wrong end of a 2-1 result in Seattle but that was easily enough to see them through to the final against New York City FC. The added bonus to the Galaxy reaching the championship game was that this year it was being held at their StubHub Centre stadium.

"I don't know if I can do it, Mr Murray." The two men sat in the corridor outside Zoe's room. "I nearly lost her and now I'm just expected to play like nothing happened. It's tough..." The emotions of the past few hours were overwhelming.

"I'm not telling you what you have to do here, Jimmy." The Scot shrugged his shoulders. "In the circumstances, we're not going to hold you to anything. But you've done something very special with this team. You've given people a reason to believe."

"That's very kind of you to say, sir, but nobody's really going to miss me. You've got Torres and the others." Jimmy looked down at his clenched hands.

"Is that so, son? So how would you explain that fans from both sides were chanting your name through the game in Seattle after the media reports explaining what happened with your family?"

"That's really nice. It's not that I don't appreciate…"

Murray interrupted. "Give it some more thought, that's all I ask, Jimmy. Take a little more time and give me a call tomorrow. Perhaps talk it over with Zoe. Either way I'll understand."

They parted with Jimmy agreeing to take 24 hours to think about his decision to walk away from the game.

Jimmy had been so clear in his mind about what he was going to do. But Wally and Murray had confused him. It didn't seem so simple anymore.

The next day the family was being driven home in a limo sent by the club and the kids were fast asleep in the back. Carl and Sarah were staying with Wally but the doctors wanted Zoe to recover in her own bed.

"So what are you going to do?" Zoe's progress had been remarkable since she'd come around and, while her monitoring would continue for a while, doctors could find no after-effects that unduly worried them.

"I just don't know if I can do it, babe." Jimmy's mind and body felt worn out, both by the emotional trauma of the past few days and the physical exertions of the past several months. The surge of energy he felt when he put on the boots was fast becoming a rather confusing memory, especially now that it seemed they never actually belonged to Duncan Edwards, after all. "It doesn't feel so important to me now."

"But you love your soccer Jimmy. Your field of broken toys and your Galaxy. I've seen the difference since you've been playing again. It lights you up." Zoe held Jimmy's hand. "It's not like you've got a long career ahead of you," she smiled. "You're 47. You might as well enjoy it while you can. And the kids love it that you're all famous."

Jimmy grinned in spite of himself. "I'm not famous!"

"Well, we can't go anywhere these days without someone asking you how many you're going to score in the next game now can we? You're all over ESPN and FOX. What's that then if it's not famous?"

The smile died on Jimmy's face. "It's because I'm a freak show. I'm an old man doing ball tricks."

"It's because you're bloody good." Zoe had taken to using the word "bloody" when she was annoyed. "You deserve it. You worked hard for it and you're an inspiration to a lot of people, me included."

Jimmy went quiet, looking out of the dark-tinted window at the countryside flashing by. "But you know the truth, Zo. It's not really me, is it? It's the boots. I don't understand it and it doesn't make any sense but I feel 30 years younger the moment I put them on and I can suddenly do things I've never tried my entire life."

Zoe moaned. "Not this again."

"I'm cheating. I'm a cheat," said Jimmy. "There's no two ways about it. Without the boots I'm nothing."

They fell silent.

"And the truth is that at least I thought I knew who I was when I was wearing them," Jimmy continued, speaking softly, embarrassed that the driver would overhear. "I thought I was the great Duncan Edwards and there was some logic in that, at least to me. He was this immense talent who died before his time and I was, like, his chance to fulfil his destiny through me. I know it sounds crazy…"

"It doesn't sound crazy…well, maybe just a little bit crazy." Zoe could see Jimmy was hurting.

"And now Wally tells me the boots weren't Duncan's at all. They were my dad's all along. So what does that mean? That I am my father? That this is some Darth Vader morality story? I really don't know, Zo, and I'm not sure I want to."

Zoe put her arms around Jimmy and pulled him close. "I know how important those boots are to you and I understand, I really do." She paused. "But I still believe this is all about you, baby. It's all to do with your relationship with your father and how he made you feel about yourself. Maybe the boots helped free your mind somehow. You said your dad thought you'd be better than this Duncan guy when you were little. I'm just saying but maybe it's taken you all this time to realize that he was right and that you were holding yourself back."

Jimmy shook his head. "I just can't explain how different it feels."

"Like you're free?"

"Maybe. Kind of. I don't know." Jimmy went quiet again, trying to digest what Zoe had said. "But it really doesn't make a difference right now because I don't know where the boots are. I think someone has taken them."

"So that makes the decision much easier then," said Zoe. She was suddenly feeling very tired. "Tell Murray that you'll play in the final and do your very best as 47-year-old happily married father-of-three Jimmy Keen, not as some tragic ghost who died before you were born.

"Do it for Wally and for your dad. But most of all, Jimmy, do it for yourself."

CHAPTER SEVENTY-ONE

There wasn't a time in Jimmy's childhood that he didn't think about this day. For as far back as he could remember anything at all, his recurring daydream saw him playing in a final. It may have been the FA Cup, what was then the League Cup or the European Cup. Every four years it would even be the World Cup. But he would always score the winner and he would invariably be carried off the field in glory.

Waking up that morning in an unfamiliar hotel bed in Carson, California, a stone's throw from the StubHub stadium, Jimmy tried to cling onto that indelible memory he thought had died the day of his knee injury. He squeezed his eyes back shut and forced himself to see the twin towers of the old Wembley; the Charlie George goal that won the 1971 FA Cup for Arsenal; Geoff Hurst's "They think it's all over…it is now" third in 1966; Carlos Alberto's pile-driver for Brazil in the 1970 World Cup Final against Italy; George Best's dribble past the keeper in the 1968 European Cup Final and Zidane's volley from outside the box in the 2002 Champions League Final. Most prized of all was Jeff Astle's left-foot goal to win the FA Cup for West Bromwich Albion in extra time against Everton in 1968.

In those boyhood dreams, it was his own face he saw as these legends turned away to celebrate. He was the one lifting the trophy and being hoisted on the shoulders of his teammates. He may have been too young to have seen most of these magical goals in person, but he'd watched his father's old VHS recordings so many times the tapes had stretched.

Jimmy was so convinced he was going to do something special in the game that his life had fallen apart when it became apparent that he wasn't. And now it appeared his own life wasn't the only one that was ruined. It was never easy for a son to disappoint his father, no matter what walk of life.

But this was the morning he'd dreamed about all those years ago. This was his opportunity to make his mark and put his face on the memories of countless boys and girls who hungered for success in the same way that he had all those years ago.

In those few moments of waking bliss, all the years of failure dropped away with the picture in his mind of a player in a Galaxy strip running to the crowd celebrating the winning goal in the MLS Cup Final. The face was his and so was the stage.

The vision lasted just long enough for another thought to stamp all over it. His boots were missing. The final was going to be a disaster. Jimmy was going to be a laughing stock. He was going to disappoint his father all over again.

It was enough to send Jimmy burrowing back under the covers. He'd been through all this with Zoe the previous day. He'd found a peace with what he planned to do. He was going to be himself, not Duncan Edwards. And he would play the best he possibly could and be comfortable with that because it would probably be his last game as a professional.

The phone rang beside his bed. It was Zoe. "How are you feeling superstar?"

"Terrified!"

"No sign of the smelly old cleats, then?" Last night, Zoe had almost convinced him he was better off without the stolen boots.

"Not a peep. I pretty much accused everyone on the team at training yesterday and nobody had a clue what I was talking about. I figured, what have I got to lose? If it was Torres that took them he wasn't going to own up to it." He paused, waiting for a reaction from Zoe that didn't come. "So basically I'm screwed."

"We've talked about this Jimmy." Zoe had her mother's patient voice on. "This is the best thing that could have happened. It's important for you to understand just how brilliant you really are."

Jimmy was never going to convince Zoe. "Okay, sure. I know. It's going to be great. I guess I'd better go and start getting ready. I'm still in bed and we've got breakfast in 10 minutes."

"One minute, Jimmy, the kids have some advice before you go." Zoe handed the phone over to Tyler.

"Hi dad. Good luck. Hope you score." He sounded excited and just hearing the little boy's voice brought a smile back on Jimmy's face. "But me and Grace and Charley have some advice that you always tell us and we really think it'll help with all those people watching and the game being on TV and everything."

There was a rustling and a little giggle from Charley. Jimmy could hear Grace whispering, one, two, three…and then all three shouted at the tops of their voices: WATCH THE BALL!!!"

CHAPTER SEVENTY-TWO

Rossi had kept them waiting right until the final minute before naming the team. He thought it gave the players who were picked an extra edge. Jimmy sensed Torres kept looking at him as they changed into their uniforms, waiting for the assistant manager to pin the team up on the wall. He wasn't sure if it was nerves or guilt. Either way, he kept his own eyes down, focusing on what he had to if he was in the team. A part of him was really hoping he wasn't.

Torres was first off his seat the moment the team was up and as he walked back to his locker his eyes settled on Jimmy and stayed there.

Jimmy waited for the scrum to part and walked slowly over to look at the scrawled list of names. He was in the starting line-up and so was Torres.

This time he held Torres' glance as he walked back and nodded: "Good luck." The Spaniard offered a scarcely perceptible nod in return. "You too, old man."

Jimmy sat back down and pulled on his new Copa Mundials. They fitted snugly on his feet and he pulled the laces tight, hoping against hope to feel a spark of energy shoot through his body. But there was nothing. Only dread.

"Hey Tank, welcome back." Terry ran over, one hand raised for a high five. "We missed you man. It's going to be awesome having you and Francesco up front. We're gonna cream them today. There's no way they're gonna stop you two guys playing together." He sat down next to Jimmy. "How's your wife doing? That was a tough break."

"She's good, thanks. Again, I'm sorry for missing the game, I…"

"Don't even think about it. I said to the guys at half-time in Seattle, 'We got to do this for Tank!' They almost took the roof off chanting your name. We believe in you."

Jimmy really wished he had those boots. He wanted to promise Terry that he had the team's back; that he could deliver. But he couldn't guarantee much beyond jogging out to the centre circle. His knees were already hurting.

Terry called the rest of the team around in a circle and told them they were winners, that this was their time and somehow the chants started quietly and built up and up. "Tank, Torres. Tank, Torres, TANK! TORRES! TANK! TORRES!"

They were still chanting as they joined the New York players and the refs in the tunnel waiting to run out into the afternoon sunshine.

At first the sun blinded Jimmy to the colour and craziness of the final. The noise was ear-blistering and never seemed to drop in pitch or power. Running slowly onto the field he tried a Duncan Edwards hop and skip to get himself going but it was more of a trip than anything else and he nearly lost his balance. Most of the games he'd played for the Galaxy had been post-season sell-outs but this was different. The stakes were so much higher for the players and the fans. Instead of feeling empowered, Jimmy felt small and insignificant in such energised surroundings. He was short of breath, not from effort, not yet, but his lungs were intimidated by the scale of the occasion.

The national anthem passed by in a blur and Jimmy picked up a sweat just shaking his opponents' hands. Over and over in his head he kept repeating Zoe's mantra, *enjoy it, enjoy it*. Moments before kick-off he sprinted over to where his wife was sitting with the kids and blew them a kiss. A smile lit up Zoe's face. It was hard to imagine that just a week earlier her life was hanging in the balance. The gesture drew a barrage of wolf whistles from the banks of his Sunday morning teammates, who were all wearing white and blue Galaxy shirts specially printed across the chest with the initials FOBD.

Jimmy waved and walked back to the centre circle where the referee was waiting to kick-off. The crowd noise had reached a crescendo, but Jimmy was trying to tune it all out. Torres tapped the ball sideways to him and he paused a second. He saw a gap he could run into but he didn't have the legs. He was like a stutterer avoiding words he couldn't say; he'd just have to find a different route to express himself. He tapped the ball back five feet to Gutierrez and slipped into the space, hoping to get the ball back. It duly came and Jimmy realised the New York players were standing off, giving him room, scared he'd run through them as he'd done in previous play-off games. That at least meant he had some time to control the ball and look for options. The years may have taken their toll on his body but his football mind was still agile. Torres made a darting run behind the right centre back and Jimmy slotted the ball in the space behind the last defender and the goalkeeper. It was perfect, with just enough weight to run into Torres' stride but not enough pace to reach the keeper. The Spaniard hit it first time, chipping high over the stranded goalie. Jimmy lost the ball momentarily in the lights and then it dropped down to land right on the line and bounce high into the back of the net.

The Galaxy was one-up after 24 seconds, the fastest goal in MLS Cup Final history. The celebrations were tempered with the knowledge of how far there still was to go but Jimmy's teammates lavished as much praise on him as with the jubilant Torres and they were both buried underneath a crush of bodies.

Just 89 minutes to go, thought Jimmy, taking his place again for the restart. *Enjoy yourself, enjoy yourself.*

Jimmy's next three touches were brief. He could see that his teammates were slightly baffled when he laid the ball off with short, crisp passes. They were waiting for something special.

Torres was buzzing around, not quite sure what to expect. Jimmy was determined not to make any mistakes and conserve his energy so he could last longer than five minutes without collapsing in an exhausted heap. He'd done much the same in training when he wasn't wearing the old boots.

With the game bogged down in midfield for the first 15 minutes, he was able to nip in and out of the action without too much burden on his 47-year-old legs. There was still a sense of anticipation in the crowd when the ball came to him.

The problems started when Jimmy stuck in a tackle just inside his own half and was surprised to come away with the ball. There was acres of space down the left hand side and he could hear the crowd roaring him on. This was the moment they had been waiting for; the Tank in full cry. He lifted his head and saw Torres about level with him and cutting in from the right touchline waving one hand in the air and screaming for the pass.

As try as Jimmy might, he couldn't break into a run. There was just too much to think about and his mind was full of possibilities. Should he run first and then pass? Or should he try and hit the angled cross-field ball right away? He still hadn't decided when a City midfielder pick-pocketed the ball and left Jimmy sprawling in the grass. Two more passes and it was in the back of the net. The wrong one.

1-1. And it was Jimmy's fault. Running back, Torres shot him a dirty look that was a little bit knowing, too. As if he'd confirmed something he already suspected.

Two minutes later, New York got a second after Jimmy was again robbed of possession and was too tired to give chase. 1-2.

Jimmy ignored Rossi screaming on the touchline. He needed to make amends somehow; he didn't want to be taken off, not yet.

Torres had clearly decided to take things into his own hands. From Jimmy's kick-off pass, he took on three players at speed, skipping through the challenges easily until he went flying just outside the penalty box after the slightest of pushes from the full back. He picked up the ball, intending to take the free kick himself, but Jimmy grabbed it from him. There was a little tussle but Jimmy had surprise on his side and wrenched the ball away. The little contretemps fit in perfectly with what he planned to do.

"What the hell?" Torres reached out again and Jimmy turned away, saying: "Be ready, Francesco. Just be ready at the back post. Hear me? Back post."

Torres mumbled and ambled over to stand by where the New York goalie was ordering his defenders into a wall.

Jimmy placed the ball on the turf and called over Mike Terry. He'd remembered a cheesy little ploy he and Carl used to try when they played for Plaistow Irons. It had only worked once, but Jimmy was desperate. "Do me a favour, Mike. Pick up the ball and then replace it as if you're going to take the kick."

"But I don't do free kicks. You know what the boss said…" Terry looked confused.

"Just pretend, Mike. And then when I bump into you just get out of the way and let me do the rest."

Terry looked even more confused and slightly alarmed. "So who's taking the kick?" He looked over his shoulder to see

Rossi going crazy in the technical area. "I think the boss wants Francesco to take it."

"Forget him." Jimmy stood back and hissed, "Take the ball!"

Terry walked over, picked up the ball and put it down again and Jimmy could see the ref glancing at his watch, irritated. The Galaxy captain looked across at Jimmy after walking back a few paces for a run-up.

Jimmy nodded.

Still unsure what was expected of him, Terry shaped up for the kick and started moving toward the ball. At the same time, Jimmy ran from the other side of the ball, bumping into his teammate before he could strike it. He heard a titter of laughter from the wall, and at that very second Jimmy kicked the ball himself, scooping it up to the far post where Torres was waiting.

Still laughing at the apparent confusion over the free-kick, the distracted defenders weren't ready for the cross, but Torres was. He met the ball perfectly, arrowing it into the roof of the goal with the keeper stranded.

2-2. It may have been the corniest trick in the Irons playbook, but it worked. Jimmy risked a look across at his coach and he looked as bemused as his captain. Hands in his pockets he was in deep conversation with his assistants, probably trying to work out what had just happened.

The goal marked a change of attitude from Torres, at least. He was on his hat-trick and grinned at Jimmy. "Nice fraud, señor!"

The goal bought Jimmy some time but he was running out of ideas…and breath. Twice he fell over as he tried to trap a simple wall pass and he was getting an earful from Rossi for failing to run back with his man when the opposing defenders went on the attack. He could hear his lungs wheezing as he made his way back upfield for a goal kick. The big boot was meant for him; he'd jumped head and shoulders above everybody when he'd had his old boots. But he couldn't get off the ground and just backed into his marker, giving away the foul. The crowd moaned. It wasn't going well and it got a whole lot worse when the free-kick was bent over the wall into the top right corner of the Galaxy goal. 2-3.

The Galaxy players were struggling not to be overrun and lucky to be only one down a minute or so before half-time. Jimmy was dead on his feet standing just inside his own team's penalty box hoping nobody came near him. With a wonderful piece of skill, City's wing back tricked his marker to get around him to the byline and pulled the ball back to where Jimmy was standing. All he wanted to do was kick the ball as far and as hard as he could and get back into the dressing room and catch his breath. Jimmy probably could have stopped the ball and pushed it out to Robbie Norton on the wing but he didn't want to risk being caught in possession again. Instead, he took a massive swipe with his left foot. As he did so his standing leg slipped out and he fell, slicing his kick. The spinning ball curled back over his shoulder, landed about ten yards out from the goal and kicked right, away from the keeper and over the line.

2-4. By the time Jimmy had rolled himself, muscle by muscle, off the grass and into a standing position and made it back to restart the game the referee put him out of his misery and blew the whistle for half-time.

CHAPTER SEVENTY-THREE

Jimmy walked head down, cursing himself for being caught on the other side of the field from the tunnel. His shirt was soaked in sweat, every muscle in his body ached and his pride had suffered a massive kick in the teeth with his final touch of the half. He managed a thin smile for his family but needed to marshal what little energy he had left to put one foot in front of the other.

He'd seen Rossi dash off the moment the whistle was blown and feared the worst. The sliced own goal could have condemned him to a second half on the bench.

The coach had already started his team talk by the time Jimmy got to the dressing room. "Nice of you to drop in." Rossi didn't turn to look at Jimmy. "But it's not a problem. You don't need to hear this."

Jimmy was too tired to protest as he shimmied around his teammates to make it over to his locker, but when he went to slump down there was a pair of boots in his seat — his old boots.

Rossi was finishing off. "Keen, you're dead on your feet. I'm taking you off for Whelan."

"But boss…" Jimmy tried to protest.

Rossi waved him away.

The room was silent and Terry looked over, shrugging his shoulders. The other players stood up and carried on with their half time routines. The message was clear; they agreed with the coach. Jimmy's incredible run was done.

"Give him 10 more minutes." The heavily accented voice was addressing Rossi. "Just 10 minutes, trust me." Torres stood up, blocking Rossi's path. "You can't take Keen off, not yet."

"I'll do what I want. Get out of my way." Rossi tried to push past but Torres refused to budge.

"If you take Keen off, I will not play." Torres crossed his arms. "I will also sit on the bench."

Rossi stood open-mouthed weighing his options. Without Torres the Galaxy's chances of winning were virtually nil. Whelan was a good target man but he was just coming back from injury and his best days were behind him. The only other striker on the bench was a kid just out of school.

"Ten minutes," he said, furiously putting both hands in Torres' face, his fingers extended. "But we have not heard last of this, Francesco. This is my team, not your team or Keen's team. You understand?"

"Okay." Torres stood aside, allowing Rossi to brush past him, and looked over at Jimmy, nodding curtly. Their eyes met momentarily. Then the Spaniard followed his coach out down the tunnel.

Jimmy took off his Copas and slowly pulled on the old boots. For a fraction of a second he worried that nothing would happen, that the magic was gone. But then a slow, delicious warmth flowed up his legs and through his entire being. It wasn't just a physical transformation; his mind felt lighter, too, as if a burden had been lifted. He stood up, expecting to creak, but bounced onto his feet and jogged over to the mirror. He thought maybe this time his looks had changed along with the way he felt but he didn't look a day younger than 47, his hair was still starting to recede and crow's feet were gathering around his eyes.

It didn't really matter what was happening on the surface. Whatever was happening to Jimmy was much deeper than that. If it wasn't magic, if these crappy old boots didn't have some weird and wonderful connection to something way beyond Jimmy's understanding then that was fine, as well. He may well be playing mind games with himself. Right now, that was okay. All he knew was that they made him feel young again.

And can anyone ask for anything more than that?

They made him the footballer he always dreamed he would be. They kind of saved him and that was all he really needed to know.

CHAPTER SEVENTY-FOUR

Coming out of the tunnel this time, Jimmy breathed it all in; the noise, the passion, the spectacle of a sporting event teetering on a knife edge.

Only now he owned it.

He tried the trademark hop. The sideline could have been the Grand Canyon and he would have leaped over it, no problem. He didn't jog over to where Zoe was sitting with the kids: he sprinted and climbed close enough to encompass them with a hug. It was only then that he noticed they weren't alone. Carl and Sarah were sitting next to Zoe…and so was Wally.

"You didn't think I was going to miss this, did you son?" The old man reached out both arms and Jimmy fell into them, a little boy again. Wally looked as frail as Jimmy had ever seen him and smelled like antiseptic and stale beer, but their connection went way deeper than the five senses. It took Jimmy all the way back to the beginning, to when he truly believed he could do anything.

The crowd wasn't sure, not yet. But Jimmy would show them. No more need for tricky little stunts; he would win this game for the Galaxy with the kind of football skills that had been thrilling fans from the days of Stanley Matthews and Ferenc Puskas through to Pele and Maradona to Messi and Ronaldo.

He would show them what Duncan Edwards was so cruelly prevented from doing. They may or not have been Duncan's boots, it didn't really matter. His spirit was right there on the pitch.

Waiting for the restart, unable to stand still, Jimmy saw Torres coming towards him.

"You and me…together. Let's do this." Torres reached out his hand and held on a little longer. "Good luck."

It wasn't an admission of guilt but it was as much as Jimmy was going to get. "Good luck, Francesco. And thanks for what you said to Rossi back there."

The whistle went, Game on. It was now or never.

New York came straight at them from the off; they'd clearly been given instructions from their coach at half-time not to rest on their lead. Torres was scythed down the first time he touched the ball and, minutes later, Jimmy was elbowed in the stomach as he went to jump for a ball on the halfway line.

The Galaxy was stuck in its own half with City playing a high press that prevented Jimmy from getting the ball. He knew he'd be fine once he'd won possession, but the clock was ticking and his 10 minutes were nearly over. Rossi already had Whelan getting warmed up on the touchline. Jimmy glanced across and saw the coach speaking with the referee's assistant, who went over and picked up the electronic substitution board. He couldn't see what number was going up but he was pretty sure it was his.

With the channels forward all closed off Jimmy decided to go all the way back and pick up the ball himself. The keeper was struggling to find an outlet so Jimmy crossed close to the corner flag and shouted for the ball. At last he had control without three players bearing down on him but as he looked up he was surrounded by opposition red shirts and none of his teammates were able to shake free. Even the route back to the goalie was closed off. Then Jimmy noticed that New York was playing such a high press that their goalkeeper was virtually on the halfway line.

Before the half, Jimmy wouldn't have contemplated a pass of much more than 10 feet but that was then. He took another, measured look at the opposing goal and lurched three steps backwards, leaving the ball suddenly alone and unprotected. Before his markers worked out what was happening, Jimmy was half way through his short run-up. He didn't even feel the contact, so sweet was the touch of laces on plastic, and the players hemming him in didn't bother to turn around, assuming they'd harried him into a purposeless clump up the field.

But Jimmy lifted his head after the strike just in time to see a look of absolute panic in the keeper's eye as he turned to begin his long, fruitless dash back to his own goal. The ball was soaring high in the sky and the entire crowd was watching its inexorable 120 yard flight goal-ward. The keeper gave up the chase as the ball flew over his shoulder. There was no bounce; it landed 1 foot over the line right in the middle of the goal and hit so hard and with such spin that it buried itself deep into the turf.

The referee blew his whistle for the goal but it took the groundsmen another 10 minutes to dig out the ball.

The crowd reaction was delayed. They had clearly given up hope of seeing anything particularly special from Jimmy so when it happened they were caught by surprise. Then the roar of approval finally exploded from all corners of the ground, including the New York section. It was 3-4.

Whelan was back in his seat and Rossi had his hands back in his pockets by the time Jimmy was back in position alongside Torres. The two men grinned at one another but their team had to soak up some more pressure from their increasingly aggressive opponents before they could really make their partnership count.

In the meantime, Jimmy was everywhere, tackling back to help his defenders, chasing down lost causes and twice clearing off the line when the keeper appeared beaten.

In the 75th minute, with their team still a goal down, Jimmy tapped a simple ball in the air to Torres, who was standing just inside the centre circle. Torres cushioned the ball on his knee and volleyed it back in the air to Jimmy, who'd run past his markers along the right touchline. Jimmy caught the ball on the instep of his right foot, knocked it up to his head and let it fall onto his left boot to dispatch to Torres, now on the right corner of the penalty box. With his back to goal, Torres kept it up three times, fending off two exasperated centre backs, and played it back a few feet to Jimmy, still in the air.

Jimmy caught the ball between his two calves and stood motionless for a second before flinging himself head-first to the ground, landing on his hands and catapulting his legs over his head to send the ball flying over the heads of the onrushing defenders. The ball was met with a scorpion kick by a diving Torres on the other edge of the box which flew like a rocket into the goal.

4-4. The game was tied.

From that point on, every time Jimmy got anywhere near the ball he was bundled over by two or maybe three New York players. The bookings were mounting up but the City players clearly had a strategy; they were taking it in turns to foul Jimmy so nobody was forced to commit a second card-able offence and get sent off. Their tactics were simple — stop Jimmy.

The Galaxy players were becoming increasingly frustrated but there was little they could do. Jimmy may ride one or two tackles but he'd eventually get clipped. Torres was getting similar, if not such unfailing, attention and the 90 minutes were almost up.

Still, with Terry driving the team on from midfield and Gutierrez trying to take advantage of the spaces left by City's obsession with Jimmy, they managed a rare excursion into New York's crowded penalty box. What happened next was so quick and unexpected that nobody saw it coming, especially not Jimmy.

He'd almost latched onto a lax City pass that missed his boot by a millimetre and the game had moved across to the right side when Denali, New York's Uruguayan midfielder, caught him with a horrendously late, studs up challenge that made contact halfway up Jimmy's shin.

There was a collective gasp from the crowd as the impact send Jimmy spinning to the ground clutching his leg. One of his feet had stuck in the grass, wrenching off his boot and he lay sprawled out fearing his bone must have broken.

The tackle was so late and so brutal that even the referee seemed shocked and slow to act. He could certainly do nothing to stop Torres hurtling across and grabbing Denali in a headlock. The two men sunk to the ground together as their teammates rushed to separate them. The team medic was already on the pitch attending to Jimmy, who was still lying face down on the grass. Players from both sides were arguing and pushing each other in a melee near the goalmouth.

The ref recovered in time to blow his whistle and point to the penalty spot. He slowly walked over to first Denali and then Torres and showed both the red card. He brandished three more yellow cards, one to a furious Rossi, before returning to check on Jimmy.

There was a deep gouge on his shin and his leg still felt numb but with his boot lying a few feet away Jimmy couldn't really judge how bad it was. Even before the tackle, his 47-year-old legs had been meted out way more punishment than they should be expected to handle.

The team medic was distracted, talking into his head mic. "The boss wants to know if you're going to come off or take the penalty?" he asked.

Jimmy looked over at his stranded boot. It had a long rip down the side where the studs raked down and across the foot. The boot he was still wearing had got caught in the grass and the rubber sole had torn free from the leather. He took it off and tried to stand in his socks. His magic boots were unwearable.

Getting slowly to his feet, Jimmy really couldn't tell if the searing ache in both legs was the result of the tackle or the previous 87 minutes. But this was the moment he'd dreamed about since he was a little kid. This was his chance to score the winning goal in a cup final. He was going to be Jeff Astle; he wasn't going to sit on the sidelines as he had done much of his life.

They'd patched over the gash in his leg; it would need stitches but not for now, and he motioned towards the bench asking for another pair of boots. The kit man ran over with a pair of green and yellow Nike Hypervenoms in three different sizes. "Couldn't find your other ones," he said. "The boss said for you to wear one of these."

Jimmy gingerly picked the size 12s and sat back down in the goalmouth to put them on. The referee was telling all the other players to get out of the box until there was just Jimmy and the keeper.

Jimmy got up really slowly; he really didn't have any choice. He jumped up and down to test the boots. They felt quite good. He glanced over at Zoe and shrugged, looking down at his feet. She smiled. It was such a big smile. And she pointed to the kids jumping up and down and screaming Jimmy's name.

I love you, she mouthed and he saw and he understood. It really was just down to him now, not any ghosts from either his past or the game he loved. This was his moment.

He looked down the row at Wally and he looked small and still in the chaos all around him. With the tiniest of movements of his right hand, the old man pointed up at the sky. He was telling Jimmy something different.

Perhaps this wasn't just his moment, after all. It was *theirs*.

The ball was already on the spot but Jimmy picked it up anyway and settled it back down. He remembered once seeing Andrea Pirlo send the goalkeeper the wrong way in an international for Italy and then tap the ball over the line with all the guile and confidence in the world and he wished right then that he had the guts to try such a thing.

But standing back, surveying the entire goal, the keeper waving his arms around trying to distract him, and the braying, bug-eyed faces of the City fans praying for him to fail, Jimmy asked himself what Duncan would have done and the answer was waiting there for him.

He took an extra couple of steps for his run-up, looked up one last time at the goal and then did the one thing he always told his kids. He watched the ball. He didn't think about placing the ball or finessing it or any of those things; he blasted it with every last effort he could muster in his sore, middle-aged, decaying body.

And he only dared lift his head what seemed an eternity after the ball had left the spot when he heard the crowd rise as one for him, Jimmy Keen, the winning goalscorer in the MLS Cup Final.

The keeper was still rooted to his spot, only he was crouched down and his head was in his hands. The ball had hit the net so hard it burst through and landed half way up the stands. *Duncan would have been proud*, thought Jimmy.

So would my dad.

CHAPTER SEVENTY-FIVE

Jimmy sat down at the bench and pulled his Hypervenom's out of his bag. He'd kept them after the final; they really were quite comfortable. The gash was clearing up on his shin and his legs were slowly turning back from black and blue to a more healthy shade of grey.

He'd got to the field at 6.35am to be sure he'd play in the first game. Even more people had been turning up since all the TV coverage but it was still the same faces who made it out early.

"Nice penalty, sir." Nermin appeared in the half-light and Jimmy gave silent thanks that the big Croatian hadn't been the one who'd tackled him in the final.

Then Pete arrived with his 84-year-old father-in-law, a scouser dressed in Liverpool red who'd come for a "run-out."

And gradually a stream of familiar faces grumbled across the stretch of grass from the parking lot to the metal bench carrying coffees, kitbags, and secretive stashes of powerful prescription drugs. They may not have had magic boots, but everyone had their own methods of making it through 90 minutes of a game that, if not beautiful, was certainly loved.

Martyn, a John Wayne with microwaved hot-pads on both knees, Paul with his Starbucks bacon and egg butty, Bill in bright gold and green and Mark all booted up and ready to play. Sean bounds over to put his name on the list before returning to his SUV for a nap, Bjorn is drinking an indefinable black liquid from a plastic cup. Along comes Andrew and Ken and Dylan, carpooling in the youth and the skill, followed by a gaggle of others who may not have the youth but remembered the skills.

All are welcome to the Field of Broken Dreams.

We talk about the Premier League and La Liga and the games played far away by players we've only seen on TV. We remember matches we've watched and players we've loved and harken back to the days of our own youths.

We talk about our wives and our kids and their sports and their partners. If we're feeling bold we may discuss politics and light a few fuses before we go out on the field and forget about our everyday lives for those few, precious minutes a week when all that matters is the passage of a simple football.

We stretch as we talk and understand that it will take more than a few replacement hips and knees for any of us to play the way we still see ourselves in our minds.

And I hold dearly onto the hope that for any of us, one day, somehow, our dreams will indeed come true.

No matter how old we are.

The stragglers are here, Frank, JC and Phil. It's 7.15 on a Sunday morning and the cones are all out.

Let's play.

THE END

David Gardner is the London Evening Standard US Correspondent, an ex-Daily Mail Foreign Correspondent and Head of Content at Football.com, Basketball.com and Trivia.com. He has had several books published, including The Last of the Hitlers, about his search to find Adolf Hitler's last living descendants in the United States; The Tom Hanks Enigma; and LEGENDS: Murder, Lies and Cover-Ups, which was published in the US by Skyhorse Publishing in May 2018. His first novel, The iCandidate, written with his wife Michelle, won a 2017 Independent Publisher Book award for national contemporary fiction. He is a regular player at the Field of Broken Dreams at age 58.

DUNCAN EDWARDS: BLACK COUNTRY BOY TO RED DEVIL

"I joined Manchester United straight from school in 1953 and I was met at the train station by Jimmy Murphy, the United assistant manager. On our way to Old Trafford Jimmy told me that we were going to see the greatest young player he had ever worked with - his name was Duncan Edwards.

"At this point in my young life I felt I could compare well with any player - that is until I saw Duncan Edwards in action on that day - I knew then that I would never be as good as him."

So begins Sir Bobby Charlton's moving tribute to his lost friend in the book, *Duncan Edwards: Black Country Boy to Red Devil*, published to mark the 60th anniversary of the United legend's death in February 1958 following the injuries he received in Munich Air Disaster that also cost the lives of many of his Manchester United team mates – The Busby Babes.

The lavishly illustrated book lovingly details Duncan's life and heritage which continues to be celebrated in the Black Country – and throughout the world – 60 years after his death.

Duncan Edwards came from a working class background in the heart of the industrial Black Country to play for Manchester United and represent England as an international player at every level of professional football.

The Book contains a collection of photographs, memorabilia, football programmes, graphic images and artifacts that shaped the life of Duncan Edwards and fuelled his iconic legacy along a path that took him from a Black Country Boy to a Red Devil.

Duncan Edwards: Black Country Boy to Red Devil
by Jim Cadman and Iain McCartney

Available online and from all good booksellers
RRP - £10.00
ISBN – 978-0-9560756-7-3

Visit the website at www.duncanedwardstribute.com Further information available from Jim Cadman - jwc@duncanedwardstribute.com

30033764R00211

Printed in Poland
by Amazon Fulfillment
Poland Sp. z o.o., Wrocław